Where Are We going?

Edited by

Allen Ashley

Where Are We Going?
Publication Date: March 2012

Copyright of the stories lies with the individual authors.

Cover Art by David Rix and Jasmin Topalusic, 2012

ISBN: 978-1-908125-13-2

www.eibonvalepress.co.uk

Contents:

Are We Nearly There Yet?

Introduction by Allen Ashley

The journey has been an essential element in human storytelling since our prehistory. As we moved down out of the trees, spread across the savannah, crossed the land-bridges, paused and built our fires – tales of our travels and tribulations became our staple bedtime story. Wars and conquest or simple acts of nomadism, exploration and new settlements enriched the genre; the invention of mythology and religion added further riches to the canon. Key works of Western literature such as "The Odyssey" or the first five books of "The Holy Bible", particularly "Exodus", are all about the trials and travails of often enforced travel. In fact, I'll let you into a little secret about my own fiction: the expulsion from Eden is the key artistic event, the fount of tragic inspiration that I return to over and over.

I cited several classics in my guidelines for this project. Examples included Jonathan Swift's "Gulliver's Travels", Joseph Conrad's "Heart of Darkness", Lewis Carroll's "Alice's Adventures in Wonderland" and Edgar Allan Poe's "The Narrative of Arthur Gordon Pym of Nantucket". These were works which thrilled, inspired, excited, educated and enthralled me as a younger man. Along with countless others, of course. Often the way of writing about one's own society is to appear to take several strides away from it and concoct a heady satire or hold up a dystopic yet still revealing mirror. This reflection – in all its senses – can be illuminating, therapeutic, controversial, beguiling… add your own adjectives. The aim is also to achieve great literature – an authorial statement worth writing and worth reading. Every creative act should start with the highest of ideals.

Then again, if one just wants to tell a good story with maybe a bit of musing or philosophy thrown in amidst the exciting events along the way, it's a classic plot template to send your protagonist(s) on a perilous, demanding journey. Rama and Sita in exile; Jesus' 40 days in the wilderness; Hansel and Gretel left deep in the Bavarian forest. In modern parlance, one has to take one's chosen characters "out of their comfort zone" or else there's no action, no conflict, no story.

Sometimes the exploration is more psychological than actual or physical – the work of Kafka springs to mind. Whatever – the enduring power of the journey template is probably that it replicates – cliché alert – the journey that is life. And yes, there's a beginning, middle and end. I think it was Confucius who said that even a trek of a thousand miles begins with one small step. So I encouraged authors to take that fictive step… and keep going.

Something that I was not looking for were quests. By this, I mean "Lord of the Rings", "King Arthur and the Holy Grail", "Elric of Melniboné" and their ilk. Don't get me wrong – I am not knocking the clear literary merits of these epics; although their derivative copyists aren't quite so appealing. One simple reason for not wanting quests is that I had a working maximum word limit of 6000 words per story; hardly enough space in trilogy land for Frodo and Bilbo to pack a picnic hamper to take to Uncle Gandalf's. Likewise, I was not seeking anything based on or derivative from computer games, be that "Black Ops" or "Assassin's Creed" or "Super Mario". Originality goes a long way with me.

Journeys; on Earth; no quests; present time or near future. Fantasy and SF or speculative elements preferred. It all seemed so straightforward on the page or posted up at a website.

With my tongue pressed firmly against the inside of my cheek (I am a writer myself, after all), I can categorically state that authors are the bane of an editor's life. I've written for several themed anthologies and have been told on occasion by a grateful editor that my effort has been the very epitome of the intended guidelines. Maybe that shows that I possess a conformist, unadventurous, one might even say *polite* streak. Other writers differ; several interpret the spec for an anthology as a challenge to see how far they can deviate from requirements and yet still get away with it. I wanted journeys, physical travel; one of these stories involves nothing much more vigorous than a city bus ride. I said stay on Earth; one of these pieces locates itself almost entirely on an alien planet, although the astronaut's body may still actually be on a couch in a NASA base on dear old Terra. Set your story in the present or near-future; but, of course, our characters are formed by their past and a revisiting of personal or imagined history can resonate effectively. I specifically edit books of short stories; I received two poems and I've taken one of them. See, I'm trying to develop my adventurous, unpredictable side!

Where are we going? Will we ever get there? Do we want to head that way or should we try to change course before it's too late?

Eighteen authors – some well-established, others still in the early glow of their careers – offer up some clues and possibilities.

It is my firm belief that themed anthologies are playing an increasingly important role in preserving, continuing and extending the function of the short story as an essential part of our literary culture. My faith in the form will never die and, on this occasion, it has been replenished and sustained by the sterling support of David Rix, my publisher, and also by the fabulous material offered to me by an array of equally fabulous authors.

Where are we going? Hold tight, we're about to find out.

\-   Allen Ashley
London, 2012

Dead Countries

by Gary Budgen

I liked dead countries. It was the possibility of completion that attracted me, the thought that I would be able to get every issue without the worry of having to keep up with all the new stuff. It's funny what you get into when you're a kid.

Eric, who lived across the street, was more of a general collector but one day he came over to my house to show me something. I answered the front door and saw his mum across the street, making sure he crossed the road safely even though there were hardly ever any cars round our way then. He nodded to me and scratched at his acne covered forehead. When we got into my room he showed me the stamps. They were a set of commemoratives showing smiling faces in cosmonauts' helmets with a rocket ship blazing in the background. The larger writing looked like angular Arabic but there was an English translation. "Heroes of our Space Program." The name of the country was confirmed in capitals. Quassia.

"Where's Quassia?" I asked. I had never heard of it.

Dear Francis.

Getting here has not been easy. Not everyone is allowed to make the journey. It has taken me a long time to be ready.

At the border I was questioned.

- Had I ever worked for a bank or in the stock market?

- Had I ever been a boss or fired someone from a job?

- Had I ever willingly trod on an ant?

Since they let me through everyone has been very friendly. I have had to join an official tour since they don't let foreigners just wander around getting the wrong idea and spreading even more vile propaganda.

The hotel is basic but decent enough. Tomorrow we are going on a coach tour to the launch sites of the space missions. The space program has been discontinued now. Apparently there are other priorities.

My favourite dead country was Latvia. I almost had a complete set of Latvian stamps. The first issued were just after the First World War and because of a paper shortage were printed on the back of old German Army field maps. I collected as many as possible of the 5 Kapeika values and would turn them over and try to find matching bits of the map. It felt as though I was reconstructing the landscape of this forgotten country.

The last issues were overprints of Russian stamps from just after the Soviet invasion of 1940.

Every Saturday I would go to the dealers in Peckham and see what I could afford out of my pocket money. Eric would be there sometimes, his mum hovering in a corner since she wouldn't let him come on his own.

When I hadn't seen him for a while I went over to his house. He was getting more and more obsessed with Quassia.

Antiquities of Southern Quassia showing the Mausoleum of the Kings.

Famous writers of Quassia.

Butterflies.

Birds.

I looked up Quassia in the encyclopaedia at school. Nothing. I checked the big atlas with a magnifying glass looking for it tucked away in some intersection of borders near Czechoslovakia, Hungary, Yugoslavia, East Germany. Then I checked South America thinking it might be near one of those countries I could never place in my mind: Paraguay, Ecuador.

I realised it must be a dead country and maybe I would have got into it if I'd carried on with stamp collecting but I was growing up, getting other interests.

14

Dear Francis,

The achievements of Quassian engineering are really something that must be seen to be believed. Elena our guide, a beautiful young woman, is so full of enthusiasm it is contagious. Today the tour party walked for miles along the top of the Albertine Dam which provides electricity for most of the capital. It is so tall that the mighty river below looks like little more than a stream.

The dam will be mothballed soon because, as Elena explained, hydroelectric power is now obsolete. They are very big on the environment here and everyone is full of hope for the future.

By the time I was fifteen I was taking the weekend's first speed at about seven o'clock on a Friday evening. There was a whole scene. We'd listen to Horizon radio for the jazz-funk then head somewhere local or up west to the Empire or the Lyceum. The river boat discos were the best. The boat would go up and down the Thames and we'd all be dancing, while the reflections of the law courts and ministries would dance with us on the water. There was nothing better than going past the Houses of Parliament and doing a line of speed as a salute to the powers that be.

One day I went over to Eric's.

"Still into stamps?" I teased.

"Not just stamps, Francis," he was straight faced. "I've been collecting photographs and books. I even get the Quassian newspaper delivered. The language isn't difficult once you've mastered the letters."

A few weeks later I took my stamp collection into the dealers. He'd always been friendly when I'd come in as a kid. I wanted money because there was an all-nighter coming up and I needed a ticket and some of this wicked sulphate that was going round.

When he finally handed over the cash it was much less than I thought the whole of Latvia was worth but I just pocketed it.

Then I blurted out: "You have anything from Quassia?"

He didn't do more than glance up from my album which he was mentally splitting into different lots.

"You've got your money, son," he said, "now get out."

Dear Francis,

Elena has taken me to meet her parents. It is wonderful here in the southern province where the farmlands are broken by dense forests and the legends of wolf-men and witches live on as ironic fairy tales. Elena and I go for long walks there; in the dark caves of leaves it feels like we are entering another world. I think I am falling in love.

Sometimes I would go round to Eric's house just because I had nowhere else to go now. He had stayed on at school, still taken there every day by his mum. I was on the dole.

"Look at this, Francis," he would say and show me album after album.

Wild Flowers of Quassia.

Ancient Churches of Quassia.

Notable Kite Makers of Quassia.

"Where do you get all this stuff?"

"I have pen-friends."

I had to remind myself that there was no Quassia. That Eric was probably making all this with stencils and Letraset.

Dear Francis,

Elena assures me that after our marriage applying for citizenship will be a formality. I know now that my decision to stay here is the right one. There is optimism about this country that is completely lacking in our own.

Young people, far from being the cynical pariahs we know, feel they are part of a great collective project. While in England there is only unemployment or a humdrum job, here there is hope and optimism.

I was living in a squat in one of the big estates up near the Elephant and Castle. It wasn't far from the terraced streets where I'd grown up but felt nothing like those.

The people there believed in a world without property or money. It was a statement to them to live like this. They were all poets or musicians or artists or revolutionaries. I didn't understand what they were talking about a lot of the time but they had electric guitars and basses. When the music throbbed through me I knew I was free.

If I went back home for the occasional Sunday roast I'd usually have to smoke a couple of joints and down a brew just to be able to handle my mum and dad.

"How's Eric?"

"Got a place at university but never went," my mum said and touched her head.

"Another bloody waster," said my dad.

Dear Francis,

For our honeymoon, we visited the eastern lakes and the ancient monuments on the shores around them. I saw the ruins that I once glimpsed on postage stamps so long ago. The Mausoleum of the Kings is built almost to a different scale to a normal building, as though made for a race of giants.

I wandered through it hand in hand with my beautiful new wife and pondered the decay of civilisations. Elena gently chided me about this melancholy. Civilisations decline because they neglect their most important resource: the well-being of the people.

This evening we dined in the hotel restaurant, simple and appetising fare. We looked out over the ruins and as the sun set they became only shadows without power, without threat.

I did horse for a while. We liked to call it horse in our crowd, we were romantics. I didn't have the balls for hard-core addiction so I settled for booze and pills and fags. Very mundane but still cost a bit. Then I was caught in HMV pushing CDs down the front of my trousers. It's a wonderful thing progress; I'd never have got a vinyl album down there.

I wasn't banged up because my mum and dad agreed to have me back which was good of them considering I was a right cunt.

There was nothing to do now, round where I'd grown up. I used to sit at my bedroom window smoking. Sometimes I'd see Eric's silhouette at his own window. One day I went over and knocked.

Eric's mum answered.

"Oh Francis," she was so glad to see me, a novel experience in those days, "won't Eric be delighted."

I went up to his room. He had a computer now and sat staring into the black screen with its green letters. His hair hung down in clumps to his shoulders and he had a ginger Jesus beard. He was in a dressing gown and the room smelt vaguely of disinfectant, semen and damp.

"Hello Francis," he said as if he'd only seen me the day before, "I'm just FTPing some documents from the mainframe of Quassia University."

"Still into all that?"

I looked around the room. Apart from the bed, every surface was covered with books, notepads, stamp-albums and those long trains of perforated paper from the computer's printer. There were drawings and hand-drawn maps pinned to the walls.

"I'm studying the technological innovations that are going on there. I've become quite an expert. There aren't many in the field."

"I'll bet."

The door bumped open and Eric's mum stood there with a tray with a jug of orange squash and two beakers. There was a little plate with biscuits arranged around it in a circle.

"What do you want?" Eric said.

"I just... I just..." she stammered and entered the room. She looked around for a place to put the tray and hesitated for a moment over the bed, then just stood there till I got up and took it from her.

"Thank you, Francis," she said.

I thought she would go then. Eric was glaring at her but she just stood there.

"I was wondering," she said at last, "why you two boys don't go out, for a walk or something."

Eric had turned back to his computer and was tapping away.

"Yeah," I said, "we could go down the pub." I reckoned she would bung us a few quid.

"Oh I'm allowed to go out without my mum am I now?" Eric said without turning. "And Francis, I don't go to pubs. I don't want to end up being a degenerate like you. Then I'd never get into Quassia."

Dear Francis,

It is with reluctance that we have left the East and our honeymoon. We took the high-speed maglev back to the capital where I am to take up my post at the university this autumn. Elena wants to make sure the apartment is comfortable for us before I start work.

They held up my dole money on some technicality so I started taking the odd fiver from my mum's purse and the Toby jug at the back of the food cupboard where they kept the emergency money.

When they kicked me out I managed to take my mum's charm bracelet and the watch my granddad had left my dad; it would have been mine one day anyway.

Some part of me knew I was breaking their hearts but mostly I just wanted a drink.

As I walked out the door I saw Eric up at his window. He waved at me.

"Prick," I said waving back.

Dear Francis,

I'm sorry it's been so long since I've written. The work at the university has kept me busy and the arrival of my twin sons has occupied all my spare time.

The project I have been involved in has borne great results. An artificial forest now covers most of the capital and my designs for energy capturing leaves have won for me great respect in society; not that there is the accompanying celebrity and excessive wealth that I hear is now such an affliction in Europe and North America.

What is most important is that we have been able to harness the energy of the sun and provide clean and almost limitless power. The trees themselves are, if I say so myself, very beautiful, like great sculptures of quartz and silver forming a canopy over our heads.

Without the need to pay excessive costs for power the price of most goods in Quassia has fallen to a level where no-one needs live in scarcity. Work can be directed toward useful social projects rather than just meeting basic needs.

There were a few rough years. I was never entirely on the streets, not for more than a few days anyway. Mostly I was in squats but the people were different now, harder; everything was done because they had to do it. There were no dreams about a better world.

The laws must have changed because we were getting thrown out more often.

I was in a house up near Waterloo. The streets were Victorian terraces being renovated by people who had somehow made shed-loads in shares and privatisation.

There were two other people in the house: a bloke and some girl. They used to moan about me using their food. They put food colouring in the milk to make it look like blood; as if that would stop me.

One night the landlord's two heavies smashed in the front door and starting chucking our stuff out the window into the rain. The other people in the squat, the bloke and the girl, seemed to have somewhere they could go. As they walked away from me, it was turning dark and the rain was getting heavier. I realised I hardly knew them at all. I got lost wandering those costume drama set streets until I found one of those upmarket off-licenses that sell mostly wine. I treated myself to a bottle of vodka and some cider.

When I found a shop doorway, I huddled down just in the shadow out of the yellow glare of the street light. I looked into the shop window through the diamond security mesh and realised it was a stamp dealer. It was the first time I'd seen one in years. There was something reassuring about the card mounts with their stamps. I saw some Latvian ones and was suddenly confused. There were the ones with the little bits of maps on the back; there were others that I recognised. But then there were a whole load that were new to me and I'd known every Latvian stamp there was. I started to laugh. They'd resurrected Latvia, hadn't they? I'd heard something about it somewhere.

Then I saw it. Picked out by the yellow light was a single stamp on a card mount of its own. It had a hand-written label saying "Very Rare £50". It showed the silhouette of a city with elegant towers. It bore the unmistakable name: Quassia.

Dear Francis,

You really must visit us sometime. The capital is more magnificent than ever. The artificial forest is now complemented by a real forest. These trees are able to absorb excessive carbon and other greenhouse gases and turn them into a hard but malleable wood that forms our main building material. The city is becoming a new Eden but one in which the inhabitants have already rejected temptation.

My mum and dad's house was dark but I wasn't interested in that right now. Eric's bedroom light was on, and from the street I could see the flicker of a computer screen.

I found a pebble in his front yard and threw it up. My aim was pretty good given how much I'd had to drink. Eric opened the window and stuck his head out. He was so hairy he looked like Captain Caveman.

"Oh it's you, Francis," he said, "you'd better come up."

A downstairs light came on and then Eric led me in. As I stumbled along the corridor his mum appeared in the kitchen door; I wondered where the tray with the orange squash was.

Eric had a different computer now. The screen was full of colour and there were images of forests and animals and crowds of people. He went over to it and clicked something and the screen changed to black with a swirling pattern. I stared at it and followed the movements for a moment.

"I've seen something," I said.

"What have you seen, Francis?"

And what was it? Through the wire mesh, through the glass in a display lit only by sickly yellow light. It danced in my head, one inch by half an inch, the silhouette of a city.

"I've seen Quassia."

He made me explain.

I begged for booze, anything, and he brought a bottle of sherry that had never been opened. He made me say everything again even as I grew even drunker propped up against the headboard of his bed.

The last thing I remember was his urgent hissing.

Are you sure? Are you sure?

Dear Francis,

It is all arranged. Your entry visa and papers have been organised and there is an open ticket for transit available that you can activate for the date that suits you best.

You can live in Quassia as you like and you will want for nothing. You could even decide to do nothing but I'm sure at some point you'll want to get involved in one of the projects. The field trips into the new forests are very rewarding. You get to catalogue the species that are evolving there. It's a bit like stamp collecting really, only much more rewarding.

So when you are ready I'll be waiting. Just find your way to the consulate and the rest is easy.

My head was run through with waves of pain and each wave frothed with nausea. I'd wet myself.

I'd had plenty of mornings like this.

A man stood over me. He was about my age with closely cropped hair and clean shaven. Even through the stench of my own piss he smelt fresh and perfumed. He was carrying a small leather valise. It was some moments before I realised.

"Eric?"

"There's a glass of water there," he pointed to the bedside table.

I tried to sit up and just about managed it.

"What's going on?"

"I hope you feel better soon. I've got to be going now."

I managed to get out of bed and followed him out of the bedroom. I reached the top of the stairs as he reached the bottom.

"Eric," I said, "where are you going?"

Then his mum appeared and silently, without fuss, she helped him get into a long woollen coat.

Eric kissed her on the forehead and looked up at me.

"I'll write," he said.

Then he was gone and his mother was already coming up the stairs, tears in her eyes.

"You can borrow some of Eric's clothes," she said as she hustled me back into the bedroom.

"Sure," I said, "yeah. I should be getting over the road, make my peace."

"What do you mean?"

"My mum and dad."

Her face went pale and she made me sit on the bed while she sat next to me. They were dead of course: Dad going quickly after Mum a couple of years before. No-one had known where I was.

"You have a bath and get changed, and I'll make a nice cup of tea. You can stay here for a bit."

I had nowhere to go. I looked around the room, at the piles of typescripts, at the hand-drawn maps pinned above the desk, at the bookshelf full of stamp-albums and scrap books. It was all here. And one day Eric would write.

A Faraway City

by Joel Lane

It wasn't just a bad dream. Kathy was used to those. They had their own shut-in logic of failure and humiliation. Getting arrested while on holiday with Steve, for a long-past crime that she'd forgotten. Being trapped in the office lift all night long and found by her colleagues in the morning. Needing to pee on a Tube train that was stuck in a tunnel. Cooking a whole salmon for a dinner-party and finding its interior was swollen with black fungus. Those were bad dreams. This was something different. Something that woke her up three times, sweating, her eyelids sticky with tears. The third time, she had to run to the bathroom and vomit.

Steve was deep in the cocoon of his own profound sleep, a low-key snore distorting his breath. She badly needed some normality, but she didn't wake him up. Sounds and images played over and over in her head. *A fist smashing into her eye. A man's face, twisted with rage. A black van full of silent women. Blood in a toilet pan. A gaunt, unpainted tower block. Pockmarked walls. A hand slapping her mouth, loosening some teeth. Three naked men waiting for her to suck them.* And the words, hissed or shouted in her ear. She didn't know the language, but she understood what they were telling her. *You're a whore. You've got it coming, bitch. You're dead. Shut the fuck up. Die.*

It wasn't just a bad dream. It was *someone else's* bad dream. This wasn't her life given a degrading twist. It was someone else trapped in a place where the worst kind of degradation was normal. There was no waking up. But she was awake – at least, she hoped she was. The alarm clock said it was ten minutes to six. Kathy had a three-hour meeting today to plan the new marketing campaign. Lack of sleep was not appropriate. But she lay awake, trembling, until the alarm went off.

Steve wasn't his real name. He'd told her before they were married. "I need a modern name. A smooth name, with no crap hanging off it. Gerard Temple isn't me. Took me thirty years to realise, but I'm not that. I can tell you what Steve Temple is doing, where he's going, what he brings in. It's the name of a player."

They'd been together for six years. Neither of them was keen to have children. They'd both worked their way up in the soft furnishings industry, late career developers, just starting to make it at the time when the former bright young things were looking to factor in babies and work-life balance. Their elegant Chelsea home required them both to be not just earning, but winning.

Not wanting to start a family didn't mean they weren't passionate. One of Kathy's worries, after eight or nine of the alien nightmares, was that the abuse she was dreaming would somehow make her damaged goods. There was desire in her normal dreams, but it wasn't consummated. Would Steve know she'd been raped in her recent dreams? If so, was it her fault? That wasn't a simple question. It wasn't like she'd been raped in real life. Even though, night after night, she was running to the bathroom to vomit. Feeling the after-effects of an unreal violation.

The nightmares came every week. Usually after Steve had been away on a sales trip. Oddly, Kathy didn't dream in his absence. As soon as he was curled up beside her, snoring gently, his sperm delivered between her thighs, the terror came. The battered, cheaply-made blocks. The vans and lorries that took frightened women through cities choked with traffic. The dark-haired men who used her viciously, or at best while locked into a bad dream of their own. Was this Eastern Europe? It wasn't anywhere she knew. And the language of what the men said to her peeled away from its meaning like a used condom.

The nightmares were a feathered cry from some part of herself she didn't recognise, now or in the past. Kathy was still wondering how to tell Steve about them when she found his notebook.

They'd been to visit friends, the night before, and Steve had drunk a little more wine than was good for him. First the clumsy innuendoes and the rants against "health and safety fascists", then the flushed face and the dry-heaving in the street. Kathy had helped him undress, though she'd drawn the line at his drowsy attempt to make love. "The drink talking is bad enough," she'd told him. To make it worse, she'd been quite in the mood – but not for his boozy groping and slobbering.

In the morning, he'd left early to get to a meeting in Richmond. Hung over more by lack of sleep than by alcohol, Kathy had chosen to work from home. And just as she couldn't start work in the morning without tidying her desk, she couldn't switch on her laptop until the house was in some kind of order. On the bedroom floor, she'd noticed a tiny key that Steve must have dropped when changing his trousers. The key to his laptop? If so, he'd surely come back. She took the key into Steve's cluttered study. Then she saw the tiny locked drawer on the right-hand side of the desk.

The notebook was slim, bound in calf leather, with white unruled pages. It was three-quarters full of notes in Steve's tiny print. His pen had scored deep into the paper. Each page was headlined with a name. *Emma, Tina, Sarah, Linda.* The most English of names, bland as afternoon tea. Under each name was a detailed account of how he had visited each woman, given her money and had sex with her. More often than not, extra services had been required. Every time, he'd noted the girl's country of origin: *Russian, Czech, Romanian, Polish.* Their names weren't real any more than his name was. Any more than his marriage was.

The descriptions stuck in her mind: a mixture of boyish excitement and cool, businesslike acronyms. 'VFM' was familiar from the office, of course; but if 'CIM' didn't mean the Chartered Institute of Marketing (and it probably didn't), what did it mean? When she realised, she had to drop the book and run once more to the bathroom to be sick. When she came back, she went on reading. The firm spikes and curves of his writing took on a sexual meaning to her. All of it hard and intense, none of it joined up.

There was a date at the end of each narrative – the last nine were this year. And it was only March. Some of the dates coincided with Steve's business trips, but some were just normal working days. Ones when he'd stayed late or driven out to a meeting. After each date was an initial or pair of initials: *MM, K, RX.* The names of brothels? There were no details of locations. The encounters could have happened in office cubicles.

Kathy locked the desk drawer, but kept the notebook. She poured herself a glass of brandy and drank it in two gulps. Switched on her laptop, but couldn't focus on the screen. Washed her glass in the sink, accidentally broke it against the tap, cut the tip of her finger, held it under cold water until her hand was white. Began to scream, but stopped when she heard herself. Sat down and cried, then stopped crying. Waited. Afraid to go to sleep in case another dream broke in.

Steve came back late, in a foul mood. He slammed the door and announced to Kathy: "You wouldn't believe what happened this afternoon. Three hours pissed up the wall because some interfering Government inspector decided to waste our time. If I run into him on a dark night, he'd better watch his own fucking health and safety, that's all." He took off his jacket, gave Kathy a swift kiss and shot her one of his practised I-feel-your-pain looks. "How was your day, love?"

Kathy handed him the notebook. "You'd better take this. Record your after-work adventures before you forget the details."

"Where did you get this?" Steve rubbed the leather binding with his fingertips as if he'd never touched it before.

"You dropped the key."

Steve looked up, dismay written across his broad face. "I thought we both believed in personal privacy. Now you raid my desk like some official from the local council, or some child who can't keep her hand out of other people's–"

"It's where you've put *your* hand that bothers me," Kathy shouted. "And where you've put something else. It's all there. You *bastard*." Her voice broke. She turned away, putting a hand to her mouth. The light in the room seemed to waver; darkness pressed in from outside, flooding the house.

Steve moved behind her and gripped her arms, very gently, like the brother she'd lost in her teens. "Darling, I never did any of those things. I've been writing porn for a webzine. It's a shameful hobby, and I didn't have the courage to tell you, but that's all it is. Just a part of my imagination that's still sixteen. I've never paid for sex. Why should I have to?" He kissed her cheek. "Can you forgive me?"

"Why are you obsessed with Eastern European girls?" she asked, still looking away from him. Her own voice sounded to her like a ghost.

"The man in the stories is a character, not me. He's a wanderer. I'm not. I know where I belong. And besides, you know how I feel about immigrants. Do you really think I'm capable of that?"

Kathy didn't answer, and he seemed to take that as a sign of acceptance. He poured them both a glass of wine, and they had a fairly normal evening. The darkness stayed outside the walls. She caught up with some of the work she'd left undone in the day, and he finished the wine while watching a DVD. They went to bed a little earlier than usual, and Steve was unusually tender with her. Kathy wondered if he was thinking about his English-named girls, real or imagined. She tried not to, but the dreams were harder to forget than the notebook. At the climax, her voice was shadowed by a hidden cry of fear.

The unreality was growing. Shopping for lunch at Waitrose, Kathy felt trapped in a model village: organic vegetables and raw seafood declaring a rural identity the shoppers would never touch. For a while she had no idea how to get out: the roads all ended in walls. Drinking with a few colleagues in a bar on the Embankment after work, she experienced a partial loss of sight. Her glass, the optics and the windows were filled with unreflecting darkness. She got her assistant to drive her home.

That night, the worst dream yet. She woke drenched with sweat, feeling a sick headache start even as the pain of the raw dream-injuries faded. A dull ache in the pit of her stomach told her she'd come on a few days early. Chaotic images pressed behind her eyes: a private party where she was viciously beaten by three other girls, one of them using a broken bottle to draw the letter S on her back. A dozen or so men in business suits, watching.

And then she was in a clinic, giving birth to the child of a nameless man. Passing out from loss of blood, coming round to find the baby had been taken away. They'd only let her have it because of the money she could bring in when pregnant. Holding onto the grief, because at least that was human.

Steve was fast asleep. It was an hour before dawn. Kathy slipped out of the bed and walked unsteadily to the bathroom, where she pulled off her sweat-soaked nightdress and washed herself until she recognised her own body. She felt weak, drained of hope and purpose. Was that how it felt when your dreams were replaced with someone else's memories? The prospect of a day at work, or even at home, seemed unreal to her.

She couldn't face either dressing or getting back into bed. Instead, she slipped into the fluffy white dressing-gown she'd bought herself years ago, and went through to her own cubicle-sized study. If she could find Steve's online erotic fantasies, that would help put her mind at rest. Maybe it would all be resolved by the time he woke up. Google searches for *Eastern European girls* and a few other strategic keywords revealed no pornographic writings, though it did bring up a few London massage parlours. That made her stop and think, her back aching from the hard chair, before refocusing her search.

On a website dedicated to customer reviews of prostitutes, she found a database whose subject fields included 'name of girl', 'location' and 'reviewer'. Kathy was impressed by the site's IT infrastructure, but that wasn't foremost in her mind. It took her less than ten minutes to find a chain of reviews, by someone called 'the wanderer', of encounters with Russian, Czech, Polish and Romanian girls who had names like Jane, Kate and Lucy – scattered over the UK, but mostly in South London. She read nine of them. They were already familiar to her.

By the time Steve woke up, Kathy was already dressed and getting ready for work. She kissed him, put a mug of coffee on the sideboard for him, said nothing about the website. It had only confirmed what she'd known since finding his notebook. He wasn't real any more. What was, she still had to find out.

The parlour was in Croydon. When Kathy had phoned, the receptionist – a young woman with a marked, possibly deliberate South London accent – had said "It'll cost extra." She'd asked for Susan. That was the last of the wanderer's reviews. The last entry in the notebook.

"That'll be fine," the voice had said, then paused. "Tell you what, darling. You don't want to come here. There's a hotel up the road, we can book a room for you. Just go in half an hour before your appointment time, pay for the room, go up there and call us. We'll sort out the rest."

It was a Friday afternoon. For all Steve knew, she was at work. The hotel, not surprisingly, was a fleapit that probably made most of its cash from hourly bookings. She checked in under her maiden name. The room, on the third floor, had grey flocked wallpaper and a brass dado rail that ended at the black-painted partition wall. At least the single bed had a fresh duvet cover.

Kathy had read in a newspaper that three-quarters of prostitutes in the UK had been trafficked. Many of the rest had come from overseas of their own accord. What were they running from? Not communism, not any more. She recalled one of Steve's wine-fuelled monologues over the table: "The laws of the economy can't be changed. What we have to do is guarantee individual freedom." But he didn't want them coming here. Or did he? Kathy stared out of the window at the broken skyline. Trying to abort the images that flooded behind her eyes. Nothing felt real. The girl she was waiting for would take her back into an unknown city. She was caught between worlds.

There was a quiet knock at the door. Kathy let in a short, dark-haired girl in a long fabric coat. "Hello, I'm Susan." Under the make-up, her face was as blank as an Expressionist sketch: a ghost of the living. She unbuttoned the coat to reveal a black slip and mini-skirt, then asked for the money. Kathy paid her. "What do you want?" the girl asked.

"Sit here and I'll tell you." She pointed to the bed. With the self-possession of a wounded cat, the girl perched on the blue duvet and waited. Kathy sat beside her and pressed a hand to her back, just above the shoulder. The scar was there, as she'd known it would be. She remembered the words in Steve's notebook: *Central European, from one of those old countries that surfaced after liberation.*

Kathy's fingers brushed the girl's cheek. Felt her sudden tension. "I want you to give me my dreams back," she said.

Susan looked at her with eyes that were broken windows. "Do dreams belong to anyone?"

"They do. And so do memories."

"I can't help you." The girl drew away from Kathy's embrace. "Don't know anything. There's not just you. Not just me. Everything…" She was crying. "Fuck this. Fuck. Fuck." Her thin hands gripped her face.

Kathy turned, feeling as if a breeze might tear her in half, and hugged the girl awkwardly. Susan muttered, "Do what you want."

"Tell me something," Kathy said. "What's your real name?"

There was maybe a minute's silence before the girl wiped her eyes and said: "I don't know. Maybe I never had one."

The airport was a model city with its own shops and bars and cafés, its own buses carrying people from one crowded place to another. Except that no-one lived here. The traveller waiting to check in glanced at her passport, as if trying to memorise her own name. The photograph didn't look much like her. She'd packed overnight, while Steve was away on a business trip, taking only her everyday clothes and a few necessities. How long would it take him to realise she wasn't coming back?

It was nearly four a.m. The airport windows were painted with darkness. The people around her had the window-dummy faces of the unslept. She didn't want to sleep again, though obviously she'd have to. The queue brought her to the check-in point and she handed over her suitcases. They felt as light as her passport.

On the way to customs, she saw a group of young men and women with narrow faces and dark eyes, tired but restless, heading for the exit. They were huddled together, but not speaking or looking at each other. None of them was holding a cigarette, but a whitish mist was drifting from their mouths and nostrils.

She walked on to the restless queue at the checkpoint. Businessmen heading for conferences. Wealthy couples going on holiday. The man in front of her was sharing his impatience with a flattened phone. "Airports are a living hell," he said. She laughed. Had these people ever been her kind?

Soon the narrow plane was drifting in a pure white city of clouds. Was it only the view that made her feel cold? She wondered briefly how Steve was taking advantage of his trip, whether he was visiting someone from the city she was flying to. But he didn't seem real to her now. It wasn't what he'd done that had made her take this flight. It was the girls with their English names, their violent dreams, the ruined but populated city they had flown out of.

Eventually, the traveller slept. And woke sweating, confused and sick, not knowing what she'd dreamed. A man with stubble on his narrow face. A black powder burning on crumpled foil, its cold smoke bringing her into a place of stillness, a sleep within sleep, a place where nothing could hurt her. Not even the bleeding she could feel inside. Her eyes opened and she saw the interior of the plane, but now it seemed ancient and frozen like an underground cave.

He was waiting at the airport, on his own. They sat in the bar and drank black coffee. The need was hollowing out her bones. Her face was a mask of sweat. The coffee burned her mouth, but she hardly felt it. "I'll call you Katrina," he said. "Because you'll make a flood." She nodded, barely listening. *How long?*

"You're older than most of the girls," he was saying. "That means you have to do something none of them will do. It's very easy. I'll provide the men. All you have to do is be dead for them." He looked at her in the way someone had a lifetime ago when he wanted her to know he was sincere. She smiled.

"I'll give you something to knock you out. You won't feel a thing. You'll be away in dreamland. Wake up a bit torn, but what's new?"

"Can I have some now?" she asked.

His face hardened. "Not here, it's too obvious. Soon. My flat's only a few miles away. Maybe we can have a rehearsal. I could do with some relaxation, Katrina. It's been a long day."

He took her arm and guided her calmly, almost tenderly, towards the concrete tunnel where the taxis waited. As she perched on the hard seat and the cab jerked forward into streets that looked unfinished in the frail sodium light, a nest of concrete fragments on a mountainside in an endless night, she had a brief sensation of another life slipping beyond her reach. A life that she'd missed. But anyone would feel the same. And it meant nothing: she couldn't break free.

Not on her own.

The Way the World Works

by Ian Sales

They flew him from Guam to the USS *Moosbrugger* in a Sikorsky SH-3 Sea King. The helicopter beat across the South Pacific, chasing its shadow across a sea of shattered sunlight. Inside the Sea King, Cavendish marvelled at the US Navy's haste. Two days ago, he'd been busy at his research in Cambridge, Massachusetts. Then a Navy lieutenant from the Pentagon had invaded his lab and commandeered him for... *this*. Cavendish initially refused, of course; but the Navy officer dropped dark hints about his funding being withdrawn. "It was 1984 last year," Cavendish snapped, "and Big Brother doesn't exist."

The naval officer was unrepentant. "You know the way the world works," he said.

Cavendish accepted defeat. He was also intrigued: what could the US Navy want with a plasma physicist? His research could never be weaponised, he was certain of that.

The USS *Moosbrugger* was one of three ships anchored in the middle of the ocean. As soon as the helicopter's wheels touched the destroyer's heli-pad, a sailor in a bright-orange vest rushed forward and dragged open the aircraft's door. Cavendish was bundled out and, deafened by the helicopter's turbines and battered by the downdraft from the rotor, followed the man into the ship's superstructure. An officer met him and led him along narrow grey gangways and down steep grey stairs into a cramped wardroom.

They told him nothing, were implacably polite as they plied him with coffee, but they proffered no explanations.

He'd thought days like this were long behind him. As a young USMC officer during his tour in Vietnam, he'd spent time aboard warships, sitting in compartments with no idea of what was going on, what was expected of him. He'd been young then, he'd trusted the military, content to wait for enlightenment. Now, a decade older and, he hoped, wiser, he found the lack of information frightening.

Later, they allowed Cavendish up on the deck. The sun beat down on the placid water, making a shifting carpet of light of the gelid waves. Several hundred feet away, a blocky ship with a white hull and superstructure kept station. On her bow were painted the letters "NOAA". Cavendish read the name painted near her stern, *Nekton*.

Now he knew where he was: Challenger Deep.

Thirty-six thousand feet below him lay the deepest part of the Pacific Ocean. There were men living down there, down in the black abyss, where no light reached and the pressure was seven tons per square inch. Challenger Base was not a secret – and for good reason: it was another propaganda victory in the Cold War with the Soviets, as impressive an achievement as the US base on the Moon.

Twenty-five years ago, two men, Lieutenant Don Walsh, USN, and Jacques Piccard, had visited the sea-floor here in a submersible called the *Trieste*. Their descent had remained a unique achievement until they'd built Challenger Base two years ago and sunk it at this spot. Six men lived and worked in the base. They were drilling holes in the ocean floor with the intention of burying nuclear waste there. Challenger Deep's floor was a subduction plate, so the radioactive waste would be slowly pulled into the planet's mantle and rendered safe

But what could be down there on the sea-floor that would require a plasma physicist? Cavendish knew nothing about the ocean depths.

"Sir?"

He turned about to find a naval officer gazing expressionlessly at him. "If you would follow me, sir?" the officer said.

He led Cavendish back into ship. They dressed him in a thick jumper and a parka, although the day was hot and bright. When they took him back up on deck, a small submarine had appeared in the water between the USS *Moosbrugger* and the NOAAS *Nekton*. It was yellow, and painted with thin and widely-spaced vertical red stripes. Cavendish was put in mind of the Beatles' film, although there was nothing cartoonish about the vessel. It had a narrow conning tower, was festooned on its upper surface with pipes and equipment, and floated low in the water.

"You're taking me down to Challenger Base, aren't you?" Cavendish asked his escort.

"Yes, sir."

"Why am I on this ship? Why not on the support ship?"

"The *Nekton* is in protective custody, sir. No one is permitted to board or disembark."

Clearly something important had happened below. And unusual – so unusual the Navy had locked up the base's crew and now required a plasma physicist. Or perhaps, it occurred to Cavendish, they needed only a physicist with technical diving experience, who was a certified aquanaut.

A swaying staircase led down the destroyer's side to the sea-surface, and at its foot Cavendish scrambled into a Zodiac inflatable boat. The Zodiac carried him across to the submarine – no, *submersible*, bouncing through the low swell, the roar of its outboard loud beneath the Pacific sun. He hung onto a rope, and sweated inside his parka. A naval officer, not the one he'd spoken to, sat opposite him, eyes hidden behind mirror shades.

When they reached the submersible, Cavendish clambered, with assistance, from the boat onto its hull. The submersible wallowed sickeningly, though the sea was flat. His arm gripped hard by a sailor, Cavendish was led to the conning-tower. It was no larger than a telephone-box and open to the front. A hatch gaped open in its floor.

"Down there?" asked Cavendish, looking down into a narrow tube with a ladder bolted to its wall. It resembled a sewer pipe, dank and filled with an aqueous blue light.

"Lieutenant Wallace is waiting below, sir," the sailor replied.

This uniform courtesy... Cavendish felt as though he were being led to the gallows.

He lowered himself through the hatch and descended the ladder. At its foot, some fifteen feet below the conning-tower, was a large window and another hatch. He looked through the window, and saw the underside of the submarine's hull, mysterious blurred shapes in the Pacific water. Opposite the window, the hatch was set in the side of a metal sphere, and was as thick as a bank-vault door. It seemed to be made of a single block of machined Plexiglass, rimmed with steel.

Cavendish slid through the open hatch. He found himself in a spherical chamber about six feet in diameter, standing on a flat floor some three feet square. To one side was a rack of batteries, oxygen bottles, and CO_2 filters; to the other, a series of panels bearing gauges and switches. In front of him, on the lower curve of the sphere, was a tiny circular window, before which a man in a Navy uniform, a parka across his knees, perched on a stool.

Cavendish gave a polite cough. "You must be Lieutenant Wallace."

The man looked back over his shoulder. "Better get settled, sir," he said. "They need to close the hatch in a minute."

There was a second stool behind Wallace. Cavendish sat on it.

The hatch swung shut behind him.

For over three hours, the bathyscaphe sank through water which faded from opalescent blue to lightless black.

Cavendish asked if the submersible had a name, and was told by Wallace, "She's a bathyscaphe, sir; and she's called the *Challenger II*." Cavendish asked if there was a *Challenger I*.

"Lost with all hands about three months ago, sir."

"Oh. I'm sorry. What happened?"

"She imploded at twenty-seven thousand feet."

Cavendish, horrified by the fate of the bathyscaphe's sister-ship, did not reply. *Twenty-seven thousand feet*? It had been over a decade since he'd last performed any technical diving, but even then he'd not gone deeper than three hundred feet.

Wallace watched the instruments and occasionally reported up to the surface on his headset. Cavendish tried not to dwell on the weight of water outside, but he couldn't shake from his mind an image of the *Challenger I* imploding.

"How deep are we?" he asked.

"Twenty thousand feet, sir."

That was ten times deeper than even the most advanced hunter/ killer submarine could dive, US or Soviet.

"What's the pressure outside?"

"About four tons per square inch." Wallace glanced at him, and then added, "The walls of the gondola are six-inch thick steel, sir. They're rated for much higher pressures than we'll experience. And the *Challenger II*'s done this trip over a dozen times. You're perfectly safe, sir."

The naval officer's assurance did not much help. If the walls failed, they'd be crushed to paste in an instant. It didn't bear thinking about. Cavendish hunted for a new topic, something to take his mind off the outside pressure. Of course: the very reason why he was here, sitting inside this metal ball:

"Surely now you can tell me what I'm doing here?"

"Not until we're below, sir," Wallace replied.

"Who can I tell? There's only you here, and you already know."

Wallace would not be persuaded. "Orders, sir," he said stolidly, and turned back to peer out of the window.

The *Challenger II* slowed its descent as it neared the floor of the Mariana Trench. Cavendish dared not guess their depth, or the pressure outside. This was not the same as spending a night in an undersea habitat one hundred feet beneath the surface. He sat hunched on his stool, and shivered inside his parka. It was cold in the gondola. And no doubt much colder in the water. What manner of creature, he thought, lived down here? What manner of creature could not survive here and yet came all the same?

As they approached Challenger Base, Wallace allowed Cavendish to look through the forward window, but he could see only a vague spherical shape lurking in the blackness just beyond the reach of the arc-light. It was like looking into a thick, heavy night; but the base was no welcome shelter.

Such a strange and dangerous place to live, marvelled Cavendish, forgetting that an atmospheric pressure over a thousand times greater than that on the surface existed beyond the six-inch steel of the gondola. US astronauts had been living on the Moon for five years now, and Soviets cosmonauts had occupied space stations in orbit for almost a decade. But the floor of the Mariana Trench was a far more dangerous environment.

Wallace piloted the *Challenger II* across to the base and, after several minutes of jockeying about, the bathyscaphe's pressure sphere settled into the docking cup on the top of base's larger pressure sphere. A series of loud clangs rang out and the gondola shook and rocked. Cavendish, overcome with fright, put a hand up to the control panel by his shoulder and gripped its edge fiercely. It was only the gondola disengaging from the hull, explained Wallace. Next came a grinding noise, as if something were chewing its way through the six inches of steel. That was the ratchets pulling the sphere as tightly as possibly into the cup, forcing out the water.

Inside the gondola, each part of the docking procedure rang out loudly, as though the two of them were sitting on a production line in a busy factory. An insistent hissing was the docking tunnel laboriously screwing itself into place over the sphere's hatch. That took fifteen minutes. Then an explosive bang signalled that the first of the base's inner hatches had opened.

Eventually, Wallace received the all-clear, and set about undogging the sphere's hatch. Cavendish shivered in his parka and tried not to think about the tons of water pressing down on each square inch of the base. He was a physicist, he belonged in a lab. When he did dive now, it was recreational diving while on holiday in the Caribbean, a scuba tank strapped to his back as he swam along thirty feet below the bright sea-surface.

Wallace preceded him out of the gondola. When Cavendish climbed out, he found himself in a dank and foul-smelling steel tunnel, electric lights in cages just above his head. At the end of its ten-foot length was another bank-vault-thick hatch. This swung open as Wallace approached, revealing a man in a thick cable-knit sweater and a watchcap. He gave a piratical grin and said, "Welcome to the bottom of the Pacific."

Despite its name, Challenger Base was not actually sited in Challenger Deep. It sat on the floor of the Mariana Trench, some five hundred feet away. So it was not quite at the deepest part of the ocean, but there was only a few hundred feet in it.

To Cavendish, the interior of the base seemed more like a tramp steamer than a research station beneath the sea. The corridor walls were beaten metal and streaked with wear; the linoleum on the floor bore scuff marks. There was a peculiar smell, not very pleasant, but not caused by people. The artificial light shone oppressively, and the base rang with strange hollow clanks and thuds. Challenger Base's manager, the man in the watchcap, led Wallace and Cavendish down a steep staircase to the floor below, through a pair of flimsy doors and into an operations centre.

Two figures rose to their feet. They had been sitting on stools around a plotting table. One wore USN uniform; the other...

"Benson?" Cavendish stepped forward, astonished at the presence of an old friend. "What in hell are you doing here?"

Benson smiled in embarrassment. "Not hell, Alan. Just the abyss."

"The hadal zone, actually," said the operations manager. "We're below the abyssal zone."

Cavendish ignored the man. "You're not working on this nuclear waste project, are you?" he asked Benson. "The last I heard, you were at –"

"– Los Alamos. Yes, I'm still there. The Navy dragged me into this, just like they did you."

The Navy officer stepped forward. Judging by his gold shoulder boards and grey buzzcut hair, he was at the very least an admiral. "It was Dr Benson," he said, "who suggested we bring you here."

Cavendish turned to him. "Why? I don't see the relevance. We're at the bottom of the Pacific Ocean."

"You have experience of underwater habitats, Dr Cavendish–"

"That was nearly fifteen years ago," Cavendish protested. He and Benson had often dived together when they were both employed in California – Benson at JPL, and Cavendish at UCLA. But then Cavendish had been drafted, and after he'd returned from 'Nam he'd ended up on the East Coast.

"There are very few people researching physics we could bring down here at short notice, Dr Cavendish."

The operations centre was a cramped space, low-ceilinged and dominated by an upright perspex map of the surrounding region of floor of the Mariana Trench and Challenger Deep. To one side of the vertical screen, with its swooping contour lines, was a plotting table, the top of which was a more detailed geological map of the area. Along one wall sat three consoles, with small steering wheels, lots of gauges, and a black and white television screen each. For one brief moment, Cavendish wondered if Challenger Base were mobile, could move about on the sea-floor. The television screens were all lit. Two displayed a murky blackness, but one bore a pattern of light greys.

The operations manager stepped forward. "Redford," he introduced himself. "What do you know about the base?"

Cavendish shrugged. "The same as everyone."

"Right." Redford pulled his watchcap from his head and scrunched it between his hands. "Obviously, we can't go out there in suits – we'd get squashed flat in a heartbeat. So we use ROVs, remotely operated vehicles, to do the surveying." He indicated the consoles with the hand holding his cap. "We run 'em from there."

Benson and the two USN officers watched Redford, silent and alert.

"Notice anything odd?" Redford asked.

"No," replied Cavendish.

"The middle monitor?" prompted Redford.

"The picture is brighter. The ROV has its lights on?"

"No. The other two do, though."

Cavendish frowned. "I don't understand." He crossed to the middle console, bent forward and peered at the picture on the screen. He could make neither head nor tail of it. A series of grey shapes, a hint of texture. Was it a wreck? Had they had found a sunken ship?

Someone appeared at his shoulder. Benson. The Los Alamos scientist bent forward. "Imagine the picture standing on its side," he suggested.

Cavendish bent his head forty-five degrees, and peered at the screen. It was a moment before he made sense of what he was seeing. "Is that... a *tree*? And some *bushes*?"

He could see it clearly now. Foliage. In shades of grey, of course. But definitely vegetation. He straightened and turned about.

Benson had returned to the plotting table. Cavendish said, "I don't understand. One of your ROVs got lost and ended up on some Pacific island? So what?"

"The ROVs run on tethers," Redford said. "About three thousand feet long."

"So that's seaweed?"

"No, Dr Cavendish," said the admiral. "You were right first time. It's a tree and some bushes. In Challenger Deep."

"Impossible."

Benson shrugged. "But there it is."

Redford nodded. "Seven tons per square inch pressure, temperature about two degrees Centigrade... You damn well don't expect to find trees and flowers down here."

"They're underwater?"

"No, it's like a bubble of air –"

The admiral interrupted Benson. "This is why we need you, Dr Cavendish. Dr Benson has explained the nature of your research in plasma physics. You're trying to create force fields. We think that bubble out there is a force field."

"Force fields?" Cavendish gave Benson a disbelieving look. "I've been experimenting with plasma windows. They're not *force fields*... and I've only managed a window ten inches in diameter. Do you know how much power it took to generate that? Two hundred kilowatts! That's enough electricity to supply sixty homes."

"Could your 'plasma window' be used to create a bubble of air?" asked the admiral.

"Not at the bottom of the ocean. It has an operating temperature of fifteen thousand Kelvin!"

"So what is it, then?" demanded Redford.

Cavendish had to take this seriously – the US Navy would not have flown him to Guam, and brought him thirty-six thousand feet below the ocean surface for a joke. But... a *force field*? If someone had found a way to generate cold plasma, then perhaps it might be possible. Certainly, given sufficient power, a plasma window could hold back the phenomenal pressure in Challenger Deep.

"How did you find it?" he asked.

"Total accident," said Redford. "Just a routine survey. Didn't see anything weird, then the ROV kind of went through this barrier and fell to the ground. With *that* on the monitor."

"You can't bring it back?"

"No, the ROV's on dry land."

"You're absolutely certain?"

"We sent another one after it." He pointed at the left-most of the three consoles. "There: if you look closely, you can see the first ROV's tether just disappearing into a black wall."

"It can't be plasma, then," Cavendish told them. "Not if the ROV went through it."

They gathered around a table in the base's wardroom. This time, the coffee came with explanations. The naval officer introduced himself as Rear Admiral Wareham. Cavendish and Benson discussed the "bubble of air". Redford had mapped its boundaries, and it was apparently a mile square.

"What's inside the bubble?" asked Cavendish.

Redford shrugged. "Plants. As far as we can make out it's filled with trees and bushes."

"Like a desert island, but on the floor of the Pacific?"

Redford shrugged once again. "I guess."

"Could it be alien?" asked Benson.

"Little green men in flying saucers?" mocked Cavendish. "You work at Los Alamos: don't tell me you believe in all that UFO crap?"

Benson shrugged. "Hey, there's some weird shit in the labs. Who knows where it comes from?"

"Not aliens," Cavendish said flatly. "There are no aliens. We'd have found evidence of them by now." He frowned. "That's not the way the world works."

"Then what's that out there?" snapped Benson. "A bubble of air, thirty-six thousand feet underwater? How do you explain that?"

"I can't."

"Dr Cavendish," said Wareham, "I wouldn't be so quick to dismiss an extraterrestrial origin. There's nothing on this planet which could create that bubble, and no earthly reason for it to exist. It's not Soviet, you can take my word for that."

It couldn't possibly be natural. Nature was incapable of such feats. Cavendish was a man of science, he knew how the world worked. Bubbles of air in Challenger Deep did not conform to the rules and laws which governed the material universe.

But there *must* be a rational explanation.

"I need to see it," Cavendish said.

"See what? The force field?" asked Wareham.

Cavendish nodded. "We can theorise all we want sitting in here, but nothing we know will explain what you've found. I need to see it, maybe then I can get a better idea of what it might be."

"I can take him there in *Challenger II*, sir," put in Wallace.

"There's only room for two in the gondola," pointed out Redford.

Benson put up both hands. "Don't worry about me. I'm not claustrophobic, but spending five hours in that steel ball on the way down here scared the crap out of me. I'm happy to stay here." He lifted his mug of coffee and toasted Cavendish mockingly.

Cavendish and Wallace returned to the bathyscaphe's pressure sphere, and for twenty minutes waited impatiently for the laborious undocking to complete.

"Clear," Wallace said at last into his headset.

The mystery had driven out all thought of the crushing pressure, of the instant death held at bay by six inches of steel. Cavendish stood by the hatch and peered through the two and half inch diameter window in its centre. As the bathyscaphe lifted from Challenger Base, he saw the pale curved flank of the base's own huge pressure sphere. The inside had been cramped, and seeing the curvature now, he guessed the base was around thirty feet in diameter.

Wallace halted their ascent twenty feet above the base, directing the vessel's propellers upwards to hold them steady. The *Challenger II* was not really designed for forward travel, she was built to go up and down. Happily, there were no obstacles this deep in the ocean and, although Wallace's field of view through the tiny window was limited, he could see well enough to pilot the bathyscaphe.

According to Redford, the air bubble was located fifteen hundred feet from the base, on the floor of Challenger Deep. The manager had warned them to be careful, as the "force field" was almost invisible, and its contents could barely be seen from outside.

The bathyscaphe moved forward, following the sea bottom, an undulating pale desert with soft rounded hills which resembled a lunar landscape. Cavendish squatted beside Wallace's stool, the two of them taking it in turns to peer through the tiny window. Suddenly, the bottom dropped away, the grey giving way to black. The yellow of the arc-light dissipated in the darkness. Wallace glanced up at the fathometer by his left shoulder. Only when the trace on the screen was level, at the known depth of Challenger Deep's floor, did he release some of the gasoline used for buoyancy from the hull. *Challenger II* began to sink.

"She can go this deep, can't she?" asked Cavendish, thinking of the two hundred thousand tons of force pressing down on the gondola.

"Much deeper, sir. She's over-engineered to withstand much greater pressures."

It was scant comfort, but Cavendish put it out of mind and continued to look through the window. Something long and white snaked across his view.

"There!" he said. "The tether."

And now he could see a second umbilical. One of the tethers led to the ROV inside the bubble of air, and the other to the ROV floating outside the bubble.

Wallace was a careful and skilled submersible pilot. Cavendish, still at the window, gave directions until a strange blocky shape loomed out of the darkness into the cone of the arc-light. It was a cuboidal frame filled with machinery, on the sides of which were a pair of ducted propellers: the remotely operated vehicle.

"Where's the bubble?" asked Cavendish. "I don't see it."

Wallace brought *Challenger II* to a halt. Cavendish urged him to continue moving forward, but the lieutenant was reluctant to do so.

"Just a few feet," insisted Cavendish. "I can't see anything."

The *Challenger II* drifted forward very slowly for a handful of seconds, then came to a halt. "That's it," Cavendish said. Now he could see the second tether. It seemed to vanish in mid-air – mid-*water* – as if cut. It was not floating, but taut and angled downwards.

The submersible floated five feet above the ocean bottom, thirty feet from the point where the ROV's tether disappeared into nothing. Cavendish, kneeling on the floor of the pressure sphere, put one eye as close to the window as he could. All he could see was a wall of night-black water, through which he could make out a suggestion of vague shapes. The bubble certainly existed, he could not deny that; but he was no closer to unravelling the mystery of its construction. A force field? It *could* be... But not one created using plasma.

"We need to get closer," he said.

"Too dangerous, sir."

"I can't see anything from here. We need to get a bit nearer."

"No, sir."

"Swing us side-on," he suggested. "Move us that way."

"Too dangerous, sir."

"For God's sake, Wallace," Cavendish snapped. "I can't see anything! This damn window is too small, and the lights out there are pathetic."

"It's still too dangerous, sir," Wallace said flatly.

"Then I'll do it my-goddamned-self."

Cavendish reached for the joystick by his shoulder. He'd watched Wallace use it to control the bathyscaphe, he knew how it worked. He gave the joystick a gentle push to the left.

Wallace swore. He grabbed Cavendish's shoulder and hauled him backwards. Cavendish toppled from his knees, his hand smacking the joystick as he fell. His head smacked against an instrument panel. He let out a yelp of pain.

Challenger II lurched. Wallace swore again. The gondola swung about, throwing Cavendish against the oxygen bottles on the other side of the sphere. Something let out a loud bang.

Challenger II fell.

The bathyscaphe dropped and hit the ground. Wallace tumbled from his stool and landed on Cavendish. The sphere rolled ponderously onto its side. Cavendish could hear rushing water outside the gondola's hatch, and the sound of metal rending.

Wallace let out a series of oaths, loudly and at length. He scrambled to his feet, and stood, one foot on a canted instrumental panel, the other on the angled floor, and gazed down at Cavendish.

"You fucking moron," he said. "*Sir.*"

Cavendish managed to get to his feet. He had hurt his leg, but thankfully it was not broken. He held onto the battery rack and watched Wallace climb up to the hatch, which was now in an upper quadrant of the pressure sphere, and look through the window.

"The antechamber is dry," he said. "And I can see blue sky through the window at the back."

"*Blue sky?*"

It would be black, surely? Light could not reach this deep.

"And grass," added Wallace.

He began to unscrew the bolt holding the hatch locked.

Cavendish reached for him. "Should you be doing that?" he demanded. "We don't know if we can survive out there!"

The naval officer looked down at him. "We can't stay in here, and *Challenger II* is going nowhere," he replied. If he was angry, he no longer showed it.

"But the pressure might be the same as in the water," Cavendish protested.

Wallace returned to unscrewing the bolt on the hatch. "I don't think so. The grass doesn't look like there's a thousand atmospheres pressing on it." He shrugged. "Besides, what have we got to lose?"

He pushed on the hatch. It was spring-loaded to make it easy to open. Once it had swung out of the way, he pulled himself up into the opening, standing on the battery-rack and grunting as he hauled himself over the coaming and out of sight. Moments later, Cavendish heard him scramble up the access tube. A strong smell of gasoline drifted into the gondola.

The petrol fumes were beginning to choke, so Cavendish followed Wallace. The access tube led up from the antechamber at an angle of around twenty degrees. The hatch at the far end was open, and bright sunlight threw a golden circle across the top of the ladder. Using the rungs, Cavendish pulled himself up the tube.

Air redolent with sweet-smelling vegetation filled the conning-tower. Cavendish sniffed experimentally, then drew in a great lungful.

Although he had not thought about the matter, on reflection he decided he had expected a jungle reek. This, however, was more like a garden: flowers, fragrant shrubs, aromatic plants...

There was no sign of Wallace.

Cavendish clambered through the hatch and out of the canted conning-tower. It was a drop of ten feet to the greensward below. He slid down the curved flank of the bathyscaphe's float, hit the grass and rolled. He rose to his feet and walked away from the wreck of the *Challenger II*.

The bathyscaphe lay bow-down, partly on her side. She was plainly damaged. Beyond her rose a black wall which shimmered like obsidian. Some fifty feet above the ground, it curved inwards and became a cloudless blue sky. Cavendish looked down at his feet. He stood upon ordinary grass. Dropping to one knee, he pulled up a handful of the plant. Green blades, with rich soil captured in a knot of roots. It smelled as though it had been freshly mown, although it had plainly never been cut.

He rose to his feet and turned about. Wallace was standing some twenty feet away, gazing down at a thicket of flowering bushes. The flowers were red, but of a rich scarlet Cavendish had never before seen in nature.

"What are they?" he called.

The naval officer glanced back over his shoulder. "Roses," he replied. "I think."

Cavendish hurried across to him. Yes, up close the flowers certainly looked like roses. But the heady waft of perfume filling the air above them was not rose-like.

"They don't have thorns," said Wallace in wonder.

Cavendish looked about him. What was this place? How did it come to be here? An alien experiment? Extraterrestrials had created an unearthly garden here in the deepest part of the ocean, where the pressure, the lightlessness, the cold, would keep them hidden and secure?

Was that it? Was that the answer?

Cavendish and Wallace spent a couple of hours exploring the garden. They followed a path in amongst the trees and shrubs. The aromas of so many species of plants, in such abundance, proved a heady mixture. Everywhere, the colours appeared sharper, more vibrant, than Cavendish remembered. But perhaps that was simply an artefact of spending so long staring at the diatomaceous ooze on the floor of the Mariana Trench and Challenger Deep.

"What the hell is this place?" asked Wallace.

"Not hell," said Cavendish.

They had just entered a small round clearing. In its centre stood a tree, gnarled and immeasurably ancient. It was not tall, no more than fifty or sixty feet from the foot of its twisted trunk to its leafy crown. It bore fruit, round and green and resembling apples.

Cavendish saw something move among the branches, something long and black and sinuous. He opened his mouth, but snapped it shut without saying a word.

He knew where he was, he knew what this place was.

"I don't understand," said Wallace. "Did aliens put all this here?"

Cavendish shook his head. "No," he replied. "It's always been here. The waters rose around it... the one place not inundated by the Deluge..." Cavendish turned about. He looked up into a sky innocent of clouds or weather or sin. "The world," he said, "it doesn't work the way we thought, after all. All my research, all those years of study – they mean nothing in the face of this."

"So you know what it is?" asked Wallace. "You know how to get out?"

"Getting out is easy," replied Cavendish with certainty. "There's one way out, and one way only."

He walked towards the tree. The lower branches were within reach of his upstretched arm. He pulled one of the apples from the tree, raised it to his mouth...

... and bit into it.

A Guide to Surviving Malabar

by Ian Shoebridge

"Have you been to Malabar before?" asked Hans, the journey ambassador from the hotel, as they walked up the jungle-fringed path to the reception lobby.

Cole shook his head.

"It's not like other islands. There are a few things you need to be careful of. Read this brochure when you get a chance. Do you know how Mackay's Point was named?"

Cole shrugged. "Named after a man named Mackay?"

"A man named Mackay *fell* off the cliff there. Fell a hundred metres to his death."

Cole gave a grim laugh. "So what about Hennessey's Bluff?"

Hans nodded. "Hennessey was an experienced hiker. That one surprised us all. So you've got the idea?"

"Sure. Keep away from the cliff edges."

Hans corrected him: "Keep away from the cliff edges that haven't been *named*. The others are mostly okay. You can't name something twice."

Alarmed, Cole decided to avoid the cliffs altogether.

"What about the beaches?"

"Actually, the beaches mostly play fair. Just don't be stupid about it. There's more than one way to die at a beach. Watch out for rip-tides and shifting sandbars. Stay out of caves, obviously. Always carry a copy of the daily tide chart. And *never* swim between the flags!"

"I'm not going to end up leaving my hotel room, if it's as bad as that," Cole thought.

It had been a hastily-organized holiday. With less than a week to forget about work and the impending gloom of his thirty-eighth birthday – probably to be spent alone, again – Cole had wanted somewhere both relaxing and exciting. He had hoped this exotic island, which even boasted of its high mortality rates in tourist brochures, might add the necessary spice of risk and fun to make him feel alive again.

But on arrival, Cole just felt old.

Given all the dangers present, Cole was surprised to see anyone on the beach at all. But there were at least eighty people, apparently enjoying themselves.

It must be like gambling, he decided. With five people a day killed on the beaches, eighty people per beach made the percentages decidedly less threatening. It was a simple case of playing the odds.

According to the island brochure, the most dangerous places were deep in the island interior: the muddy jungle and the extinct volcano. Accurate maps weren't even available for these areas; tourism was discouraged.

He saw a nearby "attraction" on the map marked as "Pumice Lake". Its statistics were listed on the brochure as a mere five deaths a year. It sounded reasonably harmless. Cole began walking along the crescent of the beach. He watched the heads of swimmers bob as the surf surged unexpectedly. The water looked beautiful, but Cole wasn't tempted.

Toward the headland, the cliffs raised themselves higher in a dark, jagged line. There was a stark warning sign posted at their base. Cole stepped closer to examine it. The message was simple:

"DANGER – FALLING ROCKS!"

Before he even had time to register the words, there was a loud crack, and a hail of debris scattered down the slope. Cole jumped back. He looked up and saw a number of large boulders – one about the size of a grand piano – tumbling down the cliff above where he'd just been standing. One especially large rock thudded into the sand right over his footprints. Cole stumbled backwards in shock. It wasn't chance. It wasn't coincidence. It was a set-up. The island had actually tried to murder him.

"What are you doing?" a voice called out. "Didn't anyone tell you to avoid the warning signs?"

Still shocked, Cole could only stammer at the man in the water, "But – How are you supposed to read what they say?"

"Don't read them! Keep away from them!" The man dived back into the water.

A woman, sunbathing nearby, added, "That's why they're called warning signs! If you don't read them, they can't do anything – because you haven't been warned!" She put her sunglasses back on as though to signify the conversation was over.

"I'll have to be even more careful with the signs that *don't* give a warning," Cole thought.

Shaken, Cole continued on. He passed a sea cave, where a bronze plaque outside the entrance bore the inscription, "Oldham's Cave. Dedicated to the memory of Lewis Oldham, who was trapped in here by the tide, Nov 1984."

It's safe, Cole remembered – it's already been named. Still, he didn't feel like exploring.

The next cave entrance bore no such plaque. It looked newer, somehow. Its opening seemed to beckon. Cole moved past it, horrified.

Pumice Lake was a large grey lagoon bed that, as its name suggested, had become filled with small pieces of pumice stranded by tides. There were some families picnicking beside it. Cole admired their ability to just relax despite awareness of the dangers, something he was finding increasingly difficult.

A woman approached him, her face curiously expressionless. "Excuse me, could you help me find my husband? He was trying to reach that backpack on the rock there, but then he slipped under."

The backpack, hanging off a rock in the middle of the lake, was packed with picnic lunches and fresh fruit. There was no way to reach it without stepping across the lake. Testing the surface of the pumice lake with a fallen branch, Cole confirmed that although it looked solid it had the consistency of quicksand. He didn't hold out hopes for the poor woman's husband. He stirred the edges of the lake with the branch but was unable to make a hole in the pumice without more pieces rolling in to fill it.

"When did it happen?" he asked the woman. It was possible a man could survive a few hours, maybe even days, in this lake of rubble – so long as he had enough air.

"Last Spring," she replied.

"I'm sorry, I can't help you," Cole said.

On his way back, the tide was out, and fantastic rock formations and coral beds were exposed all along the length of the beach. Cole stopped to admire. Whatever its dangers, he had to admit the island was beautiful. Possibly the most beautiful place he had ever been. "Well," he recalled, "it's said beauty and danger go together." Every angle offered breathtaking views of the scenery. It was just a pity the breath-taking was often permanent.

Cole looked into one of the larger rock pools. Amongst the debris of white, broken coral lay a couple of dead crabs...and some human bones. There was more than one complete skeleton here; that was, somehow, the worst part. He backed away in shock, and even as he did so, a large wave swelled up out of the previously-calm waters and washed over the pool.

Cole returned to his hotel without further scenic detours.

"I want to leave," he told the woman at reception. "Immediately. Are there any boats or flights today?"

"None until your return boat on Tuesday."

"Tuesday! I was supposed to leave on Monday."

"The boat has been delayed due to bad weather."

Cole paled, imagining a lifetime stuck here. It would be a short lifetime, at least.

He remembered the travel insurance forms the booking agent had emphatically given him with the reservation receipt. "We *strongly* recommend you purchase travel insurance..." it had advised.

Well, so what? No travel insurance would protect him against his own death.

"If you're worried about safety," Hans interjected, having moved closer to Cole during the conversation, "you could think about hiring a personal guide. I'm available as a guide, and there are many others who do weekends."

"I think that might be a good idea," Cole said.

Hans passed him a brochure detailing the hourly rates for island guides. Cole took one look and handed it back.

"I'll be all right on my own," he said.

Their prices were murder.

It would be all right. He just wouldn't leave the hotel. It was only for two more days. He strolled listlessly through the lobby. His phone had been unable to connect to a network since arrival, but he assumed the hotel must have internet access.

They did: one terminal.

"A holiday here is a holiday away from the hassles of modern life," explained the receptionist.

Suppressing a sigh, Cole paid for an internet card. He paced the courtyard until the computer was available. Then he checked his email. There were several messages from work colleagues who apparently hadn't realised he was on holiday. He felt no inclination to reply. And one from Amanda, his most recent ex. "Have you gone on one of your secret holidays again and not told anyone? Hope you're having fun wherever you are!"

Cole began to type a response, but an internal collision of emotions blocked the words. "It's great to hear...This place is not...I'm..." he wrote, and then deleted the entire thing and logged off. "At least someone will notice if I never come back," he thought morbidly.

Curiosity prompted him to do a web search for "Malabar". He found the official, heavily-whitewashed tourist website that had initially lured him, online stores selling "I survived Malabar" souvenirs, and a plethora of amateur sites offering advice on how to outwit the island, ranging from the mundane "Never go anywhere alone!" to the incorrect "Only swim between the flags!" Cole imagined the island's guides took legal action to prevent anyone publishing useful information. One site gave such maliciously misleading advice Cole wondered if the island itself had somehow written it. Cole felt a headache coming on and returned to his room.

"I'll be okay," Cole thought, as he swallowed some painkillers in a glass of water, then sat and flicked between channels. There was nothing on. "I'll acquire an interest in lifestyle and 'reality' shows," he declared. "It must be possible."

The next morning was clear and sunny. Glimpses of the shadowy mountains and verdant forests teased him through the windows. Cole had read all the books in his bag. He had rapidly tired of the formulas and genres of television. His legs ached. He needed to *move*.

"I'll just go for a short stroll," he decided. "I'll keep to the main paths – anywhere with lots of people."

He set out down a well-trodden path from the hotel to the town centre. Soon the path led him into the dark jungle, and the sounds of people died away. Cole emerged in the island's cemetery.

There was something strange about that moss-covered arena of cracked tombstones, not just the fact that it wasn't where the map said it would be, but Cole couldn't figure out what, nor did he intend to investigate. There was another trail that crossed it; he must have got them confused. He followed the other path which, according to the map, led to a quiet lookout. After passing through more dense forest, he eventually arrived on a hilltop that commanded stunning views of the entire island.

There was a seat provided to enjoy the view at leisure. Cole rested his legs. The view was so entrancing he felt he could stay here all day, just watching the scenery.

An ant bit his arm. Even the damn insects were against him! Turning to scratch it off, he saw a tarnished plaque in the middle of the seat.

"In loving memory of Edward T. Burham, who passed away peacefully on this spot."

Peacefully? That meant he hadn't fallen.

Cole thought about moving, as a precaution, but he was so comfortable, and his legs were tired from the steep hike, and there was nowhere else to rest on the way back down. He felt sleepy in the sunlight. Anyway, it already had a plaque.

A rustle in the foliage made him look over. A man emerged from the bushes. Upon seeing him, the man's jaw fell open.

"Hey!" cried the younger man. "Get off that bench – quickly!"

Cole hastened to his feet. The man grabbed him and pulled him away with melodramatic zest.

"Didn't you check the date? *Always* check the date!" The man leaned over to examine the bench. "Look, this plaque is from just three years ago! This seat could still be active!"

"I thought the plaque meant that it was safe!"

The man pointed insistently at the bench. "There's room for more than one plaque on this seat."

He had a point. But Cole couldn't quite grasp the insane logic. "So the seats *without* plaques are safe?"

"They're even worse. They still want to prove themselves. The only safe ones have three plaques, dated from the 1960s or earlier. Only those can you assume are dormant. Look, you shouldn't be roaming around here on your own, if you don't even know the basics. I'm a guide; let me give you my card."

"Thanks, but I can't afford you. This fee is more than I paid for the entire holiday."

"Well, it's your life, man. I'm not going to force you. But you're not going to last long here on your own. Try and find another holidayer to buddy up with; it'll be safer."

"If I could do that," Cole thought resignedly, "I wouldn't be here on my own to begin with."

As he returned down the path, he saw numerous other seats and benches where he could swear there hadn't been any before. It was as though they had heard about his gullibility and were all crowding in to try and take advantage of him.

One of the chairs, perched at the edge of a vertiginous drop, bore a plaque which read: "In loving memory of Samuel Beckham, after his untimely accidental death."

The tautology for some reason made him assume it must be a kind of euphemism for suicide. Was that the only alternative to letting the island take you? Or did it amount to the same thing?

Back at the hotel, bored and restless, Cole started reading the promotional brochures and pamphlets that had been left in his room. He didn't need human company as long as he had the written word.

"Malabar's vast primeval forests, distinctive-coloured beaches and cliffs, flourishing wildlife and completely unique ecosystem, are all due to the nutrient-rich soil... This unusual kind of volcanic sediment, essential to sustaining the unique ecology, is constantly being eroded by the wind, rain and sea. The modern pressures of global tourism create additional erosion problems..."

He read on, hoping for some further clue as to the twisted logic behind this insane nightmare, but the brochures were frustratingly vague, only specific when listing the myriad tours he could go on if he had the money and nerve.

Underneath the brochures, he found a strange pamphlet about a cannibal tribe that had originally settled the island and had mysteriously died out several centuries ago. Not very much was known about them except what could be deduced from remains of their dwellings and tools, plus some cave paintings near the volcano. Supposedly they had believed the island was sentient, and had worshipped the then-active volcano as essentially the *mouth* of their deity, offering it regular human sacrifices to placate its angry spirit. A god of abundance when pleased, but spewing the wrath of hellfire when displeased.

This tribe also believed that human flesh contained special properties for awakening the mind, and that cannibalism had essentially been what gave birth to human consciousness...

He dropped the pamphlet, as certain horrific notions formed in his mind, too awful to voice, too awful to dwell upon.

Cole cursed his travel agent and everyone involved in the promotion of this death-trap as a "unique" tourist destination.

He would survive – in his room. It was just a kind of solitary confinement. At least he had a TV. He flicked the remote.

The TV reception was out.

The next morning Cole asked again about his return boat.

"It *is* due tomorrow, weather permitting," answered the receptionist.

"Then I'd like to book a tour tomorrow, also," Cole said.

"You do know I can't refund your departure ticket..."

"I don't want to cancel it. I'm just betting on the weather," he said. Betting on the island. Survival was just about playing the odds. "I'd like to book the tour to the Lone Waterfall."

The receptionist looked concerned. "That's for experienced hikers. It can be quite...challenging. Are you sure?"

"Completely sure."

"That will be three hundred dollars, please."

Cole smiled to himself. There was no way the island would resist such a temptation. Cole, timid, stumbling, unfit, would undoubtedly be the first to succumb to whatever macabre challenges the Lone Waterfall hike offered.

But the tour could only operate in fine weather. And if the weather was fine, the boat home would come.

He hoped.

Now it was just a matter of staying alive one more day.

As he turned to leave, Cole saw a happy couple stroll in. They had come from an early swim at the beach and were beaming.

"How do you do it?" he asked them. "How do you manage to have a good time here?"

The man shrugged. The woman frowned. "If you don't like it here, why don't you leave?" she asked.

"I'm trying to!"

"Then you shouldn't complain. Focus on the positive! Things are always better than you imagine."

"Thanks." Cole nodded weakly. He turned to the stairs.

Both of the TV channels were still unwatchable. The internet terminal had, as usual, a long line of people waiting. Now the staff wanted him to leave his room for cleaning. He suspected it was more for revenue-raising. Survival was difficult on a tight budget. And if a tourist wasn't likely to spend money in their five-star restaurants or on their exorbitant guide services, the hospitality crew probably wanted him or her dead.

According to the map, there was a relatively safe trail to the Old Harbour. Cole decided to risk it.

The path wound through a gloomy valley, thickly-forested. Strangler Figs dominated the jungle: twisted, tangled giants of roots and vines. *"Damned nature!"* Cole thought. The natural world was composed entirely of parasites, predators and scavengers. People looked to nature for inspiration, tranquillity and beauty, but this was sheer naivety; it was all just a hideous display of slow-motion violence and covert treachery. The forest was constantly in a state of war against everything, even itself.

A wooden sign in a clearing read: "Please Do Not Feed The Trees." Cole shuddered.

The path reached the coast and the forest cleared briefly.

But the ocean was no consolation to Cole. It was engaged in its constant territorial battle against the land. The fury of its erosive power could break down any landmass, over time. And as the earth cooled, volcanoes were a dying breed. What else could birth new land? But the ocean would never die. It would eat everything if not restrained by its own weight.

He watched some seagulls resting on the rocks. A huge breaker rose up out of the sea without warning and engulfed the birds before they could fly away.

Even the beach needs to eat, he realised.

He wondered when the island had developed its insatiable appetite for human and animal flesh. Had it inspired its cannibal residents, or been inspired by them? There had always been rumours that human flesh bestowed unusual properties upon the devourer. Perhaps the soul, with all its poetry and metaphor, enhanced the nutritional value of the flesh.

Cole reached the Old Harbour, and stopped.

Hundreds of warning signs covered everything, flags wavered, plaques glinted in the sunlight, and the sea looked swollen and hungry – poised before a channel of sand that was suspiciously clear of debris. The Old Harbour was nothing more than a great death-trap. The map had deceived him in giving it such a low mortality score. The map was part of the whole insidious ploy. Cole turned around and ran.

The path turned inland, and Cole found himself, panting and exhausted, back at the island's cemetery.

"That's impossible!" he declared. He examined the map again, carefully. The path should have taken him to the other side of the ridge.

Well, if he was back here, that meant he was close to his hotel. He had been tiring of this "walk", anyway. It was 3pm; time for an early night. Cole took the shortest path that led back to the hotel.

He had been walking only a few minutes when he came across a wooden sign blocking the path.

"TRAIL CLOSED," it read, in fresh, bright red paint.

Ahead, Cole could see the path was overgrown and treacherous. Vines snaked and spider-webs glinted. Reluctantly, he turned. Clearly he had become lost. Probably there was more than one cemetery. With this island's impressively high body count, they would need several.

Returning along the path, Cole came across another sign, identical to the first, but this one with a creeper vine growing over it, to distinguish it from the former.

"TRAIL CLOSED."

Cole began to panic.

Beside him, not visible from his previous position, he could detect a faint trail running off this one at right angles, through dense jungle. It was all too easy to get lost here. Glancing back, it seemed the two wooden signs were closer.

"Damn it," he muttered. "It's got me now."

The jungle cleared as Cole arrived back at the cemetery.

Now he could see what was strange about the place. It wasn't just that so many of the tombstones were new – it was that the majority of them were blank. Even headstones that were cracked and moss-encrusted had faded to the point where any printing was no longer discernable.

So this is it, he realised grimly. I can be remembered "lovingly" on a bronze plaque for jumping off a cliff...or I can resist, and be forgotten, nameless, here. No one is remembered here. These stones just swallow bodies, digest them, and wait for the next.

He moved on toward the centre of the graveyard. He could sense the blind enmity of the stones as they sought, passively, to absorb and obliterate him, and the near-salivating hunger of the open graves, waiting for him to accidentally tread a stray foot into their gaping maws. Some of the more elaborate or angled headstones even seemed to quiver slightly – like the leaves of a Venus Fly-trap – as though holding their breath in anticipation. The whole damn island was out to get him. He didn't have a chance. Well, whatever; his fate waited for him in the centre of the graveyard.

"Slow down," called a voice. Cole hesitated.

Hans hurried through the graveyard on light feet, as though dancing over a field of thorns. He avoided the gaping holes and leaning tombstones with practiced ease. "You don't want to be *here*. How did you end up here?"

"I was just following the map." Cole said.

Hans examined the map. "Here's your problem. This is *yesterday's* map."

Bewildered, Cole asked, "How can the map be out of date?"

"Same way yesterday's weather report is out of date."

Hans guided him out of the cemetery; cautiously, yet almost oblivious to the tense, expectant atmosphere now turning poisonous with disappointment. "Pretty efficient arrangement, when you think about it," Hans remarked airily. "A self-maintaining cemetery..."

Cole was unable to speak.

Confronted with another bright red "TRAIL CLOSED" sign, Hans merely stepped around it. "These just try to look threatening. If you've got a good map you can bypass them. But your eyes need to be good at spotting a disguised trail from a false trail. The real trail is *never* straight..."

Cole felt humiliated, traumatized and exhausted.

"You know," said Hans evenly, as they reached a crossroads, "it is customary to offer a guide a tip for saving one's life..."

Cole emptied out his wallet. "This is all I have left. Just get me back to the hotel safely. My boat comes tomorrow morning."

Hans accepted the notes without modesty. "For this, I'll even take you from your hotel to the jetty tomorrow. No extra cost. We're not parasites."

The proud boat waiting in the dock was a blessed, welcome sight to Cole. He wanted to kiss its fibreglass exterior.

"Thank you," he said to Hans. "I can't say I've enjoyed it here, but thanks for your help."

"You'll be back," said Hans calmly.

Numbly, Cole shook his head. He wanted to laugh, but couldn't.

"You might not think so now, but you'll change your mind," said Hans, confidently. "I was the same as you when I first travelled here. Barely made it out alive; couldn't fathom why anyone would *live* here. But as I took other vacations, over the years, I found myself disappointed – none of them offered the same challenge or excitement. I went to some of the most spectacular places in the world and I was bored. So I came back. I wanted to study the island's tricks, learn how to outsmart it. I ended up staying here for five years, learning all the common traps, training my wits and judgement. Over time, I found I couldn't imagine living anywhere else. A normal life – barren and monotonous! How else can you truly feel alive except by testing yourself, by constantly balancing on a knife's edge over oblivion? So I became a guide. I went from wanting to master the island to...*respecting* the island."

"And if I refuse to become a guide," Cole predicted, shaking, "I'll be made compost for the island – for the 'nutrient-rich' soil."

Hans looked mildly amused. "This isn't a threat. I know you'll come back. And anyway, we need guides more than compost. The tourist trade is growing, and we need guides to accommodate for these people. The island can look after itself. It takes what it needs; often it takes whatever it can get. We lose, on average, one guide every two months. And it takes time to replace them. New guides have to prove themselves. They have to traverse Dead Man's Ravine and Suicide's Bluff before they get their full license, and that's not something you want to try without extensive preparation."

"I'm not coming back," Cole assured him. Hans shrugged. Cole stepped onto the gangway and boarded the boat. He gave a brief, nonchalant wave to Hans, who was watching him with a detached expression. The boat pulled away; soon the island was a misty green blur in the distance.

"I'm not coming back," Cole assured himself.

But he knew it was hopeless.

The Human Map

by Andrew Hook

MYANMAR

The tiger bounded out of the surf, chasing white horses. Spume frothed its mouth, but surely it was I who was mad. The sun pressed against my neck like a cigarette, as though someone was sat in the undergrowth with a mirror, scorching me as I used to scorch ants.

Paw marks larger than my own hands held together as one fist made patterns in the wet sand. Nearby, a much larger circular shape, a hollow, as though the sand had been blown out by a vacuum cleaner in reverse. Or a helicopter, I realised. But bigger. Much bigger.

The tiger wasn't interested in me. Its black and orange colours flashed across my retina, playing with my senses. After a while it was gone, mildly bedraggled. I watched it move further along the beach until it entered the jungle. Once lost, my fear increased. There was nothing, no one, other than me on the beach. I sat alone.

So I stood. My black jeans had long faded to grey, my t-shirt likewise. My Converse hugged my feet, as comfortable as slippers, as comforting as reality. I lifted one trouser leg and saw I wore no socks. Touching my forehead, grains of sand aggravated the pain. I ran my tongue around my lips. Water. I needed water. I ran my tongue around my lips again. I craved water.

Slowly, I moved away from the beach and into the shade. Palms hung heavy with coconuts. Husks littered the floor. I picked one up, the rough coarse hair prickling my skin. Repeatedly I threw it against tree trunks until it cracked and I managed to craft a drink through the fragile slit. The coconut water sweet, too sweet, the edges of the husk itself were bitter. I slept.

Waking at night the jungle sounds mingled with memories in my dreams.

Angeline sat opposite me, her feet dipping into a washing up bowl, the water moving between her toes, fluid. I remembered the scene. We had only recently bought the property in Norwich and had gone walking one summer's day to see how far we could go. It had been eight miles to Wroxham and eight miles back again. She showed me her blisters, bubbling the skin like black plague boils, but clear. I washed her feet that day, with the sound of monkeys in the trees outside the terraced house reverberating through the brick, stimulating my ears.

I shook my head.

Dreams fell out. My eyes were encrusted with sleep, with sand. I threw the coconut and it split in half. But even so my teeth could barely engage on the rim as I attempted to peel off the thin white flesh and eat.

It took me a few more hours to seriously consider what I was doing, by which time morning was up and there was a dark-skinned boy on the beach. He was sitting within the circular hole, holding a stick. I watched as he pointed the stick into the sky. Laughed.

Fearing for my sanity, my life, I wandered out of the jungle's edge and onto the sand. Danced on the hot surface. The boy noticed, stood, and ran into the jungle.

Maybe only one of us could remain on the beach at any one time.

I stood where he had sat. The circle was over fifty feet in diameter. The sand there had become glass. A polished surface. My soles blistered. I couldn't remember.

I reached into my pockets. No money, no phone, no keys. The boy returned with an older male, who wore a striped red and blue sarong over the lower half of his body.

I pointed at myself, and said in the international language: "English."

I didn't understand the language that returned to me. Guttural sounds, hard consonants. The boy touched my arm, smiled. I followed them back into the jungle. My stomach growling like the tiger.

A few days later I understood where I was. Myanmar, once Burma. On the Andaman Sea. On the Tanintharyi peninsular.

Burma.

Be Undressed Ready My Angel.

MALAYA

"Sssh."

I began to open my eyes but fingers pressed them down. Soft fingers. I wondered if they were Angeline's.

Then I heard chattering in a foreign language and realised that despite the dreams I was yet to be home.

Sounds assailed me. As though becoming aware of one sound had been a portal to hearing others. The squeaky wheels of bicycles, the shouts and grunts of market traders, the swish of rain, the steady stream of water running from a tap. And then smells: durian, mangosteen, rambutan, lychee, pineapple, banana. I knew each as it came to me, somehow. The warm chilli scent of the body lying next to me, the smell of the heat and the rain. And then the fingers were removed from my eyelids, but I still kept them closed. Afraid to open them, to see what I would see.

So Angeline returned to my vision: we had argued. Her face, her lips, were pursed to a point directed on a scuff mark on the black tiles in our kitchen. Tension, frustration, fermented inside me, but contained.

I opened my eyes. I lay on a bamboo mat, spread on the mattress of a four poster bed. Green wooden shutters were pulled against the windows. The walls were bare, plastered over the brick: cool and smooth. Upside down, I watched the smiling face of the woman who had closed my eyes. She stood, walked backwards, descended wooden steps in the corner of the room. When I sat, my head swam. There was a television in the corner, but it wasn't on.

I stood, held the banister. Moved stiffly towards the window. Gripping the ridges of the shutters, I pulled them open.

Outside was a town. Two roadways heavy with traffic. Cars and motorbikes interweaved, intertwined. Entire families rode each bike. In the distance, the sun was descending, a bright orb melting the scene as one, imbuing the atmosphere with a golden glow. I breathed in the hot air, moisture from the humidity as thick as milkshake.

Before I heard the footsteps on the stairs, I saw two things. One: all the traffic was heading out of the city. Two: a series of wooden buildings had been flattened in a circle fifty foot in diameter. Smoke rose, blackened the updraft like some American Indian signal. But this wasn't America. This was elsewhere.

A hand touched my shoulder. The girl again. She gesticulated to an older man, his hand on the top of the banister, who hauled himself into the room. Pale cream shorts offset his dark legs where feet fed into sandals. His shirt was multi-coloured, patterned with random images. But then not random, designed.

"I am Mr Pong."

His English was faltering, but within twenty minutes I had established that nothing electrical was working. Televisions, phones, the internet: everything was down.

"Since when?" I asked.

"Since you came," he said.

I was about to ask more, but then I wasn't there.

Malaya.

My Ardent Lips Await Your Arrival.

ITALY

The headache is severe. Like a migraine. But I've never had a migraine, so how do I know? Lights flash.

I'm beginning to realise that all my experiences are condensed. I stand behind Angeline as she peels potatoes and wrap my arms around her stomach, kiss her hair which smells of papaya. She moves backwards slowly, into me. We merge.

This time when I open my eyes I'm surrounded by people jabbering and pointing. They keep their distance, and if my math is anything to go by the nearest isn't closer than twenty-five feet. I'm circled. I'm at the centre of a circle. The ground under my back is blackened. I can feel the heat of it like a scorch mark through my t-shirt. There's a taste in my mouth that I don't recognise, something metallic. But not blood, maybe old money. Something alien.

I squint as the sun is reflected from the wing mirror of a scooter that pulls up at the edge of the circle, and for a moment the people are reduced to nuclear shadows.

When I look at my arms I see track marks, ley lines that terminate elsewhere on my body. I touch my forehead and a hard ridge of dried blood runs full circle, as though I've been lobotomised in some b-horror movie.

The chattering increases as I move into a sitting position. I recognise some of the language. That is, I recognise sounds, not words. Most of the men are wearing white vests. The younger women have cut-off denim shorts, t-shirts. Older women wear flowered garments. Older men have hats. As I scan the crowd I see mobile phones pointed towards me, but something's wrong, no one can get a picture.

I know where I am. This is Italy. It comes to me in a flash and in another flash I'm gone. I'm getting closer, I'm moving close to you Angeline.

Italy.

I Trust And Love You.

FRANCE

I begin to expect it when it happens. I begin to know what to expect.

Angeline is sitting on a chair with her feet on the table. *Konnichiwa* a voice says. She repeats it: "Konnichiwa". *Arigato* the voice says. "Arigato" she repeats.

From somewhere I hear my voice say, "Aligator".

She grimaces and throws something at me but it disappears before it reaches my head.

Japanese segues into French. After a brief exchange of words, French segues into English.

"Are you okay?"

I want to nod but my head hurts. Knowledge is a burden.

My tongue is thick in my head. Have I already spoken? "Where am I?" This is me.

"Limousin."

Something comes to me about the number of farmers and suicides in this region.

"I'm being used," I say.

My vision which was previously blurred now comes into view. An elderly gentleman with map-relief wrinkles on his face bends over me. He extends a hand and I rise.

"*Je ne comprends pas.*"

I look beyond him to his tractor parked in the distance. He is a wheat farmer and we're standing in a crop circle.

"I'm trying to get back to England," I say.

"England." He nods. "*Angleterre.*"

"Oui," I say, thankful for my schoolboy French. He taps my shoulder, and almost in a hug we begin to move forwards one step at a time.

He takes me to the tractor, and I sit with my back against one of its large wheels. Cradled. In the cab he removes bread, cheese, ham. We sit together, staring at the crop circle, whilst he halves the bread with a penknife and slices cheese.

"Did you see it?" I ask.

He shakes his head.

For a moment I wonder if he thinks I did this.

For a moment I wonder *if* I did this.

Memories are fragmentary.

How I've sat, my jeans have ridden up my legs. Twin circles of dried blood surround my ankles. I've been dissected, bisected.

The bread could be manna. The cheese is a bonus. But the ham sits on my tongue and stifles it.

"There's a girl," I say. "There's someone I'm trying to return to."

It doesn't seem like he understands. From a pocket he pulls out a silver bottle of water. Only it isn't water, and when it burns my tongue I find myself slipping away, being pulled back into that other space. That other space I cannot remember. Unlike France. France which I do remember.

France.

Friendship Remains And Never Can End.

HOLLAND

I'm getting closer. Angeline is pulling me back, rewinding me, like a thread from a ball of string. Only there's a cat, a tiger, also following the string. When she tugs, it jumps.

She's pulling me back through her memories.

We stand on Southwold Pier. The light is incredible here. Just an hour's drive and life is transformed. To our right, fishermen cast their lines, buckets only full of water at their feet. To our left a couple embrace. I glimpse a tongue. Angeline is taking photographs of seaside binoculars. When she shows me later the twin lenses are eyes, the ridge between them a nose, their metal casing a head. "They look like robots," she says. And I have to agree: they do.

I wake in water. It's dark. Pitch black with no moon and cold. I pull myself out of the dyke, realise my breaths are heavy. They're too heavy. Asthmatic. I reach in my pockets for my inhaler but then remember where I am. No. Not remember where I am, but remember what I am.

Or maybe, not even that.

I pause, regulate my breathing, return to normal.

I lay on my back looking up at the stars until morning comes.

As the sun shifts behind me, illuminating greenery, I find my shadow waffled: I'm sitting in a square of light. I turn and look behind me, see the windmill, sun burning squares through its slats.

It's broken. Inside smells of urine and I step around broken glass. Take the steps one at a time to the top. From a tiny window I get a good view. The dyke is fresh, the earth dark and moist around it, and the line of the dyke takes a circular route until it returns to itself. Once again, a cut in the earth, as though made in a flat plain of pastry with a cookie-cutter. In the distance I see a road. Some cyclists. I limp out of the windmill without a hope of reaching them, and that's true because before you know it there's that tug again and I'm out of here. I'm out of Holland.

Holland.

Hope Our Love Lasts And Never Dies.

WALES

It's only here where I begin to understand.

I understand that I've overshot.

They pick me up from the field and take me to the nearest pub. There's more sheep than them. I'm rural.

"What's happened to you then?"

For some reason they're suspicious. And I sense that it's more than me. There's other.

"I don't know," I say, needing to be honest, needing to find a voice.

They mutter amongst themselves.

I look around the pub. There's a television in the corner which isn't on. There's no light within the refrigerator behind the bar, and no flashing lights on the fruit machine. It's dark in here. On the surface of the bar and on the tables are candle residues. It's been a while.

"How did you get here?"

I shake my head. This could be dangerous.

"I've been travelling," I risk.

One of the men snorts and before I know it I'm being strong-armed out of the pub, two of them either side of me. I'm marched down a rough street with grass growing in the middle of it, like a green Mohican. A couple of basic shops and several small houses flank the road. Children watch me. At the end of the road is a police station. In any other situation this would be photographic. I remember Angeline and her camera.

"Come here," she says. And then, "No, there."

I walk backwards and forwards whilst the shutter clicks.

Later we pull close and she holds the camera out in front of her at arm's length, the lens facing us. That photograph is the first to grace the mantelpiece in our new Norwich home. I can see it now, superimposed over this Welsh scene. One of the older boys is running behind me, trying to kick my legs out from underneath me. I wonder if I'm going to be beaten up. Certainly friendship has faltered the closer I've gotten to home.

Home.

Hope Or My Extinction.

Inside the tiny police station there are no police officers so they put me behind a desk and leave the room. Two of them watch the door at the back, and two of them watch the door at the front. But I'm not going anywhere.

At least, not that way.

But then I do leave. I leave Wales behind.

Wales.

With A Love Eternal, Sweetheart.

NORWICH

I'm back. The experiments are over. For now.

Angeline's sitting on the corner of the bed with a smile on her face. But I'm not sure if the smile is for me or even if the smile is in the here and now.

I stand in the doorway. Rings encircle my body, as though I've entered a fancy dress competition as a lemur. Tears fall in big droplets from my eyes. I see myself reflected in them as they hit the wooden floor.

"You're back," she says.

Behind her through the window I finally see the craft, for the first and last time. It rotates like a Catherine Wheel on its side. All silver and beautiful.

"Back?" I say, "I never went away."

I don't tell her that I'm aware what Norwich stands for.

But then she turns and I see something isn't quite right.

She's transparent.

It's transparent.

Parts of me unfold like a paper animal. A reverse origami.

What are we, after all, but refractions of light interpreted by our brains? What is time, but a linear cheat? Where are we going, other than to places we have already been?

They're inside my mind, extracting the human from maps of my memories, my DNA, my future, my love.

I know where I am.

Amount of Responsive Extraterrestrial Abductees: 51.

Unlocking secrets of the human race viewed from above.

Journey to the Engine of the Earth

by Terry Grimwood

We stand on a grassed, wind-lashed slope that borders the Lemon Way estate.

"So," I say to The Visitor. "Exactly where do you want to go?"

I don't want to look at The Visitor because the hood of its parka is down. The Visitor still disturbs me, it disturbs all of us. It isn't local. Its home, as far as we've been able to work out, is a moon that orbits a gas giant in the Beta Ophiuchus system.

"That way," the Visitor says and waves towards the three, night-blackened tower blocks that dominate the estate. Its voice is husky, throaty, like someone who has smoked their vocal cords to shreds. "To the centre." To my relief it pulls up its hood and fades into parka-esque anonymity.

"Okay," I call out. "Time to move."

The others, my team I suppose you'd call them, are huddled together off to my left. I don't know what actually qualifies me to be their leader. My name is John Chamberlain and I'm a dentist, not an explorer.

But The Visitor has picked me as leader so leader I am.

The Visitor picked the whole team in fact, selecting the six of us from a thousand, thousand sets of CVs, medical records, bank statements and any other information available to brush-stroke our characters and lives. The selections it made seem random and bizarre. None of us are volunteers. We were politely but firmly roused from our beds by people who looked like police officers but weren't and brought before a panel of grim-faced men and women in some generic office in what I presume was London. The van that ferried us there had no windows.

We were introduced to our Visitor and once we had calmed down, informed that there are about five hundred of them scattered all over the Earth and God knows how many more living on their continent-sized vessel, waiting up there in geostationary orbit directly above the Great Pyramid at Cheops. Coincidence or connection? Who knows? All we do know is that their hardware is bigger and much more intimidating than anything we've got. They have asked for help in finding the Engine of the Earth and help they will be given.

Few people know about this, not even the police or army are aware. So, mouths shut and mobile phones off. There will be no calling for help if things go wrong. There was no time for any training. Two days in a hotel to get to know each other, some powerful torches and a map of the estate and that's it.

Their time-synchronised search, which begins now, will take the Visitors and their human teams into the worst places imaginable: war zones, areas wracked by natural or manmade disaster, slums and the most dangerous council estate in this country. The Visitors have given no clues as to the nature of this Engine although they have promised that when they do find it, they will simply disappear and leave us alone. Current thinking identifies it as the indomitable human spirit, survival in adversity, a sign that humanity has some worth and is not interstellar vermin. So, I'm expecting our particular quest into the desolation of Lemon Valley to uncover a courageous single-mum or heroic youth worker.

Paul speaks first. He is a big, broad, head-shaved ex-infantryman, bundled, like the rest of us, into an obligatory parka. Paul intimidates me but I'm glad he's here. I wish he'd been picked as leader.

"I'll stay at the back, keep an eye on our flank," he says. "If there's any trouble up front I'll come running."

Seems like a good idea to me.

We form into a ragged line and descend the slope via a set of rain-slippery concrete steps. The Visitor is in front of me. At my shoulder is a Cabinet Minister named Katherine Kristian. She has not been friendly and only grudgingly co-operative. I suppose she thinks she should be the leader.

Behind Katherine is Rajan Uppal, who works in Sainsbury's or Tesco's or somewhere similar. He's affable enough, and utterly terrified, though trying his best to hide the fact. Between Rajan and Paul is a High School maths teacher called Rachel Goldman. She's the one who is taking this seriously and, as far as I can see, the bravest member of Chamberlain's Marauders.

At the bottom of the stairway, we move carefully into a cut between two high grassy banks. I feel vulnerable down here. Katherine moves up beside me. "You okay?" Is this genuine concern or politics?

I nod. "What about you?"

"This seems so surreal," she says. "And this place…God knows what it must be like to live here."

"Perhaps that's what we're supposed to find out."

She nods. "You think that's what the Engine is? Humans beings forced to confront the suffering of others?"

It sounds like a speech. Embarrassed, I offer a noncommittal shrug.

The cut takes us into an underpass, which stinks of booze and piss. There are lights, though most of them are broken. In the sickly patches of illumination they do provide I see graffiti: gang boasts and threats, sexual insults, favours offered. The gibberish on the walls heightens my sense that this is the homeland of a completely separate species almost as alien as The Visitor itself.

The cut curves out of the underpass and slopes steadily upwards. I hear music. It is relentless, monotonous, some way off but malevolent enough. Someone shouts, the voice lonely, reverberating off the slab-like concrete walls of the tower blocks that now loom over us. There is a snatch of laughter, male. More shouting, glass shatters.

"You do know that there were five murders on this estate last year," Rajan informs us as we walk. He sounds nervous.

"In this *area*," Rachel corrects him. "They were not all on the estate."

"That's all right then," Rajan says and chuckles. There isn't much humour in the sound.

There are buildings on either side of us, squat and soulless. Each one is three storeys high and flat-roofed. Light spills from their curtain-concealed windows. I stop the team to consult the map, struggling to keep it flat in the rain-edged wind.

"Left," I say and hope I'm right because it feels as if we've entered a maze. The music grows louder, mingles with other nihilistic beats, fades and is replaced by more. Shrieks and shouts erupt from one of the blocks. A door slams.

Figures emerge from the shadows to our right and run across our path. I tense, not knowing whether to order a retreat or a stand. The figures move on and disappear. There is breathless laughter, male, mocking. A car erupts out of the half-dark, headlights blaze white. It hurtles past, all engine roar, exhaust stink and pulsing, skull-fracturing music. It brakes and wheel-spins behind us then swerves right and is gone. We're being watched, from the flats, from the pools of dark the street lighting cannot penetrate. I can feel it, eyes raking my skin, flaying it to the raw nerves beneath.

We press on until we reach the edge of a large, open area bordered on each of its three sides by a trio of tower blocks. They rear over us, looking as if they have erupted out of the earth rather than been built. Light punctuates their blank, brutalist frontages. They each have a name; Emerson, Lake and Palmer, which proves that there is a developer in this world who either nurses a lingering love for prog rock or is blessed with a sense of humour. I suspect the latter. Some sort of statue or sculpture sits in the middle of the area.

Another look at the map. "That thing's supposed to be the actual centre of this shit hole," I say.

"Don't call it that," Katherine sounds as if she means it.

"Why not, that's what it is." Rajan says.

"Names like that aren't helpful," Katherine tells him.

"So you think this is paradise then?"

"Don't be stupid, Rajan."

"That's enough," I say and although my rebuke sounds weak both of them stop.

"What is that thing?" Rachel asks.

"Fuck knows, looks like a big lump of concrete to me," Rajan says.

"That because you're a Philistine," Rachel tells him.

"A what?"

"I think the piece is a Gormley," Katherine says.

"Oh," says Rajan but I don't think he's any wiser.

"Is that where we're supposed to go?" I ask The Visitor.

It turns its hood-hidden face towards me. "Yes."

"Is that where the engine is?"

"Perhaps."

There is a problem.

Several cars are parked close together about halfway between us and the sculpture. Drum and Bass, or whatever it's called, throbs from the speakers in one of the hatchbacks. Even from this distance each beat is a punch to the stomach. Car-light and street light silhouette the characters lounging and playing around the cars into demonic figures, capering about the bonfires of Hell. There is something primitive about them, like the natives in some clichéd old Hollywood Tarzan film.

"Is there a way to the sculpture that doesn't involve crossing that triangle?" Katherine must be telepathic because I'm already unfolding the map.

I fumble with the flapping sheet of paper and my torch. I can't think for the noise.

"Let me have a look," says Paul. Logical idea, except I don't want him to. I'm supposed to be the leader, I'm supposed to get us to our destination. I fumble on.

"Oh for God's sake." Katherine snatches the map out of my hand. It tears. "Paul, come and do this, will you?"

I'm angry, but Paul is already peering at the diagram so protest seems futile at that moment.

"There's a path that leads, round the back of the Emerson," he says.

"Let's go then," Katherine says.

"I don't know." Why am I doing this? Caution or pride?

"I do," says Rachel. "We're asking for trouble if we attempt to cross the triangle. We should go Paul's way and take our chances."

I want her to shut up and stay out of this. I want them all to keep quiet. I can't think for the noise.

"What about you, Rajan?" Katherine asks.

"I'm not walking through that lot." Rajan nods towards the car tribe.

The mutiny is complete. I glance at The Visitor. No help there.

"Fuck," I mutter.

"What?" Rachel says.

"You win," I say. "You'd better lead, Paul, I'll watch the rear."

We enter yet another maze of narrow walkways and car-lined streets, all edged by low, cubist blocks. There's a pub, no different from the faceless concrete lumps around it. A group of smokers huddle outside. I catch a hint of wind-blown tobacco exhaust. The smokers watch us as we pass, no one speaks.

I notice that Katherine has moved up beside Paul, assuming her natural position in the order of things no doubt.

We turn a corner and blunder to a halt.

The street is like most others on the estate: concrete, tarmac, rubbish-strewn and all illuminated by orange street-light. But this one includes a large people carrier with blacked-out windows, idling by the pavement about ten metres away. A cluster of figures are gathered round it and it looks as if money is changing hands. The group are made anonymous by the abysmal light but I can almost taste their malevolence.

Drug deal. What else *can* it be?

And here *we* are, a clutch of strangers, only a few metres away, frozen like rabbits in car headlights.

"We have to go back," I move up to the front.

"No we don't," Katherine says. "We just cross over and walk past. They're not interested in us."

"We have to find another route," Rachel says. Even she sounds scared now.

"I think John's right," Rajan says.

"He's not. He's over-reacting," Katherine says. "We're too close to where we want to get to; I mean, do you really want to trudge all the way back?"

"Paul?" I say. I'm getting uneasy. The gang have seen us. They're glancing this way.

"Don't mind. Whatever you want to do, boss," he says and shrugs.

"We're going back."

"It's too far." Katherine is mounting a leadership challenge. "Everyone is cold and tired and we just want to get this whole thing over with so we can go home."

"The Visitor appointed *me* as leader." No, no, wrong. I should not have said that, too weak, too pleading. But there isn't time for niceties. This place is closing in on me. I'm breathing too fast, shaking. I press on with my defence against Katherine's coup. "And I say we go back."

Rajan nods, Rachel moves in towards me. I've done it. I've beaten down the insurgency. Now we need to get out of here because these characters and their blacked-out people carrier and huddled, dark whispering and dealing is scaring the hell out of me –

"Hey! What the fuck you lookin' at?" The voice is deep. And aggressive.

They're coming. Dear God, they're coming after *us*.

Something breaks inside me and I run. I think I shout at the others to do the same but I can't remember. All I know is that I have to get out of there. This is fear, real fear, not stage fright or some extreme sport adrenalin rush, this is survival-fear. It forces a sob from my throat, it pumps my legs and arms and snatches away my breath.

The pub, I have to get to the pub, light, people. No one is going to gun me down in front of so many witnesses. Are they? Well, *are they?* Witnesses keep their mouths shut in places like this? No one sees anything. All the Lemon Way murders are unsolved…

My team, Jesus, my team, my people.

I can't stop for them. I can't stop for anything.

The pub comes into view. I look over my shoulder. No sign of the drug dealers. They thought we were the police, they've driven away. They're racing through some short cut intent on heading us off…

My team appear, running, together, a group, a family. And here I am, away out front, the so-called leader, first off the blocks when danger rears its head.

Ashamed, I stumble to a halt and wait, panting, hands on knees. The pub smokers regard me curiously. A woman laughs. Someone coughs and spits.

We're back where we started, crouching between Emerson and Lake, watching the gang who we will have to pass to get to our – The Visitor's – destination. There is no other way. The others have separated themselves from me and who can blame them? I left them, ran away and deserted my post. No one has criticised me openly. No one has confronted me but it's there, unspoken yet deafening.

I can't tell what The Visitor feels about my failure.

"They're just kids," I say, nodding towards the car tribe that is blocking our way to the sculpture.

If I say it enough times I might believe it myself...

No one answers, no discussion so no point staying here.

"Let's go," I say and gritting my teeth, set off across the triangle. Everyone follows. Their obedience thrums with resentment.

Halfway across we're noticed. The music punches into my gut. I see figures detach themselves from the cars. I'm struck by their gauntness, their pale, pinched faces, their hunched backs, the degenerate, somehow mutated look of them, as if they have been bred into the shape and demeanour best suited for this environment. Their clothes are alien too, slovenly and cheap looking, no style or shape, but a uniform nonetheless. The shouting starts. It's not a challenge, not a demand to know who we are. They are shouting at the women; filth, obscene propositions. I hate their mindless cackle and I hate their wasted pasty skin and stupid bloody clothes and vile bloody music and my hate speeds my heart rate and drains the blood from my brain until my head roars.

"Come on lads, that's enough." Rachel's tone is non-threatening yet authoritative.

A bottle smashes on the path just ahead of me. They move away from their cars and prance, apelike, around us. Another bottle smashes. But no violence, not yet.

I keep walking, and the others are with me. I want to run, but I have to atone.

The taunting goes on; suck this, feel that. On and bloody on. A third bottle lands somewhere behind me. No one cries out, no one hurt.

One of them comes in close. He's a light-built, hyperactive little shit. He walks alongside Katherine. "Hey," Paul says. "Leave her alone."

The lad is fast, leaps out of Paul's reach in an instant. His manoeuvre is cheered by the others. Katherine keeps walking, head down, face set. The quick one darts in again.

And Katherine snaps, her rage a deafening screech of tears and fury.

"Shut up. Fucking shut up! Shut up, shut up shut up…"

One of them mimics her.

"You heard her, piss off!" Paul is at them now, his patience gone. He's shouting, spittle flies "Piss off, you worthless little shits."

The laughter stops. One of them moves in on Paul.

"Who you talkin' to?" he says.

"You, you worthless little cunt."

"Paul, no," Rachel seems to claw her way towards the face-off with dreamlike slowness. Everyone is shouting. I freeze.

Because I don't know what to do.

Rachel grabs at Paul, but it's too late. He's pushed the youth so hard the kid has fallen over. Paul drops to his knees. His arm pistons; down, up, down, up. Each descending stroke ends in a soft, fleshy thud.

The gang mill around. They shout; "Fuck, oh Christ, he's fucking killing him!" And their voices are full of terror, and yet at the same time some of them laugh. One of them pauses long enough to take photos with his phone then he bounces backwards shouting at his mates to wait for him. Another is being held back. He screams with rage, howls threats, struggles in his mates' arms then breaks away and runs. He has a pattern shaved into his close-cropped hair, a zigzag that runs along the side of his scalp.

Paul stops and slowly, almost painfully gets to his feet. He stares down at his work, motionless now. Rachel stands beside him. Her hand goes to her mouth. It seems to take me a thousand years to reach the group. The youth is curled on the ground. I can't see any details, only the black lake of blood that reaches out and around his head. Katherine kneels beside him, Rachel is clinging to Rajan's arm. I crouch beside Katherine and notice her perfume and how sensual it is and then wonder at how I can be aroused by a woman's scent while crouched beside a someone that a member of my team has just beaten almost to death.

"We have to get help," Katherine says.

I shake my head. "We can't." My voice is barely audible even to myself.

Katherine is demanding my attention and demanding that I get help. How? We haven't got any phones. We are supposed to support The Visitor at all costs. That's what we are told by the men and women in sharp and shiny suits. The needs of the many outweigh the needs of the individual.

I become aware that Paul is kneeling again. He's shaking. It doesn't take much imagination to work out why. He was a soldier, for Christ's sake. I'm scared shitless now because the big dependable ex-infantryman who watched our flanks is actually suffering from some post traumatic stress or other and right now seems to be in the grip of a panic attack.

Katherine has re-started her litany about getting help. Rajan says that she's right. I want them all to shut up. I want them all to get off my back and *shut up*.

I stumble over to The Visitor and shove my face into its impassive, inscrutable mask and yell. "What do you want? What the fuck do you want? Why don't *you* help *us*?"

"I want to find the Engine of the Earth," it answers and I want to hit the vile bloody thing but I don't because I'm too frightened.

I back away, look round and see everyone staring at me; silent, appalled, scornful.

"We're going to find a phone and get help," Rachel says. By *we*, she obviously means herself and Rajan. She is holding his arm.

I shake my head. "No, we have to stay together."

"We can't do that, John." Katherine is using her best patronising-politician's tone. "That boy is badly hurt. We can't let him die." She draws me apart. "Don't you think it wise to show ourselves as creatures of compassion?" She glances at The Visitor as if to emphasise her point.

I've failed. My team is breaking up. I'm going to be the one slammed by the media when all this finally emerges from the shadows.

"Paul." I snap. "Paul, we have to go." He ignores me, sits down, head bowed.

"Paul!"

"For Christ's sake, John," Katherine shouts at me. "We can't go. Don't you understand? *We have to help this boy.*"

"Okay, do what you bloody want?" I yell so loudly the words tear my throat. "Do what *you* think is best, don't let me stand in your way. That…That little bastard deserved what he got."

I swing round and take a step towards the sculpture.

And someone bursts out of the dark. He's shouting and screaming. I see the zigzag razored into his hair. I see the gun in his hand.

He's out of control. The gun swings around wildly and we're all frozen in place. The slightest pressure on that trigger and someone will be hurt. The youth rants, calls us murderers and filth. The others draw together, and withdraw from me. No one orders it, they just do, the action unconscious and brutal. Even Paul is part of the group and he caused this.

I have to do something. It's my role, I'm leader here. I have to confront the youth and take the gun. I have to show some worth, some act of courage to put things right.

Rachel is talking to him, so quietly I can't hear what's she's saying. She takes a step towards him, arms away from her sides, hands open. She snags the boy's attention, for a moment, long enough –

I lurch forwards, stumble against the youth, who feels surprisingly thin and small and light, and make a grab for the weapon. I hear shouts and cries and then an explosion, shocking, loud and illuminated by a dazzling flash of light.

The silence is worse.

The kid is on the ground. He scuttles back, mouth open and whimpering. I look round and see that someone else is down. Rachel. Down and still and, like Paul's victim, haloed in something dark and spreading. I grope my way towards her and feel an object under my palm.

"The gun," I say. "It's okay, I have the gun…"

It isn't okay. Nothing is okay. Sound returns, crying and shouting.

I look up to see The Visitor. Its hood is down. Something resembling a smile is screwed into its face.

"Thank you," it says.

Then I hear a police siren, growing louder. People are emerging from the flats and finally I understand what has happened here and why everyone is crying and howling and that, somehow it's my fault.

I also realise that The Visitor has gone.

The Discord of Being

by Alison J. Littlewood

Emma hadn't been to Morocco, the place her mother was buried and her father still lived, since she was little more than a child. All the same, as she stepped off the aeroplane it seemed familiar, despite the strangeness of the low, decorated terminal, the palm trees waving flag-like branches in the breeze. It was the sky, she decided. A grey covering of clouds rolled away into the distance; it was an English sky. Even so, her skin prickled with sweat as she walked towards immigration with the other passengers – holidaymakers, their children, and people going home.

In the terminal, where families waited, one man stood among the others, holding a sign that bore her name. Her father had sent a colleague to meet her, a tall, neatly dressed man named Ibrahim. She shook hands with the stranger, remembering her father's words on the telephone: *You don't need to come.* She felt he had been offering an escape route for them both.

The call had come late one night, the ring tone sounding just like any other. That was what seemed strange afterward, that the sound had carried no warning: that she hadn't known.

Disturbed, her father had said, and all Emma could think of was being pressed close to her mother's body, safe, warm. *Her grave has been disturbed. I just – I thought you should know.* And then that eternal mantra: *You don't need to come.*

The thought of it angered her. How could he have done this? For it was her father she blamed, at once and entirely. He had brought her mother here, leaving Emma to stay with an aunt, just for a little while. And then her mother died and he decided to stay, just like that, not seeing Emma save for when she came for her mother's funeral. How could he let her mother die like that? How could he have let her die *here?* And how could he live among people who would do this to her grave?

Emma opened her mouth to say something to Ibrahim, closed it again. But it was as though he read her thoughts. He turned to her with sympathy in his eyes. "The Moroccan people would not do this."

She scowled. "Then who?"

It was Ibrahim's turn to subside. He shook his head, led her to the car.

It wasn't long before they reached the foothills of the Atlas Mountains. Emma watched the colours flash by. She had imagined somewhere sepia and bleak, without growth and life; instead she found this red land, with grasses and straw and brilliant yellow flowers, everything dotted with dark green argan trees.

The engine protested as the road grew steeper, heading up towards the grey sky.

"It will rain," Ibrahim said, trying to lighten the mood. "I think you brought it from England," and she smiled back at him as he was proved right; droplets speckled the windscreen. The wipers scraped and Emma wound down the window to see a river rattling down a narrow gully, palm trees darkening in the rain.

They wound upwards until they reached a narrow track. To one side great boulders were piled atop one another, their ochre streaked with red and grey and orange. To the other was a sheer drop. Emma glimpsed the road they had travelled far below, a village nestled into the hillside beyond, the mosque's minaret towering over everything else.

In front of them, an inlet was cut into the rocks. Buildings slotted into it, filling every inch, their wooden doorways painted bright colours. One opened and a man stepped out. He wore a point-hooded djellaba and had yellow babouches on his feet. He had a grey beard and was turning something in his hand; a piece of stone. With a tremor, Emma realised it was her father.

When she turned to Ibrahim, he gave a sympathetic smile. Her father did not hold out his arms or say anything at all. Instead he raised his watery eyes, nodded, and led the way inside.

The room was dark, its concrete floor strewn with threadbare rugs. There was a simple wooden table, shelves holding rocks and grit and tools; hammers, chisels, brushes. A mobile phone lay among them, dust-covered like the rest. The room smelled of damp stone and something sweeter; honey, perhaps. Emma felt a twinge of anger. As far as she'd known, her father had left England for a good job, a prestigious job, working with the fossil mining concerns that dotted the mountains. But this – was this why he had left? Her desk at work was just one grey cubicle among many, but the walls were smooth, the floor clean. She had a computer and a telephone, air conditioning.

Then she saw a small bottle balanced on the lintel over the door, its contents dark red, muddy looking. She snatched it down and sniffed, thinking of alcohol, but the scent was of meat.

Her father looked apologetic. "It's for the djinn," he said. "It keeps them out." He shrugged.

Emma snorted, banged it back onto the ledge. "Is this it?" She could barely keep the fury out of her voice. She waved a hand around the room, encompassing everything.

Her father lifted his arms, let them fall. He still clutched something in his hand and he held it out. An ammonite, tight whorls inscribed in stone. "A new species," he said. "New to science, anyway. I saved it for you."

She reached out and his fingers closed over it. "I meant I could name it for you."

Emma shook her head. He had named her. *Her*. And then he left her for this shack with its dirt and its rocks.

Her father nodded, as though it was what he had expected. "It is good to see you, Em."

"Emma." She barked out the word, though he was right; Em was what people called her. It was what her mother had called her. Her stomach twisted.

"Emma." He nodded.

"Are you going to tell me what happened?"

"I will," he said. "But first you can get settled. We'll have tea together. I'll show you around."

Emma glanced at the room. She had seen everything already.

"No," he said. "Not in here. Out there."

The mountains swirled around them, fading into the distance. Rain still pattered down but the sun shone through it, the light soft and delicate, turning the slopes to pastel. Wild flowers sparked in brilliant pinks and yellows. And everywhere, leaning against the building, lying on the ground, were ammonites and trilobites, some of them several feet across.

Her father was talking about how the mountains had formed. Emma imagined him burrowing into the miles of fossils under his feet, chipping at the vastness until he had found each one, his home long forgotten. Out here, she could almost forget it too. The air was clean and smelled of rain, the mountains sweet, beguiling. And something he said struck her: *it was all under the sea*, and she felt a wave of vertigo, imagined fathoms of salt water above her head, stretching into the sky. She had a sense of the earth beneath her shifting and shattering, thrusting upwards over the millennia, movements on a scale impossible to imagine.

"And you study all this." She looked at the shapes on the ground, the spirals and lobes. Reminded herself they were familiar from museums and nature programmes, known, catalogued. And yet he had been here for years. He worked for a company who dug up these creatures that had turned to stone and bought and sold them.

"I study all this."

"So you understand it all."

He smiled. "No. No, I'll never understand it all."

She scowled. "What happened to my mother?"

He was silent.

"What happened?"

"She was at peace. She still is, Em."

She did not correct him. She only waited.

Her father's throat clicked as he spoke. "They dug up the ground."

"Who did?"

"We don't know."

"How far?"

He didn't answer, though Emma knew he'd understood what she meant. How far down, is what she'd wanted to ask. He said nothing, raised his hands again and let them fall. Emma remembered the fossil in his hand, the delicate life written in stone, a species never before seen or numbered. That dizziness took her again. Amazing there could be anything new left to discover. A different kind of life, long turned to rock, held for a moment in the palm of his hand.

"I want to see it," she said. "I want to see everything."

The journey passed in bursts of rain and sunshine, blue patches of sky meeting and joining as they left the mountains. Emma's father sat up front with Ibrahim. He hadn't wanted to come, but Emma insisted. She had felt like a geologist herself, fighting his reluctance, as though prising a fossil from its hole in the ground.

Now the men exchanged occasional words in Darija, the Moroccan Arabic, low and quick as though they didn't want to disturb her. Before they departed they'd packed the boot full of bags of fossils, so that Emma's things wouldn't fit; they were beside her on the seat.

Emma looked out at the horizon and saw the higher peaks of the Altas, capped with snow. She remembered that somewhere out there lay the dunes of the Sahara, home of Tuareg and Bedouin, and felt again a wave of disorientation.

Marrakesh, when they reached it, was something else again; a line of terracotta coloured rock walls. "The Red City," said Ibrahim, and she imagined it being carved from the earth, the buildings rising like something organic.

The grave was in a cemetery on the outskirts of the city, sectioned into Moslem, Jewish and Christian. The cemetery was narrow, spread around a hillside that had probably been no use for anything else. There were buildings opposite, shops with narrow alleys leading away.

Emma was suddenly reluctant, but her father held out his hand. "It's all right," he said. "I told you." She followed, glanced back to see that Ibrahim had stayed behind.

Emma was fourteen when her mother was buried, an event that was oddly and comprehensively missing from her memory, as though she'd tried to blank it out, or never really taken it in. A heart attack, they'd said; a western death in a country far from home. Now Emma stood in the cemetery, though, the recognition was strong and total, a knife in her gut. The headstones were lit by sharp, hard sunlight. She saw the one that was her mother's, but it wasn't right: it looked intact, a little crooked perhaps, but nothing to show that anything had happened. She stared at the words: *Beloved wife and mother.*

"But it's fine," she said, her voice faltering. She felt she had been robbed, as though everything should be torn and uprooted and twisted.

"It has been put right," her father said. And then, hesitant: "I'm sorry."

"I wanted to see. I wanted to know everything."

Her father sighed. "No one really knows, Emma. It happened at night. The stone was overturned, the grave–"

"Dug into."

"Yes."

"So did they find her? Did they reach the body? Did it happen to other graves, or just hers?" Emma waited, but the answer didn't come. She scowled. It was as if he didn't want to know, didn't need to know. As if something was broken and had been fixed and he had already moved on.

"It won't do any good. Look, it's all right now. No one seemed to know what happened. Sometimes – it's difficult to find things out." He sighed. "You didn't need to come. I told you."

I told you. As though that was the answer to everything.

"Did you upset someone?"

"What?" He looked surprised.

"In your job. Or whatever. Have you done something? Made someone want to hurt you – hurt my mother?"

"Of course not." He shook his head. Then, slowly: "Not like that. Sometimes I think, with the digging – we have gone too far." His voice went distant. "The djinn..."

She snorted, rolled her eyes. "For God's sake."

He paused. "So I suppose you will go now. We can take you to the airport. We have business – we will stay awhile, now we are here, Ibrahim and I. Whenever you like–"

Emma remembered the bags in the boot of the car. Of course, he had brought his work with him. Even her mother's desecration was a reason to study his precious fossils, dead things dug from the ground. She shivered as she turned from the grave. She couldn't get that out of her head: dead things, dug from the ground. She didn't know how he could bear to look at them.

Marrakesh was life and sound and noise. Emma stood at a crossroads full of cars all trying to turn at once, beeping their horns, missing each other by millimetres. Perhaps because her father seemed so willing for her to leave, she had decided to stay, until she was ready. She turned her back, passed under an arched gate set into the city walls, and entered the old town or medina. There were no cars here, but although the sounds changed, the bustle was the same. The streets were narrow and full of people: tourists, locals in colourful djellabas, women with shaylah scarves over their hair, or veiled faces. Donkey carts plodded along, unfazed by the motorcycles that gunned through it all, edging everything else out of the way.

Emma had left her father and Ibrahim at the hotel, though they had offered to show her around. She hadn't wanted to be shown around. She had wanted to walk and to think. Now she found thinking impossible. Everything was new, different. She passed a shop with brightly coloured sacks of spices on the ground, casting rich scents into the air. Another with hundreds of shoes hanging outside, forming a solid curtain.

She took a narrower turning into the souk, a roofed passageway so crowded with goods it felt like a tunnel. Stalls were hung with leather belts and babouches and wallets and bags in every colour. Everything smelled of leather. Men sat outside their shops, stitching or waiting to trade. Emma jumped out of the way of a motorcycle, the rider clutching a live chicken by its feet. Then leather gave way to lamps, every conceivable shape and size, each stall shining like a genie's grotto. Emma let the colours and sounds play over her, the constant flow of Darija and Berber and French from the crowds, the blare of a radio, the tapping of stallholders working on their wares and the bark of haggling. She felt stirred, overwhelmed, the sounds thrumming. *All of life is here,* she thought. It was naked in its intensity. People wanting to trade, needing to trade, to fleece a tourist so their children could eat.

Emma kept wading through it all, drowning in it, seeing everything and thinking of nothing: not her father, not what had happened to her mother's grave. And then someone turned in the crowd ahead, looking back so that Emma saw their face, and everything stopped.

Someone knocked into her, muttered some apology or imprecation, but Emma couldn't move. She stared at the figure, and it looked back with her mother's eyes. It *was* her mother. After a long moment the woman turned and melded with the crowd.

Emma started to push her way through, trying to keep the figure in sight. Everywhere were faces, some indignant, some curious. And then the alleyway ended and Emma stumbled into an open space. It was thronged with people. She took a step forward, looking about. What had her mother been wearing? She couldn't remember. Her breath came hard and fast. She couldn't see the woman anywhere, didn't know which way to go.

Emma stepped forward into the square, into the strains of discordant music. She knew where she was from the pictures she'd seen: Djemaa el Fna, the most famous square in Morocco, perhaps in the world. And everywhere were people. Traders sitting on stools or carpets, stalls with fairground games, storytellers' tents, people crossing from one place to another, friends meeting, kissing on the cheeks, men holding out water snakes or Barbary apes to tempt tourists to part with their dirhams. And everywhere, groups of musicians; flowerings of notes competed with throbbing drums and soothing pipes. She scanned it all, saw nothing she could recognise. The woman who had looked like her mother had gone.

Emma caught one of the city's petit taxis back to the hotel, knowing she'd never find the way on her own. She hammered on her father's door. It opened and she saw his lined face, his faded eyes. And Ibrahim, always there, a fossil and a magnifying glass held in his hands.

"I saw her," said Emma. In spite of herself she felt tears spring into her eyes.

Her father squinted, as if he hadn't yet adjusted to looking out at the world. "Who?"

"I saw *her*." Emma was suddenly furious. "I saw my mother." Then her body sagged and she leaned against the door. Her father took her arm, led her to the only chair. A foot away was his bed, tousled and scattered with fossils. "This is ridiculous," Emma snapped, and her father shrugged, helplessly.

Ibrahim stepped forward. "A little tea, perhaps," he said. "You thought you saw something. The heat, maybe. Morocco can be a strange place to those who do not know her."

Emma gave him a look, wiped at her eyes. "I saw my mother," she insisted.

"Someone who looked like her. There are many English in Marrakesh."

"I *know* that."

"She is in your heart, of course. In your thoughts." Ibrahim's voice was gentle, the kindness in it cutting through her, and Emma bit back a sob.

"A drink, perhaps," Ibrahim said again, this time to her father. Emma knew he was Moslem, wouldn't touch alcohol, and had a sudden image of what she must look like: a stupid foreigner, overwhelmed by the noise and the heat. She closed her eyes and felt her father pushing a glass into her hands. It was wine, poured into a cheap hotel tumbler.

"I'm sorry, Em." Her father said. His voice seemed different when he said it. His eyes were rheumy, the wrinkles gleaming with moisture. "I never was a good father to you."

Emma looked away, drew deeply on the wine. Her hand shook. She couldn't remember a time when he had said such things, and now, she didn't want to think about him at all; only of her mother. She remembered the face in the souk. She would have given anything to speak to her. Longed for the woman whose funeral she had attended; not this father who stood in front of her.

A crowd gathered around a tent, laughing and jeering. Emma stood on tiptoes, though she didn't stand a chance of seeing anything. Ibrahim, a head taller, looked over and laughed. "It is an old Moroccan joke," he said, "about a man and his wife. The wife is also played by a man, of course."

The crowd convulsed with laughter. And the image that sprang into Emma's head was of Punch and Judy, sitting on some frigid English beach while Mr Punch's neck grew longer and longer. She grimaced.

"It is an old tradition," Ibrahim said, and Emma nodded.

She followed him as he pointed out men rigging tents for the evening barbecues, ladies offering henna tattoos. He didn't pause, assuming she wouldn't be interested, and Emma peered down at the photographs of flowered hands and feet. She was half tempted to stay, but daunted by the women's harsh invitations.

Ibrahim had offered to show her around, and he was taking his role as tour guide seriously. "Djemaa el Fna," he said, "the centre of Marrakesh; at least, of its spirit. Hundreds of years old. Once, they sold slaves here, stolen from their homes and bound for Europe. Or the other way around."

Emma blinked. Ibrahim smiled at her. "Europeans were stolen too," he said. "Some were brought here by the corsairs. Not so many as Africans, of course."

Emma frowned, trying to understand the import of his words, but he went on. "Djemaa means congregational mosque," he said. "Fna is courtyard, or death. No one agrees what it means. It could be mosque with a courtyard. Or it could be assembly of death, place of death. You see? Morocco has many meanings." He waved a hand, taking in the snake charmers, street dentists with human teeth laid out on rugs, Moroccan teenagers buying dried apricots and figs.

"But which?" asked Emma. "What does it mean? They must know."

Ibrahim smiled. "It is for you to choose."

"No, it's not. It's–" but Emma's voice faded. She had seen someone across the field of paving slabs, someone who stood quite still amidst the movement.

"Emma?"

"It's her." Emma started walking, was jerked back when Ibrahim caught her arm.

"You mustn't," he said, urgently. "It isn't her. Do not."

Emma wriggled free and started across the square, hampered by the press of people, the haphazard placing of tents and rugs. She didn't call out, knew her mother would never hear. Then she saw that the figure had stopped. Her mother was pale, her skin white against the dark, straight hair. Her eyes were hollow, their expression impossible to make out.

Emma began to run. She had to know, to understand what her mother was trying to tell her. The woman was in a narrower part of the square now, heading for the road that marked its edge, moving easily between throngs of tourists. Emma wove in and out as people stopped in her path to check that their bags or their children were safe. She heard the road, its honking and screeching.

There. A flash of dark hair, then it was gone. Emma let out a cry, felt Ibrahim's hand close once more on her arm. She struggled and he let go, spread his hands in the air.

"Please." Ibrahim looked hurt, anxious. He glanced around to see who might be watching.

Emma clenched her hands on nothing, pressed them against her face.

"I am sorry. But you mustn't. It is not a good thing. You should not follow. You must not look for her, Emma."

"It was my *mother*." Emma choked on the words, and as she did, she knew what she needed to do. Before Ibrahim could react, she turned and ran once more for the road. A taxi was parked at the kerb, discharging passengers. Emma grabbed the open door, jumped inside. When the driver looked at her with startled eyes, she gave the name of the cemetery where her mother was buried.

Emma couldn't find the caretaker anywhere. Eventually she asked in a local shop and the shopkeeper led the way down narrow streets to a small, tumbledown house. He banged on the door until another man came, but it was the shopkeeper who asked what she needed and Emma realised he had stayed to interpret. He looked at her kindly, and tears welled in her eyes. Suddenly there was a chair, a glass of hot, sweet tea. They brought flatbreads, a dish of honey. Their generosity made everything worse.

"I have to know what happened to my mother," she said. "I have to know if the grave was empty."

They exchanged looks, spoke to each other in rapid Arabic. Eventually the shopkeeper explained. "No," he said. "Your mother's grave was not empty. But it was – opened, yes?"

Emma stared down at her glass of tea, feeling hot vapour on her cheeks. "But if she was there – what happened?"

There was more conferring. This time, the shopkeeper's voice was gentle. "He says there may have been animals," he said. "A hyena, maybe. But they did what they could for her."

"Animals?" Emma looked up. The man's eyes were fixed on hers and they were dark, almost black. She saw the message in them, and felt suddenly sick.

"He is very sorry." The man indicated the caretaker. "He would watch all the time, but he has a family. He says they took care of it."

Emma nodded. She knew they'd filled in the grave, fixed it, as her father had said. *No need for you to come.* She hesitated. "But how do you know it was my mother? And where is she now?"

This time, the translation came quickly: "But of course, it was your mother. And she is back in the ground. We buried her again."

Emma shook her head, stared at the floor. Hyenas, this close to the city? It didn't make sense. And she thought of what she had seen in the shopkeeper's eyes, when he'd said it: he was protecting her. His expression had been gentle, as though the truth he was hiding was somehow worse than his lies.

When Emma got back to the hotel, her father was waiting. He ushered her into his room. This time, Ibrahim wasn't there.

"Emma, what you did. It was reckless." He put a hand on her arm and she pulled away. "I know you think you saw your mother."

Emma turned on him, eyes fierce. "I did see her. I went to the cemetery. I know what happened."

"I am sorry." Her father didn't say if he was sorry for what happened, or sorry that Emma had found out.

"You left her for the animals. *Animals*."

Now her father looked angry. "I did *not*," he said. "I loved her. I buried her. Do you understand that?"

She was silent.

"Your mother lived, and now she is dead. It was not your mother you saw. Your mother is safe, wherever she is."

"I *saw* her."

"No. it was not your mother."

"Her ghost, then. Her spirit."

"*No*. You come here, seeing nothing." He looked away at last. "I told you of the djinn, Emma. I have – dug too much and too far. I fear I have angered them. And now one of them has come to punish me."

Emma stared, astonished.

"They are everywhere, Emma. And one of them – an evil djinn – has tasted your mother's body and now it has taken her form."

She shook her head. "You're–"

"Crazy, yes. But I know what I know. This thing has your mother's face, but it is not her. It is a grave robber, a *ghul*, Emma. And if you follow it–" he looked away. "It will take you too."

Emma lay awake, listening to the anodyne sounds of a hotel in the early morning; the clanking of the maid's cart, banging doors, the distant buzz of the lift. She pressed her hands against her face, remembering her mother as she had last seen her: dark-smudged eyes set into white skin, an expression she couldn't read. If she had been closer, perhaps she would have known what her mother had been trying to say. Would have been able to tell if her father's words were true.

She screwed her hands into fists. If she had seen her dead mother in England, would she then only have been a spirit – a ghost? Could she have spoken to her – had her father robbed her even of that, by bringing her to a place where the djinn walked?

Emma shook her head, rose, and headed for the lobby. When she reached it she heard a familiar voice. She turned to see Ibrahim, dressed smartly, a heavy-looking sample case in his hands. "Emma," he said, only that, but his tone said everything.

She shook her head. "I'm going back to the square. Just once more. And then I'm going home." She paused. "I have to understand."

Ibrahim looked at her, his gaze steady, until she had to look away. He spoke only once before picking up his case and turning to leave. "I do not think it is a place you understand," he said. "I think it is a place that you feel."

She thought of his words as she left the hotel and headed for the square. She hadn't been talking about the place, at all: it was her mother that had been in her mind. All the same, as she entered Djemaa el Fna, she knew that he was right. The bustle was there, but it was different. She saw now that the square wasn't the paving or the mosque or the buildings that marked its edge; it wasn't even its history. It was the people who filled it, selling and buying and entertaining, telling their stories, filling the air with charcoal-smoke and music, so that every moment it changed, became somewhere new. She couldn't understand this place, would never understand, because it was never the same. And if she couldn't understand this place, something man had made and torn up and remade, how would she ever understand what she had seen?

The discord of music filled her mind, confusing everything. The square was a whirl of people going about their lives, their daily dance. *All of life is here,* she thought, and remembered her mother's face looking back at her: *no. All of life and death.*

Emma started to walk. Despite her earlier resolve, she was no longer sure she wanted to see her mother. All that was left was hollowness, and a strange kind of yearning. Yet as she passed through the square, she realised her mother was there: was walking ahead of her through the throng, clearing a path for Emma to follow. This time the woman looked back and smiled, and it was the old smile, clean and good. This time no one got in Emma's way; the crowds drew back as the spirit passed, as though they saw or sensed what it was.

Emma's heart beat faster, the music around her transforming into light and air, rising and falling in perfect rhythm. This was where she was meant to be. She knew this place, belonged in this moment. She scarcely noticed as her mother entered a narrow alleyway, a shadow falling across her features. The woman pulled a layer of fabric from her dress, drawing a veil across her face; stepped back into a recess, her back to the stone, and beckoned her daughter in.

There were images behind Emma's eyes, a multitude of them: the chaos of goods in the souk, curious faces, men staring or calling out in Darija, intricate tiles on a floor or wall, donkey carts, delicately whorled stones. There were sounds, too: the deep call of the muezzin, the higher wail of the pipers. Their music no longer made sense to her. She moaned, put her hand to her forehead, trying to wipe away the things she saw or didn't see. There was pain there, but she realised it was not a headache. She touched a hand to her neck, lower down, the hollow place above her shoulder blade. She felt something dry under her fingers. When she looked at her fingertips, she found them powdered with blood.

She opened her eyes and saw the plain, blank ceiling of her hotel room. By the harsh light slashing the rectangle, she knew it must be about midday. Then a sound began to register. Someone was hammering on the door.

When she opened it her father stood there. Emma opened her mouth to greet him then closed it again. What was the use? There was no name she could call him. 'Father' was too formal, like something out of a book; 'Dad' too familiar. Instead she stared as he guided her back inside, felt her forehead. Emma caught a glimpse of herself in the mirror, her skin pale, eyes nothing but dark smudges.

Her father had her lie down, brought her water to drink, rubbed life into her hands. He kept talking, though Emma didn't listen to the words. Eventually, she spoke.

"Why did you stay here?" she asked.

This time, his words were halting. "Because I had to," he said. "Because it would have killed me not to."

Emma let his words drift over her.

"Sometimes a place takes hold of you. And you know you have to stay, because anywhere else – the homesickness–" he paused. "You are homesick for somewhere that was never your home."

For a while, there was silence. The knife of sunlight drew across the ceiling. Emma pushed herself up; found her father resting his head on his arms. He stirred, looked back at her. She put out a hand and touched the whorls of skin around his eyes, thought of the ridged curls of an ammonite.

"What did you call it?" she asked.

He looked puzzled; then he understood. "Emmaceras," he said, and smiled. "You know, Emma, ammonites are named for the Egyptian god Ammon. The god of procreation. Of life."

Emma nodded. She pushed herself up, examined her neck in the mirror. The wound was shallow, surrounded by scratches, but it was clean. Her father must have washed it.

"Do you think it's happy now?" she asked.

He merely sighed, raised and lowered his hands. He didn't try to explain, just looked at her face, his gaze steady. And then he said: "You should stay here."

Emma started. Touched a hand to her neck. She had expected him to say she should go home, get as far away from Morocco – and the square – as she could. And yet, now the words were out, she felt she understood. *All of life is here,* she thought. *And all of death.* She knew this, had been touched by it. And yet the heart of it, the sound, the chaos – it was inside her, too.

Life and death. Death and life. Vivid and loud and bright and dangerous. Not something to be ignored, to be analysed or regulated or wrapped in plastic, layers and layers of it, so that when either of them surfaced, it was frightening.

The thought made her dizzy, made her want to laugh. She looked at her father's face, felt the ties that ran between them despite the years and the distance. She caught his hand in hers, felt the thinness, the bones beneath the papery skin.

When she closed her eyes, though, what she saw was a doorway; a large, beautiful doorway in the shape of a keyhole, dusty and grimed. On the other side of it was her desk at work: clean, bare, organised. And she knew that she could step through, take her seat, resume her life. And then what? Would she turn again, look back the other way, to see – what? Already there was an odd pang in her stomach, a deep sort of longing she couldn't understand but that she could feel.

She opened her eyes and didn't know for whom or what she felt it.

Her father was watching. He smiled. "It's very simple," he said, and when she looked back into his eyes, she knew that it was true.

Xana-La

by Stephen Palmer

The fate of all those who enter Moongolia is to die.

Such assertions roam our world on the wings of song, passing from man to boy to man again; the curtailed lives of the Tuvan throat singers make them fly. But Pharaday Lemmington knew one word had been altered in the assertion he had heard a hundred times since becoming a member of the Suicide Club. Moongolia could be reached, explored. It was Xana-La that was deadly.

And so he dared the most curious of all the episodes enlivening the brief history of the Suicide Club, telling his gentlemen friends that he would find Xana-La and return with proof of its existence.

They laughed. I did, too. But I laughed quietly, for I knew something about Pharaday no-one else did, and I sat back, drinking, smoking… and I wondered.

The Bactrian Archimedean floating system favoured by Pharaday lay in its frost-limned rack on the roof of the Suicide Club, and on a dark winter morning I climbed the fire escape stair at the back of the building – six storeys in all – in order to reach the roof without my associates seeing me. There, I found Pharaday.

"Sir," I said.

He turned, but not in fright. I believe he knew I was approaching. He wore the black greatcoat and white woollen hat for which he was best known, his spectacles gleaming in the light of a Natrio-burner. "Mr Spar-Turney," he said.

"Call me Franclin."

He smiled. "What brings you here?"

"Your challenge. You mean to go to Moongolia?"

He harrumphed, like the judges with whom he jousted on a regular basis. "Any two-guinea boy may go to Moongolia, but the secret city… that is a different matter."

My heart thumped in my chest and, quite unconsciously I am sure, I folded my arms, as if to conceal my anxiety.

"Sir…"

"Pharaday," he corrected me.

"Would you need an assistant?"

He took a deep breath. "To hold the lamp when I expose the film. To tend the camels in the baking heat of the sun. To put the treasure into the treasure chests. Are these the tasks you had in mind?"

"I was serious." I frowned – I had not expected mockery. "You may have forgotten my triumphs in Dogon Escarpoture –"

"I forget *none* of the tales that return to the Suicide Club," he said. I heard an edge of annoyance in his voice. "So… you wish to accompany me to Xana-La."

"It exists?"

"Of course. All legendary places *exist*. The problem is the problem that has bedevilled man since we were apes. Getting back alive, with the tale on the tip of the tongue and ready to be told."

I nodded. "To be written down," I said.

He glanced away. "Certainly, Moongolia has something of a reputation, not least for tigers." When I said nothing he walked up to me, then once around me. "Tall," he said, looking me up and down as a toff would a racing horse, "greying at the temples, good teeth. Are you strong, Franclin? Can you pull a greased hawser, cut a leather hide with a shaving razor?"

"I can do both of those things," I said, relief flooding through me. He remembered the Dogon Witch Doctor! I shook him by the hand.

He indicated the Bactrian Archimedean machinora. "Welcome to the next flight of this old beauty."

We left at dawn one week later, on the winter solstice, which we deemed, quite wrongly, to be an auspicious date. The spitoons of two dozen of our comrades clanged in the alleys below as they marked our suicide, or journey, as we termed it.

The machinora was two-humped and thus provided with more than adequate lift, and for some days the flight went well, Parisi passing below us first, then Quinceria, Berlinzeug, Varsaw and Spi. But as we crossed the Muscovite Steppes a distant machinora appeared, one marked with the red heart of the Floating Ladies, and my own heart sank. Pharaday was notorious for his dalliances with the stronger sex.

Deciding that my best tactic would be one of honesty I challenged him, as we ate ham sandwiches and drank Somerset spritzers. "I confess I am worried," I said, "for all of us in the Suicide Club know of your… of your…"

"Oh, stop stuttering man," he said, grimacing. "My *weakness*, is that what you were going to say?"

"Yes."

He gestured at the floating bagnio. "I will have a look around – a *quick* look, mind – and then we shall be on our way. It was never my intention, Franclin, to keep my hands on the tiller for the entire flight."

I said nothing, not knowing if he had used a euphemism. By now the scented lace appurtenances of the approaching machinora were making my nose twitch, and I paced up and down, fretting. Pharaday grinned, and a thin line of drool crept down his chin.

The Floating Ladies flung out their plank and Pharaday walked across, both hands on the guide ropes because of the fierce wind (we flew at one thousand feet). Some of the women exposed their breasts in a style both shameful and attractive, but I was not to be tempted. Then a man emerged and made lewd gestures. I think the women must have sensed my outrage at this slur, because they left soon after for the velvet interior of their machinora.

"They won't speak a word of English," I muttered to myself. "It will be all vodka and condoms made of pig entrails."

Half an hour later Pharaday emerged. Standing once again at my side he hove to and dropped an aero-anchor, so that the Floating Ladies could disengage their machinora and depart.

"Fair does something to the soul, a good baste!" he said.

"For those who believe we contain a soul, maybe," I replied.

"You have the attitude of a Regency squanderer!" he roared, slapping my back and grinning like a Hindoo idol.

By the time of the next full moon our machinora flew across the black, swaying pine forests of the Turquish Main, a land I feared, not least because starlight could not save us should we fall, so bright was our Lune. I had, of course, heard of the fateful flight of the Astral Spinneret – as had we all in the Suicide Club. Even Pharaday was frightened, murmuring to himself about piercings and death by sooty needle.

Days passed. The air grew uncomfortably warm, so we activated the ice cube dolly and stripped to our knee-johns and string vests. I was most intrigued to see two tattoos on Pharaday's upper right arm, one in the form of a red half moon, the other shaped as a green flower with a white centre. He in turn examined the patterns of scarification on my chest, made when I was in the hands of the Ouagadougou torturers.

"The hairs do not grow there any more," I remarked.

He nodded. "You are a fine man," he said. "I chose my assistant well."

"Africa," I said, "is a dark continent indeed. But not so dark as where we go."

"Indeed not. And, now that we are close to the Orient, Franclin, I do not mind telling you that I am rather anxious about our fate. This was a somewhat…" He struggled for words, then sighed and said, "*ironic* challenge to undertake."

I did not know it then, but that word signified our respective fortunes.

We floated at speed across the lands of the West Iranian Pashas, and thence into Far Northern Indoo, which lay below us like a fabric of emerald green and blue – a more entrancing land difficult to imagine. We ate poached eggs on toast enlivened with Durham sauce, and we drank perry from glass goblets. But all the while we looked ahead, and thought of the doom that was ours.

Balmy days passed. We floated ever east, ever on, as the snowy cranes flapped over our heads and the tigers roared far below. That white-peaked mountain chain beloved of the Suicide Club, the Himalayas, rose far to the icy north; and then the jungled hills of Burmeer.

The sun lay low as we approached the mountain range that Pharaday claimed marked the site of the concealed city: Chin'a to the north and east, the Desert of Gobi too near for comfort. We landed the machinora and let it graze the wind-rippled grass plains of the region, packing our backpacks then setting forth, with walking sticks in our right hands and binoculars in our left. Vultures followed us, but we did not speak their tongue, so we ignored them.

"Those bald-headed varmints don't know our fate," Pharaday reassured me. "They just like to show off. Pesky, if you ask me."

I looked at him. "You have been here before, have you not?"

He sensed the current lurking beneath my sentence, and he frowned, then uttered a single cough of embarrassment. "What do you mean?"

"I know you have no belly button, sir."

"What?"

"It is true. I know it. I suspect the fact lies close to your motive for this journey."

He said nothing for a long, long while. We tramped along a lane of high grasses set with silver trees, alive with twittering birds and copper-green butterflies. At last he said, "How do you know?"

"When I joined the Suicide Club," I explained, "I was nothing more than a naïve lad, not even twenty – pushed forward by my father in those last months remaining before the Patagonian Cancer got him."

Pharaday sighed. "He was a marvellous chap, your father."

"One night I was taking the air outdoors upon a balcony, watching painted ladies in the street, when I noticed a bright yellow lamp switch on at the window beside me. This was accidental, I promise you. I looked in, and saw you and a naked girl – the black one with the beads in her hair."

"Heléne Formidablé."

"I know not her name. You were dressed only in pantaloons and… the red silk sash around your waist that, so the girls gossip, you never take off. But you walked forward and raised your arms to close the curtains, and as you did the sash rose, revealing your abdomen. There was no belly button."

"I see."

"This is why I knew I had to come on your journey. I knew it would be like no other."

"I am glad that you have been honest with me," he said. "I was minded never to tell you – though, often at nights as I wrestled with my conscience, I wondered if it would be better to let you know. But… hah! You already knew."

I nodded. I knew then that he would tell me the reason why he had chosen Xana-La as his destination.

"I have many, many dreams of Xana-La," he said. "They seem so real to me. But there is something else too."

"What?"

"Franclin," he said, "we are not the first to have set out for the secret city."

"But surely," I said, "nobody has come back? We would know! Never mind our club, the *whole world* would know!"

"You would think so," he replied. "But the man who went to Xana-La and returned brought only three words back with him. Just three words, Franclin, yet they energised me like nothing else."

"What words were they?" I whispered.

"*You were there. You were there.* He whispered that to me as he landed his pluvial machinora in the yard behind the club. I rushed out to rescue him from the deluge, but he drowned. And you know? I wonder if Xana-La did that… I wonder if the mystical power of that city reached out over Asia all the way to our little club in London to drown my uncle."

I gasped. "Lextor the First? He was your uncle?"

"My family has never been one for settling down to the quiet life."

"But… you are saying that *you* live in Xana-La? Another Pharaday?"

"So I understand. And I will find out. Oh, I mean to find out."

I nodded. "And I will stand beside you. And we will return, to tell the greatest tale of our age."

"You fill me with hope, dear fellow."

We trekked into the foothills of the mountains. They were, Pharaday assured me, called the Spirallo Mountains because from high orbit a traveller could see their helical form. "What the Moongols call them I've no idea," he laughed. "Doesn't really matter, I suppose."

"We should respect their cultures," I replied, "if only through their tongue and music."

He glanced at me as though I were raving. "If you say so… and I suppose you may have a point. Be difficult to escape their clutches if we couldn't speak a few words of the lingo."

By now we were ascending fast, the air cooling, our breath coming hard and deep. My shins ached, my eyes stung, and I stank of sweat. In a rippling, ice-cold river we bathed, then carried on, taking a path of stone laid out between ochre boulders.

Pharaday pointed to the indigo evening sky. "See those bustards? They mark the secret way." He smiled and raised a forefinger into the air. "A clue, you see, one I learned from talking to the Hindoo fakirs who occasionally come this way." He grinned. "For the emeralds, you know. Fair sends them into gem-lust."

"Bustards?" I replied.

"Yes. Tricky bird, the bustard, but what is not generally known is that they migrate annually in and out of the valley in which Xana-La was built. I paid sixteen Chin'a slaves to acquire that particular clue."

I whistled. "Expensive."

"Shhh!" he hissed. "*Never* whistle around here. You don't know if listening tigers are about."

We walked on. After an uncomfortable night we passed an uncomfortable day, and then another one, until, climbing an escarpment, we found ourselves looking across a plateau: ice-covered, rocky and harsh. We had long ago put on woollen sweaters and hats, and changed our knee-johns for long-johns, but still the freezing wind robbed us of our bodily warmth. And we were exhausted.

Pharaday, however, spoke happily. "Not far to go now," he said, cleaning his spectacles with spit and tissues. "We shall follow the line of the golden bustard, it being the leader of the family. Only the golden bird will lead you to the secret valley entrance."

So began the most difficult part of our adventure. To follow the flight of the golden bustard we had to dodge between snow-shrouded boulders, through ravines, across ice-edged streams and along narrow ledges, sometimes beneath bright blue skies, more often through snow and hail. We never spoke, we shouted – and still the wind tore our words away.

Exhaustion and defeat seemed the most likely prospect as we sheltered from a blizzard in a narrow defile. I looked over my shoulder, hoping to find a deeper part of the cave where, perhaps, we could light a fire; but there was no wood fuel and my lighter had run out of petrozine.

Then I espied a light. In fact it was no light, it was a gap in the rear wall of the defile. I staggered across to it, to peer through.

A most incredible spectacle. "We have found it!" I cried. "Pharaday, we are here!"

Yes. We had arrived. For at the rear of the cave lay a low crack leading out to a ledge, and thence to a path.

"My sweet felinus," Pharaday said, as the tears rolled down his face.

The Xana-La valley lay before us. Green and pleasant, set with white and pink trees, and scented like the rose garden at Kew, it rolled downwards and away from us for mile after mile, the sky windswept above, but lined to an extraordinary height by encircling peaks. It was cool, certainly, but calm. Falling snow from high above was transformed into a mild, dewy mist.

We sat at rest for a while, drinking stream water and eating cold pork chops and pickle, until we felt strong enough to walk on.

And the secret city of Xana-La awaited us. I felt beaten down by its majesty. In truth I almost fell to my knees and prayed, but some remnant of my London manners restrained me from that embarrassment. Pharaday, however, wept like a girl.

Xana-La rose in white encrusted towers from innumerable blocks built like sugarloaf cubes into the stone of the mountains. These towers entwined one another like tendrils, and all were pierced with windows, tall and narrow, like those of Welsh castles. Bridges and rope ladders joined different quarters of the city, and from every parapet a flag flew, emblazoned with a white-centred green flower on a sable background.

As we approached I heard the mystical sound of choral music, which I guessed came from chambers within the city. Even I, hard-hearted it has been said, was moved; and the shivers played up and down my spine.

We reached a great door made of beaten copper, in which a design of tigers chasing men had been etched. Rubies and emeralds marked the eyes of every figure, while the clouds were inlaid mother-of-pearl.

A single man stood at the entrance. He was ancient, with a white moustache, beard and hair. He wore a tunic of leather and a long skirt of orange cotton.

"You have come to visit Xana-La?" he said, in perfect, albeit accented, English.

"We have indeed," Pharaday replied.

The man nodded. "There is only one rule. Do not touch any tiger."

We both nodded, at which point the door opened a couple of feet, allowing us entrance.

We had arrived!

Inside, the city was a maze of passages, scented courtyards and long, twisted alleys. It was quite beautiful: natural, claustrophobic, idyllic, overcrowded. The green leaves were almost too green to bear, the scent of the flowers enough to make one drunk, the music too profound to grasp. It bustled too, with a vast range of people: beggars, labourers, women and children, and quite a number of more important folk – judging by their bejewelled fingers and fur-lined cloaks.

The people looked at us, stared at us even, but we were never molested or stopped. I guessed that visitors to Xana-La were either accepted without concern or, possibly, were more common than I had realised.

We lodged in a small inn called the *"Tigris Fang"*. Pharaday paid with gold coins loosened from the clutches of his South African relations.

"This will last an hour or two," he said, nudging me in the side with his elbow. "Time to explore!"

"And find… *you*," I said.

He looked embarrassed. "Perhaps, Franclin," he said. "Perhaps."

I glanced away. Now that we stood inside the fabled city I felt uncomfortable, as though hidden layers of Pharaday's personality were being revealed. His libertine ways I knew, but much less did I know of his deeper character; and of course the enigma of his physique remained unresolved. I decided to watch the man and stay alert for trouble.

As expected, Pharaday insisted we visit the disreputable quarter of the city, which lay in the lower levels, and, not wishing to lose sight of him, I agreed to trot along too. He was surprised and, I think, pleased. The ladies of the quaintest bordello were oriental, though some seemed to have Indoo blood, and two or three African. Choosing the darkest skinned moll (blackamoors were his feminine ideal) Pharaday disappeared, leaving me alone.

One of the other dark ladies approached me. I believe she may have felt sorry for me – perhaps recognising that I was, in a sense, Pharaday's chaperone. Or perhaps she was curious. Whatever her motive and thoughts, a minute or so later I found myself in her room. "Just to talk," she said. "Nothing more than that. I'm Panthera."

"You are very kind," I said, as she poured camomile tea into porcelain cups. "Tell me, did you walk here, to the valley, and then decide to stay?"

"Oh no," she said, "I rode here on a zephyr. A lot of us girls did. Tell me… who is that man you came with?"

"Do you smoke?"

She smiled. "Yes!"

I handed her an exotic cigarette, which she took, and lit with a match.

"He is my associate," I explained.

"Is he?"

A thought occurred to me then. This was a lady of Xana-La. She would *know* things. I glanced around the room, which was small but luxurious in its décor, and seemed secure; then with a conspiratorial glance I went to sit on the bed. Panthera joined me, a smile on her ruby lips.

"He is called Pharaday Lemmington," I said, "and he is an acquaintance of mine from London." I related several of the tales of Pharaday in Asia, Pharaday in Zulu-land, Pharaday crushing diluvial rebels on the Amazon, then went to the side table and prepared two dishes of biscuits, and more tea. These I took back to the bed, my intention to ask a favour of Panthera; but I was at once halted by her look of sorrow.

"Oh, you are so kind, and so well mannered," she said. A tear welled up in the corner of one eye.

"Are you quite well, Panthera?" I asked.

She began to weep, and then to my surprise flung her arms around me. "You're in terrible danger! There is another Pharaday here. He is a mean, shifty man, and nobody likes him. He treats me badly when he visits me, and the other girls too. He will deceive you! Do not eat the food here. He will try to mesmerise you by tainting your supper with the nectar of the Viridio Flower, and then you will never leave Xana-La… oh, and there are worse secrets I dare not tell…"

Shocked by this confession, and overcome with sympathy, I hugged Panthera to me as I would a lamenting child.

"There, there," I said. "I will take care. You surely are a lady of good character to warn me so."

She smiled and nodded, and then, in the swiftest of gestures, pulled down the thick cotton tunic she wore. Her nipples, already erect, were extraordinarily long.

Yes, I did engage in furtive relations with Panthera. But I also told her of my plan. And she agreed to be part of it.

Pharaday spent most of the night with one or other of the dark skinned ladies, emerging, tottering like a drunk, at some unholy hour of the morning.

"Wretched girls have exhausted me," he said. "My legs feel tenderised."

I had been half-asleep in a chair: now I jumped up, awake and nervous. "Pharaday! Come back to the inn, I insist. We have spent far too long in the company of these ladies."

He staggered up to me and examined my cravat. "Tied differently," he said. "So you have been playing butter the teacake as well. Most excellent! But I am so tired I can hardly walk. You must allow me to lean on you, Franclin."

We returned to the inn, entering with our pass key, and moments later we lay in our rooms, fast asleep beneath crisp, white sheets.

I soon discovered the truth of Panthera's assertions. While Pharaday explored the mercantile quarter of the city I took all the remaining food in our backpacks and secreted it under my bed. Pharaday had trumpeted his intention to eat at all the best inns of the city; he would not be interested in British beef and roly-poly puddington with raisins on top. Then, anxious once again, I left the inn and walked to a courtyard I had earlier noticed, where I took the cool air and tried to relax.

Some time later Pharaday chanced upon me. "You, sir," he said, his manner terse. "Are you meant to be here?"

"Pharaday," I replied, "I do not believe this to be a private courtyard."

He stared at me, and I realised he had not expected me to speak quite so familiarly with him. He said, "Yes, well, hmm, are you enjoying your time here?"

"Tolerably. After the immense journey we undertook…"

"Indeed. And the inn… you like it?"

I shrugged. "It smells of yoghurt and the floorboards creak fit to wake lettuce-sellers as far as Shanhai, but it is pleasant enough."

"Yoghurt," he said. "Floorboards… yes, yes. Well, I must be off. I shall see you later."

I watched him depart. A vision of Panthera's face rose up before me and I grasped the truth of her words. But what were these worse secrets she had mentioned?

I realised I had to take my chance. Pulling my coat about me, I followed Pharaday, lurking sometimes ten yards, sometimes fifty behind him, following as he ascended the steps and crooked passages of the city, until, half a mile above the plain, he halted at a door. I was not surprised to see a red half moon painted upon it.

I raced back to the inn. My Pharaday bought gewgaws in the markets still. At top speed I sprinted down to the bordello and sought Panthera, who, luckily, was not engaged with a client.

Without delay I said, "What is the place of the red half moon, high atop the city?"

"Oh Franclin!" she said, her face twisted with shock. "Never go there! I beg! You are too good a man, too sweet and decent to go there."

I took her in my arms and comforted her, telling her that I would not return to the place. At the time I believed myself, I really did. But then I left, returned to the *"Tigris Fang"* and entered my room. Subtly, carefully, somebody had been through my belongings. Downstairs I asked the doorkeeper if Pharaday had returned. He nodded. "And gone again," he remarked.

But I knew *my* Pharaday had not yet returned.

At once I leaped steps and vaulted railings, ascending through silver afternoon light to the place of the red half moon, where I halted. The walls stood devoid of windows, the door shut: silent, forbidding. I stood alone. But I was not to be defeated. Spying a series of balustrades falling in graceful arcs from the bath-house next door, I clambered up to them by means of guttering, then crawled, like an alley cat, to their very end. From that eyrie I saw a skylight in the roof of my goal: the building of the red half moon. I jumped. I landed awkwardly and almost slipped, but pulled myself to safety by means of hairy ivy.

Moments later I opened the skylight and peered down. The sweet, heady scent of incense came to my nostrils and I heard faint chanting. A floor of wooden boards lay six feet below me. The attic lay empty, so I lowered myself in.

My only weapon was the dirk given to me at the beginning of the journey by Pharaday. I loosened it in its sheath.

I had no plan in mind. But I knew something sinister, perhaps something terrible, lurked inside the building, that related to Pharaday and his curious life, and so I decided I must move on to discover the truth. I crept to the attic door and listened. The sound of chanting, faint, though distinct, did not alter, and I guessed it had its source some distance away. I hoped the upper reaches of the building would be dusty and empty, as were the upper reaches of most buildings.

I opened the door and slipped through. The corridor I found myself in was dark and cobwebbed, empty and silent. I crept on, found a staircase, descended, entered another corridor, walked to its end to find a second staircase… and the incense-choked chamber at the bottom of those steps led me to a concealed balcony from which I was able to observe a bizarre scene in the hall below.

It was some kind of shrine. At one end stood two thrones, on which sat a human man and a tiger, hand in hand like king and queen, and wearing silver crowns. A dozen people stood in various attitudes before the royal pair, some seated, some standing. Incense rose in thick clouds from lines of thuribles set on silver poles; I closed my mouth, trying to breathe shallow, knowing a cough would betray me.

And then I saw Pharaday. But I did not know which Pharaday it was.

He spoke to the king in rough tones. "This is a poor state of affairs, your felinuship. You tell me that I must take the place of my embodiment and leave this city – my home – and yet you will keep the embodiment of the other one?"

"This is my desire, Lemmington," replied the king. "You will do as you are bid."

"But why? I need answers, your felinuship."

I judged from the bile of the man that this was not the Pharaday I knew from the Suicide Club. In a menacing voice the king said, "The presence of your embodiment, returned to Xana-La, means the intruder who escaped managed to return to London. My plan is to…" He chuckled, then continued, "… *amend* the embodiment of the other man, then utilise him appropriately."

I swallowed: mouth dry. I knew they meant me. The intruder I supposed to be Lextor the First. Some awful plot was moving here that threatened civilised society in London, and a shiver ran up my spine.

"Show me this amendment," Pharaday said.

The king hesitated, glancing at the tiger beside him. As one they rose, the tiger balancing without difficulty on her back legs, then walked to whatever chamber lay behind the throne. Seeing that the balcony on which I perched continued behind the rear wall of the hall I wondered if I might be able to see more.

Yes – I did see more. The chamber behind the hall was large, filled with huge iron vats, glass vials, steam and macabre black implements. And there on a table, laid out like a damp corpse, I saw myself.

And my other self had no belly button.

I almost fainted from horror. I stared again at myself. There was a great hole in the left side of my chest, bloodless and inanimate, or so it seemed, with the ribs skewed back and held by means of threads and pins. A scene too macabre for me to grasp.

Then I saw still more. Tiger bodies in carts – a dozen at least.

"Ah!" I heard Pharaday say. I glanced over the edge of the balcony to see him. "Now I understand the meaning of your phrase, your felinuship."

"My phrase?"

"Indeed – 'to put some heart into the embodiments' you said. Your felinuship, I must apologise, I imagined you used *heart* as a metaphor, like the British do to mean enthusiasm. Why…" and he laughed for a moment, then wiped his lips, "… I did not realise you intended using real tiger hearts. Most ingenious!"

The upright tiger – the king's queen, or so I imagined – gave a blood curdling yowl. And that is when the horror got the better of me, for an involuntary cry escaped my own lips.

The tiger's ears flicked. One pointed in my direction. Then she turned her head and looked up, straight into my eyes.

Her second yowl was more of a shriek. Pharaday and the king turned to stare up at me.

I ran for my life.

Clattering up the stairs, shouts behind me, heavy bootsteps: but what I feared was warm breath on the back of my neck, sharp teeth breaking my spine. Tiger jaws. Gasping for breath I staggered into the attic, my legs hardly fit for escape; like jellies they were. I turned. Nobody at the door. With my last energy I grasped the edges of the skylight and heaved myself up, managing to get an elbow upon the roof – a ploy that saved me. As my legs dangled and my strength faded, I bent one leg up and used it to lever myself out. Then, like a beached fish, I lay on the roof, shutting the skylight as my final effort.

I knew I did not have long to live. The tiger queen would emerge from the building, ascend and capture me, if she did not kill me. I rolled onto my back, tears in my eyes, and murmured, "I did not wish to go like this. Oh, I did not…"

There came a fluster of feathers, a smell of mountain air, then something enormous landed beside me, making the roof tiles vibrate. A bird!

"Franclin! There is yet time to escape. Show me freedom, I beg, and I will show you love!"

"Panthera!"

The monster bird – some species of auric bustard I believe – lowered its head to glare at me with one fulvous eye. A saddle lay upon its back, Panthera astride it. I struggled to my feet and, taking hold of the pommel, dragged myself up, raising and moving my right leg as Panthera leaned back to facilitate my inelegant mounting, so that moments later I sat before her, facing forwards. The delicious warmth of her body progressed through my clothes to my own skin – a kind of mystical protection it seemed.

Then there came a chilling yowl from the far edge of the roof. "The tiger queen!" I cried.

The bustard raised its wings and jumped off the roof just in time; I glanced over my shoulder to see the tiger queen, tail thrashing, one paw raised clutching feathers.

Panthera wailed and hugged me. "I thought you were doomed," she said.

I kissed the back of her hand. "Take us to the head of the valley," I said, "and I will show you your freedom."

We walk the lanes and pleasant green alleys of London, Panthera and I, daring the looks of our neighbours, who think that a British man should never marry a woman with dark skin. But we do not care. We know love. And we consider ourselves trailblazers in more than one sense.

But I watch my neighbours, kin and colleagues with an almost fanatical fervour, for I know that one day, perhaps this year, maybe in the new decade to come, I will stroll down a street and see myself walking towards me; and I will know that this other self has no belly button and the fierce heart of a tiger. Ah… it is only love that tempers fear.

And if you, dear reader, are perusing this tale, then Panthera and I are gone, to who knows what fate – for I have caused this document to be held in the vaults of "The Times", to be published in the event of my vanishment.

At the Rail

by Andrew Coburn

On a starlit deck of a luxury liner, a man named Beckwith eyed a woman poised determinedly at the rail. Who was she? Beckwith didn't want to know. If she intended killing herself, that was her business, none of his.

Another man, name of Swain, closed his eyes and locked the woman in his mind, for she had the bearing of someone he'd known years ago, a colleague. The last time he had seen her he had tried to read her body as if it were literature. He had loved her, but she left him for another. A pity. They could have grown old together.

Mists from the ocean enfolded the woman at the rail, threatened to etherealize her . . . and did. Where was she? Where'd she go? The two men converged. Neither knew the other. Each was traveling alone.

Beckwith said, "I was afraid she'd do something like that."

Swain was alarmed. "Do what?"

"You know."

The two men stared at each other. Beckwith had pronounced features too big for his face. Swain's face was a sort of diagram, lines streaking this way and that, the eyes squinting as if to make sense of themselves.

"No, I don't."

But he did. Unnerved by the woman's ominous absence, he gazed into the sky at silent stars, their distance belied by their brilliance. The moon loomed unreasonably close, awesomely stark, chillingly supernatural.

"Something funny about the way she kept to herself," Beckwith said, his sunburnt nose peeling in the moonlight.

Swain had happened upon her several times, but they had not spoken, merely nodded, her only companion a book, quite enough in his mind to launch a harmony between them. With a shudder he wondered if she were floating, as if living on the ocean's surface.

"Don't know how old she was, but she had a nice body," Beckwith said.

"I saw her at the pool." A widower, Beckwith had missed his wife miserably for a month, then not at all. "But a snooty type, that's my take."

"Not snooty. No, not at all." Swain spoke as if from personal knowledge.

As if the woman were beside him, a spectral presence. Or more than that, a murmur in his brain.

Suddenly Beckwith pointed. "Look!"

Much farther down the deck, the woman partially reappeared through holes in the mists, her black hair shot with silver, her reality nearly a fact. The lines in Swain's face quivered.

"Thank God," he said. And began to cry.

Surprising Beckwith, who said, "What the fuck?"

She was named Cleo, after a grandmother. Mr. and Mrs. Giosakis were Old World, Cleo their only child, with classical Greek features evident from the start. Her mother wore black dresses and her hair in a bun. Her father ruled the roost.

At age four she attended preschool classes at Hellenic Orthodox Church, an easy walk from where she lived, a tenement house with a backyard, a part of which her father had turned into a garden. Mrs. Giosakis tended the vegetables, and little Cleo watered the flowers. Bees made the rose trellis a lyre.

At five she entered first grade, where she was a quiet presence and a prize pupil, gold stars on her papers. Her father screened her infrequent playmates to make sure all were Greek and none were boys. Boys, he told her, could not be trusted. Her mother, marginalized, seemed to agree.

136

By the time she started eighth grade she was considered a beauty. Boys stole looks at her, and the janitor did so openly, none of which would have surprised her father. "Remember what I told you," he warned. The only boy about whom she had secret thoughts was Tobias Chapman, who hated his given name and refused to acknowledge it, which annoyed the teacher.

"I'm talking to you, young man!"

"Sorry, Miss Kiley. I don't know any Tobias." He paused theatrically, with a quizzical look. "Do you mean *Toby*?"

That may have been when Cleo fell in love with him.

When she started Haverhill High her father warned her about male desire, and her mother nodded solemnly. Pointing a finger, he said that school was for hard study, not for monkey business. Unbeknownst to her, Mr. Katsaros, an English teacher, kept an eye on her and rendered weekly reports to Mr. Giosakis on the steps of Hellenic Orthodox Church.

"If only all my students were as good as your Cleo."

"Not easy raising a daughter," Mr. Giosakis said. "I work hard."

Cleo's name was regularly posted on the high honor roll, automatically earning her entry into the love-of-learning Philomathean Club. She was a member of the Girls Chorus and the Student Executive Council, but mostly she kept to herself, to her studies, to her diary. In her diary, on a frigid December Sunday, she wrote, *The frost on the window says something I can't read.*

She seldom caught sight of Toby, for they were sharing no classes, not even the same lunch period, though once they came face to face on a stairway. Her whole body tried to speak to him, but failed. *Since much was understood, nothing was said,* she wrote in her diary and then tore the page out, fearing her father might read it.

Toby went to school dances, she didn't. Fully aware what her father's reaction would be, she didn't ask, though she was tempted when the sophomore class held its spring dance. Jealousy made her heart beat fast the following year when she learned Toby's date for the junior prom was Sally Boone, who showed herself off in tight sweaters. *Is that really what you want, Tobias? Someone like that?* Later that page was ripped away too.

In their senior year they were assigned to the same home room and even had the same lunch period. For Cleo, it was as if they were back in Winter Street School, Miss Kiley's room, and she was careful to call him Toby, not Tobias, which she preferred. Twice during the year he was suspended, first for cutting classes, then for smoking marijuana in the boys' lav. In the meanwhile his grades suffered, which concerned her.

"If you're not careful, you won't graduate."

"Sure I will," he said. "If you help me."

During free periods they met in the library, and in whispers she coached him in calculus and Roman history. During lunchtime over their plastic trays she quizzed him, which precipitated chatter they were a couple. Mr. Katsaros, who was not blind, spoke to her in private.

"I'd stay away from him if I were you, Cleo. He's not someone who would please your family."

She felt heat in her face. "He's not bad, Mr. Katsaros."

"He doesn't apply himself. Odds are he never will. Besides, there's the larger question of your heritage."

She trembled. "Please don't tell my father."

In the library Toby smiled at her. His eyes were as blue as hers were brown, his hair as fair as hers was dark. Girls grabbed looks at him the way boys did at her. The senior prom was a month away. Yes, she knew that. Many girls already had their gowns. "Will you go with me?" he asked.

She was stunned. Her skin felt too tight for her face.

He waited. "Well?"

How could she tell him she could not go out with boys, especially not him? Wasn't fair. He was a god, why couldn't she be a goddess? If not Aphrodite, then a lesser divinity, a nymph. Or he could be Paris and she Helen of Haverhill. *Rescue me!*

"Is it because I'm not Greek?"

She nodded, the best she could do. All she could do.

He grinned at her over pages detailing Hannibal's defeat by the Romans. "I was going to ask you to marry me, but I guess that's out too."

Cleo graduated with high honors and a full scholarship to Wellesley College. Toby, she was told, was joining the navy. In her diary she wrote, *Life is wondering what's next. What will be, what won't be, and what will never be.*

She kept the page intact.

Despite Dramamine, Beckwith succumbed to nausea and convalesced in his cabin. Swain roamed the deck with his lungs awash in sea air and an eye out for the woman. Not until afternoon did he spot her sitting at a small table in one of the quieter lounges, a small drink in front of her. His approach was tentative, almost on tiptoes.

"I thought you were dead," he whispered. When she looked up at him queerly, he raised his voice. "Hard to explain."

"Then maybe you shouldn't."

"I'm John Swain. May I?" When she offered no objection, he dropped into the table's other chair, and a waiter in a white steward's jacket arrived almost instantly. She was drinking sherry. He ordered the same. "I don't know your name," he said.

"Any reason you should?"

They were silent while the waiter delivered his sherry. He smiled while openly admiring her features, which he deemed classical. She stared intently as if the lines in his face formed fragments of sentences she could almost read.

"My name is Cleo Pantos. Why did you think I was dead?"

"We saw you on deck last night. At the rail. Then you seemed to dissolve in the mist. For a moment we thought . . . well, you know." Her looks were coloring his mind.

"Why are you staring?"

"You're a beautiful woman."

"Once, maybe. What is it that you want, Mr. Swain?"

He wanted Love . . . Life. He wanted his youth back, from which he felt far removed, as if that part of him had never existed. And he wanted a front seat at the show with a woman like her. The sherry tickled his throat. "What we all want," he said. "Everything."

"You've come to the wrong table."

Perhaps she feared he was trying to glom onto her, sap her strength, feed off her worth. "I'll leave if you like."

Moments passed. "What do you do, Mr. Swain?"

"I teach. Not always with success."

"I considered teaching. Instead I raised three sons, two very much like their father."

Dare he ask? Could he hope? "Are you a widow?"

"A wanderer."

Agitated, he sipped more sherry, applied a napkin to his mouth, and took a bold chance. "There's a dance tonight. I wonder–"

"I don't dance, Mr. Swain. But we could dine together."

I have died and gone to heaven. He trembled. "Please. May we use first names?"

Amused, she smiled. "Me, Cleo. You, John."

Her father said, "Mr. Pantos is a lawyer. An attorney at law."

"Please, call me George."

George Pantos, his heavy eyes appraising her, had a broad forehead and a neatly crisp moustache and wore a suit obviously made to measure. Cleo guessed he was closer to her father's age than to hers, and she knew the reason he'd been invited for Sunday dinner. Her father said, "Cleo's in her last year at Wellesley. Top of her class."

George Pantos scrutinized her. "You do your father proud."

With effort, she thought of him romantically and pictured him poised over her with dignity and performing the bedroom act with rhythmic decorum. She also imagined herself with a baby at her breast.

Later she confided to her mother, "I don't love him."

"Pretend you do," her mother whispered. "In time you might."

Her father appeared. "What do you think?"

"Give her time," her mother said.

"Don't take too much," her father said gruffly, "he's a catch."

He was a lawyer. An attorney at law. Her father was only a shoe worker. Yes, she knew that.

She was glad to get back to Wellesley, but there was no escape. Each time she returned home on holiday or seasonal break, George Pantos was a dinner guest, his place at the table across from hers, his heavy eyes aware of her every movement, signs of his approval or disapproval held in reserve. Was it a game he was playing? Was she playing it too? *God, I hope not.*

Licking his lips, he said, "The baklava is delicious."

"Cleo made it," Mr. Giosakis said.

"With no help from me," Mrs. Giosakis added.

Cleo graduated summa cum laude from Wellesley and a month later married George Pantos in a lavish celebration that left her father flat broke but, paradoxically, feeling like a man of substance, a solid figure in the community.

Cleo's wedding night was not as she'd imagined. Out of his clothes, George Pantos was primitive, hairy, and overweight. His mouth smothered hers as if to do harm. His breath was medicated, too much Listerine, and his penis – she'd never seen one in the flesh before – was a blunt instrument he seemed unduly proud of. On her, he was a ton of huff and puff. She didn't cry, but God knows she wanted to.

They moved into the city's Bradford section, into a large colonial he had bought in anticipation of marriage and a large family. At civic dinners, her beauty and intelligence made her a prized possession, an asset on his arm, added proof of his worth. She said she'd like to do something with her education and mentioned teaching. "You're my wife," he said, tapping his thick fingers on the dining-room table. "Your place is here."

He wanted children. He wouldn't mind a daughter but really wanted sons, the more the better. She soon gave him one, then a second, then a third. Each delivery was difficult, particularly the third, which was touch and go. He named the first child George, after himself, and the second Alexander. The third he named Phidias.

Cleo, nursing Phidias, said, "I'd like to hold off for a while before having more children – all right, George?"

He patted her shoulder. "We'll see."

She lay face-up in her cabin, open-eyed, and questioned herself. *Am I too old for this?*

John Swain, who had reluctantly and gradually disengaged from her, now lay on his side gazing at her, loving her from his depths, idolizing her as if she were from a higher realm. "I feel honored."

She raised a hand and patted his hip. "As well you should."

"Are you making fun of me?"

"I would never do that." Turning her head, she gazed at him. His wrinkles brought to mind the British actor, John Hurt, whose face bespoke vulnerability, heartache, weariness. In a movie, John Hurt uncovered a decades-old telephone directory and hunted up relatives and friends long dead, which made him wonder... *If I ring up the numbers, will their former selves answer?*

John Swain stirred. "Is our relationship going to grow?"

"What would you call this?"

John Hurt. *Is that you, Dad? Dad, it's me, John.*

John Swain distrusted irony as much as he did subtleties. He liked things simple and straight-forward. And he dearly wanted a woman to wear her feelings on her face the way he wore his. "I love you," he stated.

She pretended to half hear him. "So you never married?"

"It's never too late," he said quickly.

Marrying for the second time, she would feel repossessed, the new owner exerting control. She would be taking hundreds of steps backwards.

John Hurt's father. *I miss navy coffee. I miss stew eaten at sea. I miss ports of call. Beyond that, I don't miss much at all.*

John Swain closed his eyes. "I hope we never reach Port au Prince."

Her fourth pregnancy ended with a miscarriage, after which she secretly went to a doctor, not Greek, and had her tubes tied. Her first act of rebellion gave her alternating moments of exhilaration and trembling fear. Her husband, worried she was suffering postpartum depression, speculated on whether she should see a shrink.

"You have sons to raise," he reminded her.

George Junior and Alexander vied for their father's attention and approval and were not above lying and cheating to get an upper hand on the other. Both were prone to tantrums, though never in their father's presence. Bearing his likeness, they were his favorites, while he was ambivalent about his third-born. Phidias's face was neat and exact, a gift from his mother. George Junior was a bully and Alexander a schemer. Phidias, sweet Phidias, was a dreamer. Taunted by his brothers, he kept close to his mother.

From early spring through fall Cleo spent much time in her garden, in which spiders spun webs and garter snakes abounded. The notes of birds and the beating wings of bees gave her a lift. She loved earthworms because they defecated every ten seconds and kept the soil fertile. She cringed when George Junior's heavy step devastated daffodils. On purpose? She hoped not, though Alexander claimed he had.

The boys went to private school, where George Junior was a behavioral problem and nearly booted out. Alexander was reprimanded twice for cheating while Phidias was teased for being teacher's pet. Disconcerting to Cleo, who daily chauffeured them to school and other places, was George Junior's addressing her in his father's peremptory voice, with Alexander following suit. Her attempts at discipline were futile because their father could overrule her and frequently did. He was the supreme being.

George Pantos said, "Not my fault you can't handle our sons."

"Our sons, George? Don't you mean yours?" She held back tears. "I need to get out of the house. I want to get a job."

"Don't talk nonsense."

"I feel useless."

"Perhaps you are," he said.

She felt cheated when her father died. So much she'd wanted to say to him and never had and now never would. Some weeks after the funeral, she looked into her mother's eyes. "You knew I didn't want to marry George Pantos. Why didn't you help me?"

"Help?" her mother said. "How?"

Cleo found herself in the presence of a man in Bermuda shorts, with erectile hairs on the ball of his sunburned nose, and a camera hanging from his shoulder on a brightly braided strap.

"Beckwith," he said. "Earl Beckwith."

She knew he wandered the ship taking pictures of passengers when they weren't looking, and she suspected she'd been one of them, quite likely when at the pool. John Swain stood beside her near the rail, and together they watched him saunter off with his Bermudas snagged in his behind, held there as if by suction.

"I don't like the way he looked at me," she said.

"He saw me leaving your cabin this morning and called me a lucky bastard. Are you embarrassed?"

"I don't have to be. No man is in charge of me anymore." Dark glasses shielded her eyes from the blinding sun. With sea air filling her lungs, she smiled. "I feel free enough to fly away."

They moved along from one deck level to another and, though neither had any interest in the game, paused to watch people playing shuffleboard. Swain said, "We know so little about each other."

"That's how shipboard romances operate."

"Have you had many?"

"I'm an amateur, John. New to the game." She stretched her spine. "My back hurts. The bed wasn't made for two."

They moved to the rail. The sea was uncannily smooth and dyed a dramatic blue, to which the sun added sheen. John Swain said, "It's not a game for me."

She adjusted her glasses. "I don't know exactly what it is for me, John, but certainly something different."

"You've given me more than you'll ever know."

Later, for brunch, they served themselves from silver chafing dishes of scrambled eggs, bacon, sausages, warm rolls, and sliced fruit. Each had second helpings. John Swain, slender like John Hurt, said, "We're lucky we don't have to worry about our weight."

"But I do, John."

A delicate-featured youth in a mess jacket offered them coffee and gave them a start. He brought to mind her son, Phidias. Phidias helping her in the garden. John Swain mentioned predicted rain in Port-au-Prince. Her smile was big, bright. After a rain the garden was in a high state of arousal. Bees and butterflies were everywhere, even in her hair. Foliage opened, flowers gushed their colors and scents.

"Absolutely." She lifted her coffee cup. "Did you always want to be a teacher, John?"

"Yes." He was trying to look deep into her eyes. "What did you want to be when you were little?"

"A goddess."

George Junior, treasurer of his high school class, was intoxicated when he lost control of his Ford Mustang, a birthday gift from his father, who was furious but thankful his namesake walked away from the wreck with only abrasions. In court, the case was filed without a finding, and George Junior was soon back on the road with another Mustang, despite objections from his mother.

George Senior was jubilant when his second son Alexander made the varsity basketball team but alarmed when in a twisting move Alexander was banged to the floor and carried off the court with a fractured ankle, a picture of which was printed on page one of the local paper.

Phidias was another matter. Phidias was a sophomore and would have been a better student had he been more intellectual than dreamy and had his raging hormones not racked him with turmoil that came to light when George Junior called him "a fucking fag" at the supper table. His father went white. His mother, horrified by the language, told George Junior to go to his room.

George Senior said, "Stay!"

George Junior said, "Ask little Phid what he was doing on his knees in the boys' lav."

"Everybody go!" George Senior exploded. "Phidias, you stay!"

In the middle of the night, Cleo Pantos tiptoed into the dim of her youngest son's room and whispered, "I know you're still awake." Sitting on the bed's edge, she stroked his hair.

"I couldn't help it, Mummy."

"I know."

"Dad says I'm not fit to live in his house."

"As long as I'm here you are."

She and her husband spoke privately the next day. Each had slept little. "It's not as if it's terribly unusual," she said. "He's Greek, isn't he?"

George Pantos appeared insulted. "What's that got to do with anything?"

"How many boys do you think Socrates buggered?" she said, surprising and frightening herself but not stopping. "What do you think Plato was up to at those symposiums? And how many fellows did Alexander the Great take into his tent?"

George Pantos wanted to punch her, but held back, just barely.

She began looking back at her life. Why had she never sorted herself out, had never held her own, never thrown open all the doors to her mind? Why had she never extended her arms like wings and flown? She glanced in the hall mirror with no real sense of recognition. *If I don't recognize myself, how will anyone else?*

But someone did, a week later as she was descending the stone steps of the post office. After so many years, despite his obvious hair loss, she recognized him in the instant. And he, her. "Cleo. I'll be damned."

He asked her to have coffee with him. Yes. Yes, of course.

Tobias Chapman. Retired from the navy after 20 years in. Chief petty officer, if you please. Married to a Filippino woman, four children, two of each. Pictures in his wallet. Living up in Maine now. He was back in town because his mother had died, the funeral tomorrow. She learned all this before they reached the coffee shop. Over coffee, she told him about herself, what little there was to bring him up to date on. He was impressed.

"Married a lawyer, did you?"

She was staring hard at him, remembering him sprawled behind his desk in Winter Street School and then his smiling into her face in high school as she explained why she couldn't accept his invitation to the prom. Suddenly, without meaning to, she blurted, "I loved you, Toby."

He was taken aback only for a second. "Back then, I loved all the good-looking girls, especially you."

"Did you really want to marry me?"

He was honest. "No, I wanted to see the world."

"I don't know what the world is."

When she returned home, she found an ambulance in the drive and a boy being lugged out the front door on a stretcher. When she screamed, George Junior appeared on the front steps, Alexander behind him. Alexander shouted, "It's all right, Mum. They say he's gonna be OK."

"He only got sick," George Junior said. "It was all for show."

All in all, Phidias attempted suicide three times, the first time by overdosing on aspirin and his father's blood-pressure pills and the second by cutting himself with a razor. The third time, using a rope, he succeeded.

Moonlight endowed the sea surface with ghostly goings-on. Staring out at the drama, Cleo stood unanchored, her hair blowing, a stiff breeze rocking her, before she gripped the rail from a fear of being whipped away. But what would she lose? Her identity? She could easily toss it overboard. No! She had spent too many years without one.

Startling her, a voice said, "Mind?" And Earl Beckwith joined her at the rail. "Port-au-Prince tomorrow," he said, "Stay away from the *Marche en fer.* That means Iron Market. Vendors will be all over you like flies, and if you don't know what you're doing, you'll pay through the nose."

"You've been there?"

"No, but I've been told. A nice place to visit is the National Palace."

"Yes, I've read the brochure."

High in the sky a jetliner squirted red signals. Beyond that was the moon, on which Neil Armstrong had disturbed dust. She was aware that Earl Beckwith was staring at her.

"Mind if I say something personal, Mrs. Pantos?"

She suspected he'd been drinking. Something in his voice. He leaned toward her confidentially, and she wondered whether she was being inched into a game without fixed rules.

"I know you and Swain have something going, but for the life of me I don't know what you see in Prune Face."

Cleo's gaze was skyward. "And I don't know the odds of your being struck by a falling star, Mr. Beckwith, but you'd be much safer back in your cabin."

If looks could kill.

A little later she joined John Swain in the lounge, where he had already ordered her a drink, a mild martini. Without intending to, she began talking about Phidias. No note on his first two tries and not much of one on his third. Only three words. *Mummy I'm sorry.* "Broke my heart." She picked the olive from her drink, began eating it, and felt a little sick in the process. "I didn't protect him enough. When he was little his brothers called him 'Hideous Phidias', and others started doing it as well."

"Children can be cruel."

"Not only children. His father thought it was funny. Hilarious."

"I'm sorry."

"I don't know what's worse. Losing a child or never having one to lose. Maybe you can answer that, John."

"I can't."

They listened to the piano player's rendition of a Sinatra standard. Cleo said, "Is there any song Sinatra *didn't* sing?"

"I used to listen to him on *Your Hit Parade.* That tells you how old I am. People of my generation never thought he'd die. I mean, his presence and his voice were too vital."

"Growing up, I was not allowed to listen to popular music," she said and finished her martini, or most of it. When he gave her a meaningful look, she said, "No, not tonight, John. Port-au-Prince tomorrow."

"What does one have to do with the other?" he asked.

"Nothing."

He went to his cabin, she delayed going to hers. She wanted to see more of the moon, more of the ghostly doings on the water, and leaned hard against the rail. The moon was the lord of the night sky, the stars his vassals. Was it the sea or the night itself that had a soft purr to it? For a lovely moment she felt she had the power to skirt the borders of this world and glimpse another. A voice scattered her musings.

"It's me again."

Earl Beckwith. Damn it, he was drunk. He grabbed hold of the rail for balance and grinned at her.

"No disrespect, Mrs. Pantos, but I'd really like to know something." He giggled.

Please don't giggle.

"Does your ass shine in the dark?"

She held her own. "You're not going to be a nuisance, are you, Mr. Beckwith?"

His voice and breath touched her. "I'm a lonely man. Aren't you lonely too, Mrs. Pantos? Isn't that why you're on this cruise?"

Her back heel raised, she was ready to run, but she didn't think it would be necessary. He seemed a man without meaning, partly the consequence of too much to drink.

"I'm older than you, but I'm healthy, Mrs. Pantos. If you married me, I'd do everything to make you happy. And I'd put that in writing."

She imagined a dog licking her hand. "I've already had a husband, and I'm the mother of three sons, two of them deceased."

"I'm sorry." His eyes filled up. "I truly am."

"Please don't cry!"

But he did.

It was not a good summer.

Before leaving to play golf, George Pantos swabbed his brow, surveyed the garden, and said, "You've let it go to hell."

Cleo readily agreed. She was standing in the midst of it. "It's taken on a will of its own and won't behave," she explained. "Some flowers hog the sunlight, some wander where they have no business, and some are bullies that overrun their neighbors. It's become survival of the weediest."

He looked at her oddly. "I'll hire a professional gardener."

"Do as you please."

He continued to gaze at her. "All right, Cleo. Whatever it is, get it off your chest."

"It's my garden. I like it as it is."

"All right. What else is bothering you?"

"I don't have a life. I don't even have a job."

He was exasperated. "You're almost fifty years old. Who's going to hire you?"

"You're right, George. You always are."

Later that summer, on the Massachusetts Turnpike, when a Ford Mustang passed their van at a reckless speed, a woman said to her aunt, "Someone's going to get killed." Several miles later the Mustang struck something hard and flew apart. "Jesus, what a mess," the investigating state trooper said to the emergency medical technician. "College boys."

George Junior, the driver, somehow survived, but Alexander didn't.

George Senior was at once inconsolable and angry. Cleo tried to comfort him, but he shrugged her off, as if the loss were something beyond her ken.

Only one son left. At least it was his namesake. Did he *really* say that? He didn't mean to. "We should've had more children."

"That wasn't possible," she told him.

His head snapped around. "What do you mean?"

She told him about the procedure performed long ago by the doctor who wasn't Greek. So much bubbled up inside him. Did he mean to strike her? No. He couldn't help himself.

George Junior rushed into the room. "Jeez, Dad, why'd you do that?"

In August, a week before his surviving son was to return to college, Attorney George Pantos played eighteen holes in the dense heat, walked with a heavy step toward the clubhouse, and dropped dead at the door.

150

Birds hovering over it, the cruise ship was docked at Port-au-Prince, but no one allowed to debark. A passenger was missing.

"Who?"

John Swain cleared his throat. "Earl Beckwith."

For no rational reason, only an emotional one, she was not surprised. Nothing really surprised her anymore. In the diary she no longer kept except in her mind, she began writing. *Tragedy is woven so widely into human life that its edges are always showing. It becomes terribly natural and unbearably normal. It . . .*

"The captain is looking for the last person to see him."

"That may have been me,"   she said.

"You mean after we left the…"

"Yes."

"Do you think he… no… people don't go on cruises to do that, do they?"

"Probably not the people you know, John." A child in a sailor suit skipped between them, and in her mind she likened him to the boy on the Cracker Jack box. "I may not have seen him. Maybe it was a dream waiting for me to dream it."

"What?"

"It may be that Mr. Beckwith imploded and we'll find only his skin, like an old empty suit left for Goodwill."

He gazed at her as if he didn't understand, and yet did.

"I'm sorry, John. I didn't sleep well last night. Maybe it would have been better if you'd been there, despite the small bed."

He saw an opening, a huge one. "I'm selfish, Cleo, I'm expecting too much, but I want to live a real life. You're my only chance. Will you marry me?"

Her second marriage proposal in fewer than twenty-four hours. For a passing moment she was a goddess. Or, if she were younger, a nymph. OK, she imagined herself younger and Toby with all his hair, some of it falling in his face. The sound of chalk on the blackboard. All wishful thinking.

"I can't do it, John. I have a son who needs looking after. He's grown, but not so you'd know it. He's struggling with guilt from the deaths of his brothers, the loss of his father. He needs me."

The lines in John Swain's face groped with his emotions. "It doesn't mean you and I can't marry."

"It means I don't want to. I'm sorry."

A figure was emerging through the mist rolling over the deck, a man in shirtsleeves fishing through the unclear wash of the Caribbean morning. The pronounced features were unmistakable. John Swain said, "We thought – "

"I know what you thought," Earl Beckwith said. "Maybe I wanted you to."

"I don't understand."

Earl Beckwith stared at Cleo. "Maybe you do, Mrs. Pantos. I left my wallet on the deck by the rail – no money in it, I took that out – but what were people supposed to think when they saw it lying on my neatly folded jacket?" He winked. "I made myself scarce, and they thought what I wanted them to."

John Swain was not amused. "You'd better notify the captain."

Earl Beckwith shot a smile at Cleo, as if they were in it together, kindred souls, lovers. In his fantasies Cleo was sure she had been, as Tobias Chapman had been in hers.

"Since my wife died, I haven't been anybody. Everybody wants to be somebody. Can't blame me for that, can you, Mrs. Pantos?"

George Pantos periodically appeared in her dreams, complaining, demanding, still trying to hold her accountable. The dead should know their place. George Pantos, she reasoned, didn't.

Earl Beckwith was triumphant. "Now the whole damn ship's looking for me. Imagine that?"

John Swain was disgusted.

Cleo understood. Horrible to be nobody, fun to be somebody. She began to laugh. She had never been so happy – and so sad.

"What's so funny?"

A great joke on the three of them.

I'm a nymph, and these two old goats are satyrs.

The Bridge

by A.J Kirby

Tiny splinters of white light explode in front of my eyes; or is it behind my eyes? Whatever. All I know is that the world as I see it is suddenly suffering interference. The clear picture is interrupted by these fizzing lines which look like the individual strands from tinsel. I've seen them before, these splinters; they're usually a pretty good indication that I'm about to black-out. It's as though my eyes are always the first to go. Perhaps they don't want to see what comes after. I know I don't.

This time I don't go on over to the other side though. There's no waking up covered in unidentified blood or vomit, no wondering if it is me or someone else that the excretions have come from. Instead, I manage to drag myself back somehow. Back from the bridge.

I feel the knife in my hand; the tubi-grip that I've put around the handle is greasy with my sweat. I see the other boy's eyes now; wide-open in fear, or is it pain? Have I already used the knife?

My eyes dart around his body, but I can't see any blood. It will take a while to seep through his Michelin-Man jacket and thick jeans, perhaps.

I know him, this boy. He's called Benni, or Benson (after the cigs) and I've always thought of him as borderline evil. He's like a hyena in the way that he kind of slinks around corners, all hunched shoulders and bristling anger. His pinched face looks cruel and mocking.

Not now, it doesn't. I can stare deep into him and wrap myself around his heart and choke the life out of it. And he knows it. Even now, at the end, or the beginning of everything, he knows that he underestimated me. When I get angry, I'm a cobra, man. He just couldn't see it before. No damn respect; that's Benni's problem.

I feel the edge of the knife cutting into my first finger – my trigger finger – where the tubi-grip runs out. It's not even a proper knife, my knife, being pretty much one hundred percent blade. But that's what you get when you can only get twenty-five ding together at short notice. I'd probably have been better with ma's kitchen blade, or one of those cleavers. If I'd had one of those cleavers, Benni's head would have been rolling about the pavement by now, right at home amongst the sneering, curling dog-muck and the discarded roaches. No word of a lie.

Benni screams something at me, and it comes out like one of those roars you'd hear from a dinosaur being sucked into a tar-pit. It lasts far too long; so long, in fact, that it finally hits me that I am actually seeing all this in slow motion. Something's gone wrong with the laws of physics or time or chemistry or history. I don't even pretend to understand it. All I know is that somehow, the bridge has been pulled away. I haven't blacked-out and gone over to the other side. I'm still here, only everything's arse-ways. I'm suddenly scared.

I pull the knife back and tuck it into the folds of my jacket. I hear the blade sing as it tickles the quality fabric. And then I start to step away from him, hearing the rushing sounds of shouting in my ears as I walk. I can't make out what they say. It's like they are speaking a foreign language, or they're shouting up at me from the bottom of a well.

My eyes suddenly click out of the tunnel-vision and I see that Benni's got quite a few of his black-coat crew behind him, at a not necessarily safe distance. They are all waving and gesturing, posturing and glaring. But, for some reason, I walk backwards away from them. None of them think it is weird, this walking away backwards malarkey, but then I've always had a reputation as a bit of a weirdo around the estate. They probably think it's just like me to pull a knife on someone and then just walk away from them in comedy style as though nothing's happened.

I continue to walk away from them and none follow as I round a corner and put them out of sight. I take a moment and lean against the grey wall, tracing my hand over the rough pebbledash; grasping for reality. Drained, depressed faces stare at me out of drained, depressed windows. I decide that I have to press on. One of these watchers might call the police. I might have already been caught on the CCTV. One of the black-coat crew might finally get up the nerve to follow me.

When I start walking, it's backwards again. Very strange. And what's more, there's a real purpose to my stride. I keep feeling that at any moment, I'll fall over or crash into a lamp-post. I don't even look where I'm going, but somehow, I seem aware of the contours of the land; where the roads are, when to step around the old woman's tartan shopping trolley, where to turn for the steps onto the second level.

Up on the second level, most of the flats are boarded up. They've boarded up the boards, too, because people like Benni tend to like to smash things. And he likes to spray-paint his nonsense name on whatever he can see. As I'm walking backwards, it takes me a moment to realise that I've approached one of the most dilapidated flats. Sure enough, right there on the plywood front door is Benni's tag, decorated with that stupid crown, right above the 'i'. Someone has crossed out the name though. They've scratched over the blue paint with fierce, criss-cross lines from a knife or something. And for no reason at all, I pull out my knife from the folds in my jacket and I start to try to cancel out these lines. I'm frantic, masturbatory in my desire to see the door cleaned of the scratch marks.

Remarkably, when I stop to rest, I see that the scratches have all-but disappeared. No word of a lie. All that remains is Benni's name again, complete with that stupid crown above the 'i'. I feel almost like I've done my good deed for the day and with a new spring in my arse-about-tit step, I walk on. I want to whistle. The sound would complement the echo of my footsteps as it bounces back off the concrete.

I walk past the old drunk in the stairwell and pause for a moment. Sometimes, I like to reach into the old flat cap that he leaves on the floor. I like to riffle through his dirty collection of coins. Once my fingers close around a thick one – I can judge a pound coin simply from the slightly serrated edge – I usually take it. Old drunk can do nothing about it. He's too drunk, too weak, too scared. Probably, people like Benni take more than me, but everyone takes from this sad specimen of a man.

So it surprises me that I reach in my pocket for a squid coin and then lean over to put it in his cap. I feel around a bit, for good measure, but leave it in there. Ma would be so proud. Old drunk's not pleased at all, however. He moans something to me through those morbid yellow lips. I tell him that he should be grateful and forbid him to spend the money on more booze. As if in answer, he lifts his blue plastic bottle of white cider and he spits a hefty mouthful of drink back into it.

I wish I could take my eyes off Old Drunk as I walk up the steps to the third level, but I'm still walking in reverse. As the steps lead me up, I watch him spitting yet more of his stinking brew back into the three-litre bottle. And he must be even drunker than usual, because right at the moment that I turn onto the third level, he catches my eye once more and he actually jumps. It's as though he's forgotten all about me giving him the squid, and he's suddenly scared that I'm about to come straight back down there and rob off him again. I catch myself grinning; poor Old Drunk; his version of the world must be so screwed up now that he doesn't know whether he's coming or going. I've probably robbed him of his last vestiges of clarity, what with my funny walk and charity.

So anyway, I'm up on the third level now, where ma lives and I do sometimes. And have a guess who the first person I see is? It's only Daniel-San. He's our estate's answer to the karate kid, only he's way more useless. He *does* know a bit about martial arts though, and about where to get weapons from. I've a good mind to show him the damage that his crappy blade has done to my fingers, although they don't even feel cut now.

Daniel-San walks up to me wearing this massive grin like he's just won the lottery or something. And in a way he has, getting twenty-five ding off me for that piece of rubbish. But what's even stranger is when he starts to talk to me. I start to think that maybe he'd got so engrossed in one of those kick-boxing flicks that he watches all the time, that he'd turned Thai on me. As he speaks, his face performs all these weird twitches and things that I don't understand. I don't *want* to understand them.

And then he hands me my twenty-five nicker back. Just like that; no word of a lie. If taking things back is as easy as this, I'd give back that games console that I booted into touch after failing to complete a level. I'd go straight to Key-Ring out the back of the pub and I'd just wait for my moulah. No word of a lie; I'd return the white stuff that I got from Bilbo. The white stuff that turned out to be chalk dust.

So, seeing as though we're being so honourable and business-like about this business transaction, I pull the knife out of my jacket and remove the tubi-grip, which I pocket, for some reason. Then I hand it back to Daniel-San, feeling the warm glow of having made a profit and done a good thing. It wouldn't do to have the blade on me if anyone came a-knocking. I almost feel like giving Daniel-San a real nice reference that he could use for his other customers. I hadn't even needed to ask him. Maybe he feels guilty about the nature of his shoddy goods.

Before I forget though, there is one aspect of Daniel-San's customer service technique which requires a bit of work. Almost as soon as I'd hand him the knife back, he simply strolls away from me. He doesn't even think of passing a remark about the weather, or about Old Drunk, or about what had happened with Benni. Transaction complete, he goes about his day.

And another thing; as he walks away from me, he walks backwards too. For a moment, I feel like pulling him up for taking the piss out of me, but then I think about the knife. He had it now, didn't he? There was nothing to stop him coming back and using it on me, was there?

I say nothing to him then. Zilch. Diddley-squat. This is a new me; a me that doesn't take offence at stuff like that. It's a weird, wild world and I'm not cut out for judging other people. Not when I walk backwards all the time and hand over money to tramps and clean up graffiti. When nobody even got me on community service to do so...

Evidently ma doesn't think much of the new me though, because before I know it, she's screaming some incomprehensible nonsense into my ear. I hadn't even seen her come up behind me, but maybe she's seen the whole thing with Daniel-San and misinterpreted it. For about the first time in my life though, I don't scream back at her. She looks worn out, like. She still has the curlers in her hair – honestly, who else apart from my ma has curlers? – and all her make-up is smudged all over the shop. The words 'hedge', 'backward', and 'dragged' are on the tip of my tongue, but I bite them back. Who am I to talk about backwards?

When I don't shout back at ma, I discover, she soon burns herself out. Tears stop, nose stops running, hell, even her make-up starts to look normal again. But for some reason, when I try to hug her, she pushes me away. From out of nowhere she dashes back to the flat, slippered feet slapping against the concrete. Without realising I'm doing it, I'm soon following her, running myself now.

Things are starting to happen fast; too fast. I see that my mobile is in my hand. Now, it's wedged against my ear. I half-recognise Daniel-San's strange new voice on the other end. Now, I'm charging backwards through our front door. The smell of chip fat and cigarettes is everywhere. But there's another smell too. It's something ripe and sweet. Chemical. I pause my mad-dash to kick a broken mug out of the way on the kitchen floor, but soon I'm back on the thick shag-pile carpet of the front room. And I'm staring at the front room wall where the big picture of da used to be. In its place is blue paint. A tag; Benni's. The crown on top of the 'i' feels mocking.

But as I feel the anger bubbling up inside me once again; as I think about calling Daniel-San back and getting that knife again, something very strange happens. The boy himself barges past me into my front room. He must have followed me all the way back up here. He is clutching the blue spray-paint to his chest. It couldn't be more incriminating.

Somehow, I manage to tear myself away. I move out of the front room, through the hallway and into the bedroom. As I leave, I notice that he's already started to remove his tag. Strangely, he does this by spraying more of the blue paint on the wall.

And it's only when I get back into my room and lie back down on my bed that the weirdest thing about the whole day occurs. I start to drift off to sleep. As I do so, I notice that I don't feel angry at all any more. In fact, I'm sort of happy that it's all over. Benni, I start to remember, is my kid brother after all, and all he needs is a break.

The Chain

by Frank Roger

The old man looked up as he grew aware of Mario's presence at his side and smiled. He was still clutching the empty Coke can he had just picked up from the gutter, like a treasure he had stumbled onto and desperately wanted to claim as his property.

"May I ask you a few questions?" Mario asked. He noted the old man's frown of puzzlement and added:

"My name is Mario Freeman. I'm a freelance journalist doing a series of articles on modern urban myths. I saw you walk down the street and pick up all the empty cans people have thrown away."

The man nodded. "That's right. I just hate it when people litter the streets with rubbish. Especially empty cans."

"So you're picking them all up and then you get rid of them?"

The man chuckled. "Oh, no, I'm not throwing any of them away. I keep them stored at home." He put the can away into his shopping bag, and resumed his tour of inspection, his eyes scanning the pavement for more trophies.

"Look there! Another one." Mario followed him, saw how he picked up a crushed beer can, dropped it into his bag and kept going. This was clearly a routine. "You should see my apartment," the man went on. "I've got cans stacked all over the place."

"So you're collecting them?"

"Yes, but I'm collecting them for a specific purpose. I've got this big project in mind, you see."

"Tell me about it."

"It's an art project. As soon as I have enough cans, I'll assemble them all into this gigantic sculpture. It'll be a symbol of our consumerist society. Scrap metal turned into fine art. It's my way of protesting against our throwaway economy. In a sense people won't have thrown all those cans away for nothing, as they will all end up in my sculpture. I'm not quite sure yet what it will look like. Still, I think I'll produce a powerful and significant work, something of lasting value I can rightly be proud of. Now if you'll excuse me."

"Thanks for your time," Mario said. The man shot him another smile and walked on, picking up every can he noticed, however dirty or crushed. Was he a nutcase or a budding artist? Would he indeed produce a stunning piece of art one day? Maybe he shouldn't be the judge of that, and limit himself to recording the facts.

He halted and remarked that a clothes store across the street was unusually crowded. Was something going on there? Why didn't he check it out? He crossed the street and entered the store. He saw right away that most customers weren't here to buy clothes, but were staring at a dozen or so TV screens spread all over the place. On the screens a movie was showing featuring naked actors. It was not a pornographic movie; if it hadn't been for the nudity, it might have passed for an ordinary low budget film.

It was hard to keep track of the story or catch the dialogue because of the street noise and the brouhaha inside, but he couldn't help noticing the actors switched from archaic English to some obscure dialect. All the scenes appeared to be shot in the same studio, with stage props limited to the bare essentials. This was a bizarre and very low budget affair indeed.

He studied the audience, a motley collection of boys and older men, and only a few women. These people were obviously neither movie buffs nor customers looking for fancy clothes. In a way they reminded him of pilgrims, gathered to attend a religious ceremony, ignoring the racks of clothes as if they were shrines with holy attributes they were not supposed to soil with their sight or touch. The brouhaha they produced might pass for quietly chanted mantras.

He watched for a few more minutes, then walked over to a counter where a shop assistant was patiently waiting for customers.

"Can I ask you something? What's the idea behind this movie that's shown here?"

The girl flashed him a bright smile and said: "It's an idea of the manager. He wanted to do something special that would bring us publicity, make us the talk of the town and boost our sales."

"And is it working?"

"Lots of people are coming in each time we're screening the movie. When it's finished, we wait half an hour before running it again, and then another crowd pours in. So far there doesn't seem to be a boost in sales, though. The manager was hoping the contrast between the nudity and the clothes on display would spark off some interesting reaction. We'll see."

"Do you happen to know something about the movie?"

"It's *Lysistrata*, some kind of cult classic, made by a guy called Ludo Mich. I believe it's about a sex strike."

"A sex strike?"

"Yeah."

"Well, thanks for the information." He turned back to one of the screens, but by then the shop was so crowded he no longer felt comfortable and left. He crossed the street again and hung around until the movie was finished. He could tell because everyone tried to leave the store at once. Very few "real" customers remained inside. It was clear the manager would soon learn the difference between ways of attracting people and boosting sales.

Mario walked on until his attention was drawn to the window of a closed shop. The blinds had apparently been covered with graffiti, but someone had overlaid most of the graffiti with words, painted or sprayed on a white background through which the original motifs were still faintly visible. He took a few steps closer to study this palimpsest-like effort from nearby. He read the words, but they didn't make sense. Warning, imminent doom and prophecy seemed to be key words. He had the impression they were merely fragments of a text, pieces of a verbal jigsaw puzzle, begging to be assembled. Was this the idea, were there indeed other fragments elsewhere? And if so, where could he find them?

In the bottom right corner he spotted the tagger's signature, a hieroglyph-like symbol. He peered closer and found a series of numbers under the signature in very small print. Now what could this mean? Was it a clue of some sort? Did the numbers have a meaning?

He studied the words again, but they remained meaningless. Wait a second, he thought. He peered from close by and found there were a few more numbers embedded in the text. They just had to be there for a reason. He took out his notebook and jotted down the three sets of numbers. Should he put them in a certain order?

He took a good look at the numbers and had an idea. Could it be that the tagger had not only identified his work by his signature, but had also added some information for those who would like to get in touch with him? Could the sets of digits refer to a cell phone number? He counted the digits and nodded. This might well be the case. Now there were a few possibilities, depending on how he arranged the three sets of numbers. He noted them all down and felt he was making progress.

He took out his cell phone and formed the first combination. The number didn't exist, so he tried his second option. This proved more successful and he heard a voice at the other end.

"Yes?"

He thought about how to start this conversation, then simply read the words off the wall in front of him.

"I know where you are now," the voice said. "By the way, you're the first one to get my clues. Congratulations."

"Thank you. This text here isn't complete, is it?"

"You're absolutely right. It's just a fragment of a large epic. Its parts are spread all over town."

"Tell me all about it."

"I just hate the graffiti that turns up everywhere. It's meaningless shit, a waste of paint. I felt I had to do something about it, wanted to fight its spread before it smothers us. So I decided to tackle this issue my way. This is my crusade."

"You cover it all with words."

"Not just words, buddy. It's a large epic poem that I cut up into pieces and post at random all over the place. If you want to see the entire text, you'll have to track down all the parts. Then you put them in the right order and everything will become clear to you. It's deeply meaningful, you can peel away layer after layer until you reach its essence. You'll see. Good luck, pal."

The line went dead. He looked again at the words on the wall, jotted them down in his notebook and decided to move on. He would look out for other graffiti covered with parts of this epic, and try to assemble it completely. Who knew what he had stumbled onto here?

He walked on, scanning the walls for more evidence of the lone crusader's poetic talents. Across the street he saw someone with a large shopping bag, and thought he recognised the guy who picked up all the cans littering the gutter. As the man suddenly turned his face in his direction, he noticed it was not the can collector. There was just some superficial resemblance. The man entered a shop, and on the spur of the moment Mario decided to follow him. It was the Dog-Eared Copy Shop, a place selling second hand books. There were only a handful of customers around, quietly browsing. Mario slowly made his way through the aisles, and frowned as he saw how his target opened his shopping bag, took out a few books and put them on a shelf.

Mario shot a glance at the shop owner, who was sitting behind his counter, reading his newspaper. He hadn't seen a thing. He turned his attention to the offender again, and noticed he was still emptying his bag and adding books to the shelves. He edged closer to this remarkable shoplifter-in-reverse and whispered, so the shop owner wouldn't hear: "Excuse me, can I ask you a few questions?"

The man looked up, startled.

"I saw how you took books from your bag and put them on the shelves. What's that supposed to mean?"

The man smiled sheepishly. "It's yin and yang," he whispered back and seemed to consider the discussion closed, as he prepared to walk off.

"Wait a second," Mario said, grabbing the man by his arm. "I need to know more about this. What's the yin and what's the yang? And is the shop owner aware of your activities?"

The man cast a glance at the owner, afraid he might have overheard the conversation. Then he looked Mario in the eyes and explained: "You know, shops like this one have a theft problem. There's lots of cheap stuff here, but still some people can't refrain from stealing books. I've seen it with my own eyes. I just can't stand it and feel it's my duty to restore the balance by putting books I no longer need on the shelves here. You may think this is trivial, but it's my contribution to the fight against the forces of evil."

"Yes, I see, but why don't you simply offer the books to the guy who runs the shop? He'll probably buy them from you."

"You're missing the point completely. That wouldn't cancel the theft. My action may be modest and symbolical, it doesn't solve the crime problem, but at least it restores the balance somewhat. I think it's important. As I said, it's yin and yang."

"Some books that aren't paid for disappear from the shelves, but they're replaced by others that needn't be bought."

"Exactly. I'm what you might call a shop unlifter. By the way, why are those people filming us? Did you arrange that? I'm not taking this. I'm leaving."

Mario looked behind him and saw that two men had indeed recorded their conversation with a small camera. He turned around again to explain to the shop unlifter that he had nothing to do with this, but the guy was already gone. He walked up to the two men and said: "What's all this supposed to mean?"

"We can't talk in here," one of them replied. "Let's go outside." A few moments later they were back on the street and Mario demanded an explanation.

"We're doing a feature for a local TV station. We started out with the guy who's covering all the graffiti and replacing them with what he calls his epic poem. One night we caught him in the act and did a nice interview. We've tracked down a large part of his poem by now, and we begin to see patterns. For instance, there's talk about a prophecy and references to books and bad stuff coming our way. And then we spotted this guy picking up cans from the gutter, and you know what we found here in this bookstore?"

The man reached into his pocket and held up a paperback. Its cover showed a worn and dented soft drink can.

"This is one of the books the guy you just spoke to put on the shelf. So that means there seem to be links between all these persons and their activities. When we spotted you talking to the can collector, studying the graffiti and entering this shop, we concluded you were part of all this. Are you?"

"No, I'm not," Mario said.

"Maybe you are now," the man countered. "How did you get involved?"

"I'm a freelance journalist doing a series of articles on modern urban myths. I simply stumbled onto the guys you just mentioned. I had no idea this was a chain of elements forming a big plan. I'm only beginning to see the contours of it. Is all this perhaps a set-up?"

"That's what we thought, and we assumed you were part of it."

"I could say the same thing about you. You know, you're not very convincing. For one thing, I don't think you look like a regular TV camera crew."

"True enough, we don't and we're not supposed to. We're shooting images with a small hand-held camera, because that's the only practical way in these circumstances."

"Look, this conversation is getting us nowhere. Why don't we work together? We can make more progress this way, especially as you seem to have gathered more material already than I."

The two men shook their head. "I'm afraid that's out of the question. Firstly, we don't know to what extent you're involved in this game. And secondly, we're not supposed to work together with anyone. I'm sorry. Now, we really have to go. Good luck with your research."

"Wait," Mario said, but the two men turned around and crossed the street. He wanted to follow them, but had to stop for a bus just driving by. On its side he saw an ad for 7 Up featuring a large can, and next to it graffiti that had been covered with text. He didn't have the time to read all of it, caught just a few words, "imminent", "metal" and "apocalypse". Then the bus was gone, and there was no trace of the two men anymore. He took his notebook and wrote down the words he had glimpsed. They fit the tone of what he had noted so far.

It was too bad he had lost sight of the two TV guys. It would have been interesting to see the images they had shot of all the graffiti. It would have saved him a lot of time. Now he would have to do all the research himself. He still didn't know whether this was a game or something to be taken seriously.

He felt tired and decided to call it a day. He needed to take a break, and would continue his work tomorrow. So he headed for the nearest subway station and a few minutes later he was on his way home. Each time the subway car slowed down as it entered a station, he looked out for graffiti covered with parts of the scattered poem. He caught glimpses of several bits ("deluge", "metal", "doom"), but couldn't read them properly as people were walking by in front of them. It was tantalising, maddening. Maybe he should take a ride on the subway late in the evening, when fewer people were about. And he should take a camera, so he might study the footage at ease later on.

At the last stop but one, a young woman carrying several bags lost her balance as she made her way to the exit, and a few items spilled onto the ground at his feet. She apologised, grabbed her bags and hurried to get out before the doors closed again. He tried to draw her attention to the stuff she had lost, but it was too late already. The woman disappeared amid the throng of people on the platform, and the car got moving again.

At his feet were a can of Coke Light and a dog-eared paperback. He kicked aside the can and picked up the book, flipped through the yellowed pages. It was a volume in the Pantheon Classic Library, *"The Plays of Aristophanes"*. He glanced at the table of contents and noticed one of the plays was titled *"Lysistrata"*. Could this be a coincidence? There just had been too many coincidences today. This element had to be part of the game or whatever it was, the woman was probably involved and had dropped the items in front of him on purpose. So the ones in charge must know (or at least have guessed) he would be here at this hour. It was clear the plot was thickening. What cursed labyrinth had he ventured into?

Back home he took a shower, had a quick meal and went over the notes he had made, but he grew tired with it all and put his notebook aside. Later that night he watched some TV, switching at random between channels until he stumbled onto something that caught his interest. Suddenly he sat upright as he saw something familiar. Images of the text-covered graffiti, at various places all over town. Snippets of an interview with the man collecting cans, conducted in his apartment, which was literally crammed with cans.

Was this the feature the TV crew he had talked to had been making? Or a preview of it, as this series of fast-cut fragments couldn't be the finished programme? His jaw dropped as he saw a glimpse of himself, talking to the shop unlifter in the used book store. Why had he been singled out to participate in this game against his will? Why had he allowed himself, however unwittingly, to become involved in this plan? And what was it all about? He was still groping in the dark.

A string of commercials followed the preview, and then something else entirely started. He had just seen a teaser that yielded no answers and gave rise to many more questions. He went back to his notebook, trying to make sense of it all. He saw the poet's cell phone number, and decided to call him again.

A whispering voice told him: "I've done all I could. I did my very best. It's over now. I've reached the end of the line. Now I hope that someone else will carry on and finish my work. Before it's too late. What about you? Good luck."

Then there was silence. There was no one at the other end. This had been a pre-recorded message. Just to be sure he called the number again, and got the same message. What the hell was all this supposed to mean? Was this a game, or was there really a menace looming on the horizon? Should he call the police? Would they believe his paranoid story? He decided it would be better to get a good night's sleep and tackle the issue tomorrow with a clear mind.

The next morning he had breakfast and went out again, eager to continue his work.

As he arrived downtown, he noticed that city workers were hard at work removing graffiti, including the poem fragments he was hoping to gather and analyse. Were they trying to prevent him from doing research and grasping the full meaning of the epic, were they part of this conspiracy? Was this a big cover-up operation, did this mean even the city council was involved? Perhaps the police as well?

Or was this simply standard procedure, did they remove all graffiti on a regular basis, say once a week, and was there absolutely no ground for his rising suspicion? Maybe the entire situation, everything he had seen so far, could be reduced to his attitude: he saw patterns and links where there weren't any, he got carried away by his own enthusiasm. He was too much "into" this urban myth project, explained the purest coincidence as evidence for a major plot, allowed stress and his overheated imagination to rule where level-headedness and reason should dominate.

A bus drove by, its side ornamented by graffiti, in its turn covered with words. He was able to catch "deluge" and "prophecy", and then the bus was swallowed by the traffic. Apparently they hadn't found the time yet to clean up everything. The doomed poet's magnum opus had not yet been obliterated completely.

Let's try out a few things, he thought. He took his cell phone and called the poet again, but there was no reply, not even the recorded message. I have to calm down, he said. Maybe there's a simple explanation for all this. What if there's a prankster playing tricks on me? Or maybe everything I've experienced so far was filmed for some reality TV show, which will be revealed at one point soon. I shouldn't panic so easily.

There's no hard evidence for the theory that the poet had somehow been eliminated, that they were removing his epic for another purpose than a routine cleaning chore. There was no prophecy at the basis of this whole episode. He should try to get these silly notions out of his mind, tackle his project with a fresh, unbiased attitude.

So let's get this straight: there's no relation between the guy picking up cans, the books, the movie in the store, the TV guys, or the epic scattered all over the city. I should simply study these phenomena as separate items.

His train of thought was interrupted as he noticed two cops ahead, coming in his direction. He looked behind him, and saw two more cops were following him. Were they closing in on him? Had he been right all along, were they indeed eliminating all those involved in this game or conspiracy, and was it now his turn? Or were they just doing their rounds here? For a split second he considered his options. Wouldn't it be better not to take any chances and get the hell out of here?

When he heard a screeching sound he panicked and ran, choosing a direction at random. The moment he noticed the shrill noise was produced by a car braking abruptly, it was too late already. A truck driver could not avoid the car, made a desperate manoeuvre and spilled part of his cargo of soft drink cans onto the tarmac. Mario saw the tidal wave of cans coming, as if in slow motion, and realised there was no escaping his fate. He ended up sprawling on the ground, covered by a deluge of metal. Deluge? Metal? My God! The prophecy! The mad poet had been right all the time! Would he meet his death here on the street, crushed and suffocating under tons of cans? Would this be his own personal apocalypse?

He cursed himself for becoming embroiled in this unwholesome affair, closed his eyes and waited for the end to come.

Later that same day he was released from the hospital, as he had only suffered some mild bruises. He had been told to take it easy for a while, and he would follow that advice. The urban myth project could wait. He considered the case closed and had no intention to go out on the street and hunt for information for the time being. It was all over, and now that the menace-ridden epic had been erased, there was nothing that would remind him of this fearful episode.

That night he watched the news on a regional TV station, and smiled as he saw a short report on the traffic accident which had involved him. He could see how he was "rescued" from the mountain of cans and driven off in an ambulance.

He smiled and thought, until recently I would have considered this proof that someone is still shadowing me and recording what I'm doing. Of course we all know that there's always a guy around with a camera these days, so it's only natural that a TV station had access to this footage. There's really nothing to worry about.

The coverage of "his" accident was pretty short, and other local news followed. His cell phone beeped, and he reached out for it.

He frowned as he saw it was a simple text message, sent by an unknown source, without any identification. The message informed him that the prophecy would run its course, that he had only savoured his first taste of doom, and that fragments of the all-explaining epic poem would now reach him through high-tech media, as traditional venues had been closed off. He had not managed to avoid the apocalypse, as he may have thought, it was inexorably edging closer and would descend upon him and everyone else as predicted.

Mario leaned back. So it wasn't over. The chain had been interrupted, but not broken. The style of the message was unmistakably that of the damned poet. That could only mean he had not been eliminated, unless these messages had been pre-recorded and programmed too. He would undoubtedly find out, whether he wanted to or not. He had better accept the fact that he was becoming inextricably entangled in this affair, and that he would have to live the experience until the end.

Until the very end, as the prophecy had it.

Our Island

by Ralph Robert Moore

Our island is the only island in the world.

In the wide waters, only it is land. There is the sky, the ocean, our island.

It is a fortunate island, with an abundance of apples, and other foods. In the main bay, in the deep blue sea water, is a gray Navy destroyer.

The island takes five hours to walk its length, two hours to walk its width.

Stone and Gwen play by the southern shore, climbing over the black rocks. Down where the green and white waters gutter between the roughness of the rocks, splashes rising five feet, Stone's muscular legs guide his bare feet down the pocks, his blue eyes looking up, looking up, to make sure Gwen, twisting the long, black seaweed of her hair away from her face, is safe. At the bottom of the climb, both children waist-deep in the cold swirls and popping white bubbles, they find a large pink sea shell. It is extraordinarily complex in its colors and its shape, as complex as a bird's beak, a kernel of corn, the orange translucence of a shrimp's peeled-off shell. But whatever little hunchback once carried the shell above its red and yellow claws has abandoned this beautiful weight, is gone.

Both are thirteen. They spend all their days together, side by side, helping to harvest the crops, repair the fishing nets, gather warm eggs from the chickens.

This evening, after a dinner of roasted snapper and raw apple slices, all thirty-seven members of the island sit around the tall red campfire, rags under them so their bare bottoms don't rest directly on the dirt.

For Stone and Gwen, this is always the best part of the day, when everyone has a full stomach and can relax, chores done, just before sleep, singing songs.

Alice, as usual, selects the first song.

In her high voice she sings:

On a summer day in the month of May a burly bum came hiking
Down a shady lane through the sugar cane, he was looking for his liking.
As he roamed along he sang a song of the land of milk and honey
Where a bum can stay for many a day, and he won't need any money
Oh the buzzin' of the bees in the cigarette trees near the soda water fountain,
At the lemonade springs where the bluebird sings on the Big Rock Candy
Mountains.

Stone and Gwen sing along happily, leaning their upper arms into each other, sharing the vibrations of their voices, even though they understand so few words in the song, it might as well be in a foreign language.

After the songs, before bed, Stone and Gwen walk hand in hand past the trunks of the dark palm trees, down to the gleam of the shore. Leaving behind footprints in the wet sand, under the yellow moon, they bathe in the cool green waters, bare bodies goose-bumped, washing off the sweat of their work. Returning an hour later, to a campfire now orange and black, they snuggle against each other in their tent, limbs around limbs, the air cooling, each feeling the heat from the other's small body, smelling the brine in the other's hair and skin.

It is a perfect life, especially if you know no other life.

As they start to nod off, eyes heavy-lidded, their tent flap is raised. Alice bends over in the exposed triangle, smiling.

"Tomorrow, after prayers, the three of us will leave the island." She raises an amused hand at their alarm. "We'll return in two days. And neither of you will ever have to leave the island again."

Gwen, lying on the mat with Stone's arms around her, lets out a whimper. Stone can feel her heart beating against his wrist. "Where are we going?"

Alice squeezes the child's ankle. "Both of you are old enough now for your Facts of Life talk."

Everyone on the island gathers at the shore to say goodbye to Stone, Gwen and Alice.

Anchored in the rolling green waves is a white boat ten times larger, and much taller in the water, than the rowboats the islanders use for fishing. A tall metal mast, like a tree, sticks straight up from the center of the boat.

One by one, Gwen first, then Stone, then Alice, climb the wet rope ladder on the left side of the boat, stepping up onto the boat's firm deck, feet shifting to maintain balance.

The children soon discover, behind the tall mast, worn stairs leading downward.

Alice smiles, long gray and black hair blowing in the shore breeze. "You can go down. We want you to explore."

Stone goes first, eyes wide. As he reaches the bottom step, he bends his knees, quickly looking around in the boxed dimness.

A musty smell. A table for eating, with a bench on either side. He twists his head around on his neck to see if Gwen has noticed. Nostrils flared, she nods at him.

Beyond that, a hallway.

Within the hallway, on either side, bunks for sleeping. Gwen presses her outstretched five fingers down on one of the thin mattresses. Lifts her chin to Stone. "Softer than the mats."

"We have to go topside now, to launch."

The children follow Alice back up the dark stairs, out once again into the blue sky, islanders standing knee-deep in the waves, happy.

Alice walks to the front of the boat. Stands behind a steering wheel. Reaches down, presses a button.

From below the boat, a loud rumble starts up.

She grins at Stone and Gwen, who have followed her. "It's okay, children. That noise is an engine. You remember reading about engines, right?"

She pushes a lever forward. "Go to the back of the boat, and wave goodbye to your friends. But remember, you'll be seeing them again in just two days, and you'll never, ever have to leave the island after this."

They do what they're told. All those familiar faces, waving at them, smiling. Stone and Gwen clutch each other's hand, using their free hand to wave back, as the people in the waves get smaller and smaller.

Soon, they can't see the people at the shore. Soon, their island itself is swallowed up by the flat horizon.

Gwen keeps waving at the disappearance, warm tears on her cheeks. "Goodbye, old friend."

Terrified, knees shaky, they make their way back to the front of the boat, to Alice, all that's left of their island.

She lets go of the steering wheel. "I need your help now."

Alice directing, she has the two of them unfurl a tall triangle of white cloth that stretches from the top of the white metal mast down to the boat's deck. Once it is unfurled, the tall sail immediately puffs out, flapping noisily in the wind.

Alice goes back to the steering wheel, flips a switch, and the deep rumbling under them goes away.

Now there is only the loud flapping of the sail, and otherwise, ocean silence.

Stone looks around anxiously. There's the sky, the sea, and their boat. No land.

Gwen comes over, hugs him.

Alice, setting the steering wheel, walks over in the cool breeze to the two of them. "Let's sit on the front deck. Remember all the questions you've had over the years, where people would tell you, wait until your Facts of Life talk? Well, now you can ask all those questions. And I will answer every single one of them."

Gwen goes first, out of urgency. "Where are you taking us?"

"You'll soon see. It would be foolish to tell you now, because you have no context to understand what I would say."

"Are we going back to the island?"

"Absolutely! And then everything will go back to the way it was before, except you'll know more." Alice smiles at them. "Let me show you something." She reaches into a black bag on the deck. Pulls out a long rag. "Can you guess what this is?"

Stone, with his eyes, asks permission to take the rag from Alice. He unravels the cloth in his rising hands. There's a left side to it, and a right side, both sides joined together at the bottom. "Is it a rag for two people to sit on? Like Gwen and me? Is it a present?"

The fingers of Alice's right hand ask for the rag back. Standing up, she holds the rag upside-down, with the joined section in front of her black and gray pubic hair. "A long time ago, people used to wear clothes. Clothes were rags they wore over their bodies. This rag was known as pants. Watch."

She holds the rag down by her feet, then steps into each side. Pulls both sides up, until they reach her waist, covering both her legs.

Gwen observes with snub-nosed wonder. "Why did they wear rags?"

"To keep warm. And for other reasons. There were also rags they wore to cover the tops of their bodies, from the waist to the neck, but we don't have any of those left to show you. But you do see, people used to be a little different in what they'd do, a long time ago? Different than what we do now?"

Both children nod, even though it is unlikely, at this point, that they really understand the point Alice is making.

"So, any other questions? About anything?"

Gwen looks at Stone. He looks back at her.

Stone wets his lips. "Why don't we wear rags now?"

"We don't have any. None that are in good enough shape to still be worn. And we don't have the equipment or the raw materials to make any more."

"Did you wear rags when you were younger, before we were born?"

"No. All the 'clothes' that people used to wear turned to rags long before my time. The rags we sit on, when we sit on the ground? They were all at one time clothes." Alice smiles. "That's a lot to take in, so maybe we should just relax, and enjoy our ride for a while."

As nighttime rises in darkness from the waves tossing around their boat, Alice offers each of the children two apples for dinner. "We can't cook on this boat, like we can on the island, but this will at least put something in your stomachs."

Halfway through her second apple, Gwen has a question. "Will I have a baby someday?"

"We all hope so. You'll probably have your first baby with Stone. When a young couple like you and Stone decide to have a baby, all you have to do is let Stone put his penis inside your vagina. It'll hurt the first time, but after that, you may find you actually enjoy it. After you have a baby with Stone, you'll be asked to have babies with other boys on the island around your age, just like Stone will be asked to have babies with different girls on the island about his age. We want the two of you to have as many babies as possible."

Gwen's eyes go inwards. After obviously framing the same question over and over in her mind she asks Alice, "What if I only want to have a baby with Stone, and I only want Stone to have a baby with me?"

Alice shakes her head. A deal breaker. "We can't do that. We need lots and lots of babies. You'll have to try to have babies with most of the men on the island, just like Stone will need to try to have babies with most of the women on the island, including me. Because some of the babies won't be good babies. You and Stone are first cousins. So when your baby is born, it may not be a good baby, which means we won't be able to keep it. We can only feed so many mouths. And the mouths we do feed need to grow up to be strong, healthy children who can have more babies. When we came to the island, a long, long time ago, there were two hundred and fifty four of us. Now there are only thirty-seven. So we have to keep making babies, or else there won't be anyone else left on the island! You wouldn't want that, right?"

"No. I guess not."

"But that doesn't mean you and Stone can't still spend most of your time together, like you do now. You'll still have a very special relationship with each other."

The three of them lie down on the deck, looking up at the night sky.

Stone, secretively, looks sideways at Alice's body to see if he gets an erection like when he looks at Gwen's body. He does. So at least he can do what's asked of him. But he likes that he can spend most of his time with Gwen.

180

Alice, aware of Stone's assessment of her, points a bare arm up at the sky. "See the moon?"

Stone nods. "Is that another island?"

"In a way. Except there are no fish between here and the moon. People like us used to live on the moon, about one hundred years ago."

"Do people live there now?"

She shakes her gray and black hair. "No. They all died. They went blind because we could no longer send them medical supplies to protect their eyes from getting tiny cuts from moon dust, then they starved to death, because we could no longer send them food."

They decide to sleep on the deck, under the stars, because it's cooler than the humid bunks below decks. Stone and Gwen cuddle against each other. Alice sleeps a distance away.

The next morning, after eating some more apples, they watch the flat horizon they're heading into.

Around mid-morning, they see a brown dot in the center of the blue and green horizon. Once the sun is high up in the sky, the dot has spread across the horizon.

Gwen stretches up on the balls of her feet. "Is that our island?"

Alice rubs the top of the girl's head. "You really miss our island, don't you?"

Gwen, teary-eyed, nods. Stone takes Gwen's hand in his. Squeezes.

Alice points. "Look how wide that land ahead of us is. And we're still so far away from it. Do you children remember when we saw our island as we left? It was much smaller than what's in front of us, right?"

Stone watches the land widen, tense. "Are there people on this island?"

Alice looks at the growing shape. "Not really." Puts a smile on her face. "Do you know what that's called? What we're heading towards? It's called Texas."

Gwen stares suspiciously at the Texas coastline as it gets impossibly wide, filling the entire horizon. "How big is Texas?"

"It's very, very big. You see how its length takes up everything in front of us. You can walk the depth of our island in four hours. Do you know how long it would take to walk the depth of Texas?"

Stone shifts his bare feet on the deck. "Two days?"

"Much, much longer than that! It would take months."

Both children jerk up their heads. Stone wants to say something, but can't think of what.

Alice gives them a sad smile. "Even then, Texas isn't an island. If you spent months walking the depth of Texas, when you reached the other side, know what you'd find?"

Stone knew the answer. "Water."

"No. You'd find more land. Oklahoma, then Kansas, Nebraska, South Dakota, and North Dakota. Walking all the way up through those lands would take years. But even then there still wouldn't be ocean. There'd be Canada, which would take more years to walk." She watched their eyes, letting the enormity of that growing shoreline sink in. "And all that land, that would take all those years to cross – and that doesn't even include the years it would take to cross the length of that land – that land is just a small part of the land out there. There are other lands farther away from here, that are almost as large, or even larger. Europe. Asia. Australia. Africa. Antarctica. How many square miles to our island?"

Stone was embarrassed he got the first question wrong, so Gwen answers instead. "90 square miles."

"That's right! Well, all the land I just mentioned, it's over 57,000,000 square miles."

Stone blinks his eyes. "So why don't we live there?"

Alice draws her right index finger across her throat. "Because we can't."

She hands each child a telescope. "Tell me what you see."

Their sailboat is close enough to the Texas shoreline now that they can discern buildings even without the telescope. But the buildings are much higher than the one-story huts on the island. These buildings rise up taller than trees, taller than trees growing on top of trees growing on top of trees. And still taller.

Stone puts the telescope to his blue eye. Takes a moment to adjust the focus, the bottom of a beige building swaying up into detail. In that magnified circle, he sees only the building's base. Then movement.

Resting his elbow on the rim of the boat's half wall, he swivels the circle ever so slightly left, blurring. Then back in sharp focus. Bald, naked men and women shuffling silently towards the edge of the building, long red scars across their stomachs, chests, necks, scalps. Bending. Fixing their teeth to the concrete. Eating.

Gwen pulls the telescope away from her eye. "They look like termites."

"That's good! See those huge piles of rubble to the right?" The children don't need the telescopes to spot the piles.

"Those used to be tall buildings too. Just as tall as the ones still standing. But the termites chewed and chewed on them over the years, and eventually they fell."

Stone rubs his nose. "Why are they chewing everything?"

"They can't help it. A long, long time ago, long before you were born, long before your parents were born, or your grandparents, everybody used to live on that vast stretch of land in front of you, and the other vast stretches of land, and they were all happy. But then one day something went wrong, a small little spot, and someone in that land bit another person, and he or she bit a lot more people, and so on. The different governments tried everything they could to destroy the biting people. Chemicals, radiation attacks, trying to cut the infected areas away from the healthy people, but none of it worked. Eventually, all the people who weren't bitten had to hide from the growing number of people who had been bitten.

"They hid in houses, and stores, and sewer drains and trees, but the biting people found them, surrounded them, and no matter how hard the unbitten people tried, they couldn't stop the biters from crawling in and biting them.

"A few people – a very few, considering how many we once were – escaped to islands. There used to be communities of unbitten people like us living on islands off New York City, Georgia, Florida, our own island off Texas, California, and England. In the early days, we all used to communicate with each other by shortwave radio, trying to figure out how we could go back to the lands we had left, and make them ours again. But it was impossible. There were just too many biters, and not enough of us. The world had become a mouth. Eventually, one by one, over the decades, the other islands winked out. Until only our island was left."

The children say nothing for a long time, as the sailboat glides a safe distance along the shoreline.

Alice watches them absorb what they've learned, as she has with other children over the years. "I'm sure you're both feeling a lot of emotions. It's normal to deny the reality of what I've just told you, but of course you can see it with your own eyes. The fact we've lost so much might make you angry, but there's nothing we can do to change what is. We can't bargain with the biters. They don't talk, and they can't hear. Which is depressing, but it's something we, the ones left still unbitten, have to accept."

"Can we kill them?" Stone talking.

"No. We tried, those early years. Bomb them, shoot them in the head, burn them, douse them with poison, set them on fire. Nothing kills them."

"Are they dead?"

"I don't know. They're moving, so I guess in some ways they're alive. In some ways, the problem is they're too much life. Life that lost its modest aims. Life that became too aggressive."

They spend another night aboard the sailboat, on the deck, anchored a safe distance from the eaten shoreline. As Stone and Gwen huddle against each other, not talking, they hear, rising from the nibbled shore, the rage and violence of the biters. It takes them a long time to fall asleep.

The next morning, Alice tells them, "Now you know the Facts of Life. Now we go back to our island."

Gwen stands up on tiptoe, clapping excitedly.

On the voyage home, Stone, who had watched Texas slowly disappear on the horizon, asks a question that had been troubling him. "Is it possible the biters might find our island?"

Alice smiles. "I was wondering when one of you would ask that question. No, it doesn't seem that likely. Because if they could, surely they would have by now." She hesitates. "But in some ways, it really isn't necessary that they find our island, is it?"

Alice can see Stone doesn't really understand what she's just said. But that's okay.

All the islanders are waiting for them, up to their knees in the waves, when they return.

Gwen hops off the side of the boat, into the cool green water. Swims to shore with elegant overhand swings of her bare arms. Her father is there to greet her. Gives her a hug. "Now you know. Now your eyes are like our eyes."

Everyone that night gathers around the fire for a meal of roasted snapper and raw apple slices, Stone and Gwen sitting next to each other. They watch the three children on the island younger than themselves chasing after each other, laughing, once dinner is done.

Alice, as always, leads the islanders in a song:

Reach out your hand if your cup be empty
If your cup is full may it be again
Let it be known there is a fountain
That was not made by the hands of men

There is a road, no simple highway
Between the dawn and the dark of night
And if you go no one may follow
That path is for your steps alone

After the song, Stone and Gwen decide to sleep away from the others this night, down by the shore.

For the first time, they make love. Pain, as Alice said there would be, but pleasure.

After the upset of everything they had learned, but heads now calm after orgasm, they decide to wander down the wet sand, to the southern shore.

The moon is big and yellow, so much closer than the distant tiny white stars, as they climb over and down the black rocks, to the wave lappings they can, in the darkness, hear better than see.

At the bottom of the rough rocks, a spit of dry sand on which they can sleep.

The tide is going out. Two orange fish swim in circles in the phosphorescent waters of a tide pool cut off from the ocean, the level of the small pool slowly lowering.

Gwen backs her bare body into Stone's, spine against stomach, sea into cove.

The two children fall asleep, eyes drooping, to the reassuring sounds (waves, breeze, palm tree bendings), that have always been here, that will be here forever, on our island.

Underpass

by Daniella Geary

> *"It seemed that out of battle I escaped*
> *Down some profound dull tunnel, long since scooped*
> *Through granites which titanic wars had groined.*
> *Yet also there encumbered sleepers groaned,*
> *Too fast in thought or death to be bestirred…"*

– Wilfred Owen, *Strange Meeting*.

We think we know our cities. So many streets and routes and blocks, exquisite patterning, worn and polished, transfigured over time into strange organic artworks, Venice being the best. But all are fantastical really, beneath a veneer of grey familiarity. Remember when you first visited your nearest city as a child, the terror of becoming lost? You overcame this, and still do, by a simple remedy: a city of your mind, an invisible construct that you carry everywhere, marked with monuments and landmarks, favourite places, quickest or safest ways from here to there. And thus, although we all share a city, it can only ever be an abstract concept, an unknown, vague and nebulous thing, through which we sleepwalk, having each arrived from different directions, occasionally bumping into each other, co-inhabiting, almost coincidentally, the same geographic space with contrary intentions.

But what of tunnels? Our cities, and this is the eeriest thought of all, were built by dead people, people whom we can no longer really know or ask any questions of. But they left maps. Of course they did, but you'd be surprised how few people ever consult them. The city of my birth is by no means the largest in the country, but within it I know of countless disused Victorian railway tunnels, lost and forgotten beneath the surface. They are mostly rather carefully boarded-up now, closed over with iron railings and grim warnings of penalties and death. We suppose that they are very dark and probably full of rats and worse, with numerous opportunities for unfortunate and lonely deaths. Only fools would venture down them. But of course, children are just such fools.

When I was fourteen, a friend and I dared each other to break into the Parkhead Tunnel, which it was rumoured passed all the way under the city centre and out into an opposing suburb, a distance of perhaps twelve miles. Someone had claimed to have "done" the whole thing several years before, but this "someone", upon closer examination, turned out only to have been a friend of a friend, someone's older cousin, a flimsy thread, in other words, on which to hang your life. But hang it we did.

We took a girl with us, like true survivalists, although she didn't seem much like one at the time. Brenda Maxwell, *Maxi*, as she was universally known, was the ultimate tomboy in our school, a fierce fighter and no mean footballer, with whom nobody ever "messed", as much because of her own physical prowess as that of her two infamous elder brothers. You didn't do anything "girly" with Maxi, no sweet talk or chatting up. Nobody had ever kissed her. You accept these things with surprising respect as children, much more so, sadly, than in the case of their male equivalents. But I don't mean to insinuate, not that it would matter. Maxi will have children and a husband and all the rest if it by now, for all I know. Whatever that proves.

The instigator of our adventure however, the setter of the dare, was my best friend at the time, Robert Williams, known only, and for reasons already by then lost in the mists of time, as *Dicey*. Then again, in light of what happened, looking back, maybe the reasons were always self-evident.

190

Getting into the Parkhead tunnel was no easy feat on any normal day, but Dicey had gained a key piece of recent intelligence: that some mysterious maintenance work, only ever carried out once every ten years or so, was currently underway at the entrance near the river at the north end of Ramsay Park. This entrance was normally sealed tight with huge rusting steel doors, but sure enough when we got there we found that one of these was half open, with a couple of council vans parked outside.

We hatched a plan to hang around until near nightfall then slip in the door before the workmen left and conceal ourselves in the shadows inside. For this escapade, clearly a packed lunch and blankets would be necessary, and Maxi's house was nearby, hence the brainwave of involving her. It was the summer holidays, and various parents absent or drunk, mine included. My father had returned on leave from the oil rigs the previous week and settled into his usual pattern of drunkenness, late returns home, and verbal and physical abuse of myself and my mother. In such phases, we had developed a contingency whereby I would be sent to stay with my uncle in the city centre, and such was my presumed location today. But my mother, no stranger to the bottle herself, had increasingly lost track, lost the impulse to phone, and so I often found myself free to roam, unaccounted for, a street urchin of sorts, for days or a week at a time.

The situation for Dicey and Maxi was both less and more complicated. Their parents simply cared very little what they did or where they slept from one night to the next. This was the 1970's remember, and paedophile paranoia had not yet set into the public psyche and made every child the prisoner of centrally-heated homes and 4 x 4 people carriers. We were, in short, used to looking after ourselves, because for years nobody else had. Feral children? Maybe, but somehow not. We were just kids grown adult before our time. Or so we thought.

Getting into the tunnel actually proved scarily easy, as it turned out. There were bushes nearby and the daylight was failing, the workmen tired and careless, as we scarpered past behind their backs, like something out of "The Great Escape". Crazy really, because it was the opposite of that: we were seeking imprisonment, not fleeing it. Getting into, not out of, a tunnel system, with all the claustrophobia and risk they tend to entail.

When the steel doors finally slammed shut and locked behind us, the reality hit home and I shivered with more than the cold. We had been smart enough to take spare batteries, but this made us foolhardy. That first night, to keep us warm, or out of excitement and fear, we kept walking for mile after mile, burning up electricity. The place was a real mess and spookier than you can imagine. Dripping wet, black stalactites hanging from the stone vaults overhead. Piles of rubble to clamber over. Stinking debris and bird shit and worse: rats. We only heard them at first, then Maxi spotted one. I found some old cast-iron railings, and pulled a single bar out of it. A makeshift spear, with a sharp point that had once stuck into the ground, and at the other end: an ornate fleuron. With this we pursued rats, but Maxi's lobbed bricks were more effective. We squashed them flat and poked their guts around and scared each other witless throwing bits of them at each other.

Finally, we got tired and we huddled up together on a dry-ish pile of old wood, trying not to think about the rats, ears alert for any of their tell-tale little noises. When Dicey started snoring, to my surprise Maxi turned and kissed me on the lips. Too surprised to speak, I just played possum as she put her hand down the front of my trousers and rummaged around there. She made me do the same to her and her breathing started changing. Shortly afterwards, Dicey woke up and I felt cheated that Maxi hadn't yet completed her mysterious work on me.

It didn't seem like long before it was daylight, or what passed for it down there. We realised then that there was an airshaft nearby, and in the light I saw that Maxi's face was abstract, nonchalant, as if nothing had happened between us. But I saw it differently. I was confused. I suppose, as I know now, I am a romantic at heart. I expected what her hands had done to signify some kind of admiration or interest in me, but looking back now it seemed more like idle curiosity, like playing with her pet dog. Nonetheless, I felt good that it seemed like some kind of secret, and Dicey wasn't in on it. That made me feel strange and special, kind of fluttering inside.

It was easier to walk with the patches of light now coming down. The underground routes in our city were all built on the cut-and-cover principle, unlike London, meaning they were all formed as shallow troughs near the surface then vaulted over, not deep bore, in a sense not true tunnels at all, although the danger and evidence of collapse were just as real and evident around us.

As we walked and explored, we wondered at what parts of the city we were passing under. Occasionally we would glimpse a church spire or hear distant crowds or buses or cars and feel set apart and exhilarated, brave and unique. Few people, we believed, had dared to attempt this route as we were. The question of how we would ever get out added a note of terror that the daylight glimpses somehow ameliorated. Foolhardy doesn't cover it.

I wanted to get Maxi talking, to bring her closer to me than to Dicey, a conversational equivalent of what had happened during the night, but she was hard to reach somehow. What would we do when we left school, was our great debate. Maxi said she was leaving early after the next term, to help her dad out in his scrapyard. Dicey said he didn't care. "A drug addict or a footballer. How the hell should I know, Larky? My dad's never worked, why the fuck should I? Are you soft or something? You've been a bit of a sooky swat this last year, mathematical genius boy. That Miss Watson wants to blow your weeny while you recite the nine times table backwards…"

"Fuck off," Maxi said. This was what I wanted. She was defending me at last. Something warm caught fire inside me. A girl was standing up for me, sticking her neck out. "Just 'cos he's smarter than you, just 'cos you're a thick-headed dope fiend like your dad, deadbeat Dicey…"

He spat and went quiet at that. He didn't like it, but I couldn't imagine the two of them fighting, not then, at the age they were at, boy and girl. Was what Maxi had done with her hands like fighting? –Or like love? I scarcely knew the meaning of that word, in any sense. It probably hadn't even been affection. Dicey kicked a few stones over at me, like I was a rat to be squashed, and Maxi stopped and turned. She slapped me across the face and took my spear from me. "Here, soft boy, I'll show you what you ought to be doing with this…" She jabbed Dicey in the arse with it then held the spike under his chin, up against the tunnel wall. She turned to look at me, laughing. "See? You understand? I'm just a fucking girl. Use your balls and put this *mother* in his place. He likes that, *sadomasochist* style. There's a far too big word for you, eh Dicey?"

He went berserk at that and broke free and we both ran off as he roared and started lobbing more bricks and stones after us. There were side tunnels and passageways. I thought I'd run up the same one as Maxi, but I became disorientated in the half-light. About to turn back, I nearly jumped out of my skin when something moved on the floor in front of me. "Maxi!" I cried out like a child, but it wasn't even her. I nearly peed myself in fear. It was an old down-and-out, waking up from under his piles of bedding on an old station platform. His eyes shone white, and his mouth opened, a wet red triangle from which issued a trail of hoarse words, strange as broken glass.

"Where are you going, son? You got a map?"

"Who are you? How did you get in here? Is there a way up around here, a doorway, a staircase?" I was answering questions with questions, stupidly, dazed.

"No way out for me, son. For you, maybe. Lost your little friends, have you?" he sneered.

"No. They're just back there…" I noticed it was now oddly quiet behind me. I almost wondered if Dicey and Maxi had caught up and were listening at the entrance, but when I swung my torch back the way I'd come, the tunnel was empty.

194

"Come down here alone? No, I don't think any lad's as daft as that, not even you."

"I'm not daft." I protested. "What do you eat down here? Rats? You must have a way up to the surface…"

"If I did, I'd use it, don't you reckon? This is my home and you've just bolted in without even knocking, now isn't that rude?" He advanced towards me and I instinctively stepped back. "Oh touchy! I don't bite! You're not scared of little old me, are you?" Of course, this made me even more scared. I brandished my iron spear and backed away.

"You're going the wrong way, son. Do you hear me? You need to turn around, to change your way. You get that? You get what I'm telling you?"

I shook my head, hands tensing on the spear, and he opened his mouth and bared his jagged old teeth like a wild animal. Then he howled like a wolf. "Lonesome boy…" he sang, "lost in the underworld, you need to slay your dragon to impress a girl, not just slop around in the devil's guts so…" His hands reached out for me and I turned and ran, tripping, scrabbling, out of breath. His laughter echoed off the dripping walls around me.

Backtracking, I found nothing. Running ahead, hearing voices, I caught up with Dicey and Maxi. They were friends again now, and both laughing as if they had been exchanging jokes about me. "What happened to you, Larky? You had us worried, thought you'd been eaten by an extra large deluxe king-size rat. A super rat. You look like you saw a ghost. You alright?"

"An old guy…" I stammered, then steadied my voice, sounding too rattled in front of Maxi. "A tramp, a wino, living in one of the side tunnels."

"Yer arse…" Dicey laughed, "you pishing in our boots?"

"Honest. Scout's honour," I said, "…on my mother's life."

"Boy's ready to sell his mother for a tramp, Maxi. He should be studying Economics, what d'ye think?"

"I think he's telling the truth, aren't you, Larky? Or I'll beat the shit out of you for pulling our chains…"

Dicey tittered: "Oh, that raises the stakes nicely. You still telling us you found an old guy back there? If you're right then maybe Maxi will jack you off."

I nodded my head, embarrassed, while Maxi slapped Dicey across the head. But just then we began to hear voices, not behind us but in front. Some torches came bouncing into view, blades of light cutting through a billowing cloud of dust up ahead.

It was the Saracen Street gang, or the Townhead Yung Fleet, to give them their official moniker. I realised too late that I'd been spotting their signature graffiti in amongst the gloom for the last half mile. *"The Observer's Book Of Gangs"*… has anybody written that one yet? The Fleet were about the most feared outfit in the central belt. They were legendary. I had never met any of them, only seen a few pointed out at a distance, heard their nicknames mouthed in hushed tones. Dicey had claimed to have some kind of connection to them through a cousin twice removed; twice removed by Social Services probably. The crazy thought occurred to me that Dicey had set this coincidence up for some reason, to be appraised by, or inducted into, their gang.

Fortunately, they didn't all spill out across the tunnel in police formation or we'd have been really stuffed, a confrontation situation. Everything depends on how people stand in relation to each other, posture is everything. Maybe the whole world is a ballet of indefinitely postponed violence, latent, dry tinder waiting for the spark. There were seven or eight of them, but they didn't face off, they mingled, in a predatory sort of way, sniffing us, while their leader, the infamous *Tyro*, sounded off: "You're a long way from home turf, Dicey, ma man! Who's this you've brought with you?"

"It's a girl!" one of his cohorts sniggered, "he's brought a fucking lassie…"

But the boy regretted this remark within seconds. Maxi put him in a headlock, and drew blood then tears. I even saw her punching his genitals, and counted myself lucky she'd been a little more gentle than that with me the night before. This seemed to shift the power in our favour briefly, through sheer novelty and shock value, and though outnumbered, Dicey leapt into the breach to drive home any possible advantage. Unfortunately, his devious mind fixed on me as a prop. "Hey, this is Larky; psycho boy we call him. He found a tramp back there, an old jakey, down-and-out, old scumbag, living alone down here. He wanted to do him, but you know how it is, one leader to another. Ah reined him in. Psycho boy needs kept on a leash, know what ah mean? Maxi here will bite your balls off, but Larky psycho boy, he'll take your heed off with a chib and play football with it, three and in…"

Nobody had ever called me *Psycho Boy* before. This was utter improvisation. Tyro turned his attention to me and sidled up. My heart sank, but I resolved not to show any fear, to sublimate it into something else, anything. "A Jakey you say, mental boy? What d'you say we all do him? D'ye fancy that? Grand slam, gang slaughter? No one's ever gonna know down here, are they?"

I shivered, and Tyro's rapacious eyes widened in surprise for a moment, then he probably put it down to the epileptic fit of a borderline lunatic. I decided to play the part, with an unearthly howl and beating my iron spear off the tunnel walls until fragments of mortar came crumbling down.

"Easy, psycho boy…" Tyro purred and I laughed, insanely he thought, but really to myself about how easy he was to delude into an opinion. Even Dicey looked at me, impressed at that point, and a little worried. Maxi's expression was lost in shadow. But the game Dicey had bounced me into went quickly out of hand. Before I knew it I was being nudged down the tunnel, at the head of a deranged procession, Tyro's new bloodhound on loan, baying wolves panting behind me.

As we all trotted like little pygmy tribesmen, I felt some new sickness falling through my stomach like quick-setting concrete. Dicey had done it again, somehow wrong-footed me into a bad situation which could only get worse. I saw at that moment what a talent the boy had, a talent for evil, if I had to put a name to it. Contrary to what people think, such evil is much more common in children and juveniles than in adults, and has much more opportunity to get out.

I thought of leading them the wrong way, to a different spot, but I'd have looked stupid or false. Then it actually started worrying me that we wouldn't find him at all, God forgive me. If only we hadn't. We turned up the side tunnel I'd seen him in and with a couple of quick sweeps of the torch, there he was: a bag of ragged clothes on the ground, and that grey matted hair and skeletal face, bloodshot eyes wide and shocked then closing, doubling over in pain.

I kicked the old guy around a few times, but nothing too hard. Nothing was breaking, but he was squealing like a pig. I could feel Tyro near me in the shadows, hear him shouting, "Kill 'em, do 'em, psycho boy". But he knew I was holding back, my credibility was crumbling, something was going to have to give. One of Tyro's neds was grabbing the old guy's shoulders by this point, and Tyro was reaching for his feet. Moss gleamed, water dripped from the sweating stone vaults around us, puddles glinted off across rusty rails and sleepers, dark figures shifted, in that eternal instant in which my soul hung in the balance. Someone shone a torch beam onto the old guy's face and he looked up at me and our eyes locked in a fateful moment of anguish and despair, and something flipped inside me.

Almost without thinking or really deciding anything, I had spun my spear around, lashed its end across the head of the kneeling demon in front of me, then lunged its sharp tip backwards with maximum force into the figure behind me: Tyro. Roars and screams splashed across the wall, torches flickered away in panicked blades of confusion. I could hear scuttling somewhere at my feet, creeping me out. I hoped it was the old man sliding away like a crab. The ned in front was still moving, holding his head. So I proceeded to give him everything I had contemplated for a moment for the old man. He beat a hasty retreat, then I turned back towards Tyro, groping in the growing darkness, unsure what he was capable of, or of what I had done to him.

Dicey and Maxi were calling out to me from the darkness. I heard sobbing, tears. Could that be Maxi, a stereotypical girl after all? "Larky... we better run, mate. You've killed him, you fuckin' psycho. His mob's probably coming back for you, re-grouping, getting reinforcements..."

I was getting tired of his clichés, and to my surprise found myself asserting authority over him. "Shut the fuck up, Dicey. I'm trying to listen for his breathing. Shine a light this way..."

I found the end of my spear in the dark and followed it with my hands, seeking out whatever it had impaled. At the last moment, Dicey mastered the torch situation and threw a cone of illumination onto the face now only inches from my own. I nearly screamed like a girl myself and jumped backwards. Tyro let out a groan, a kind of gurgling roar, but much more pathetic than that word implies. His grimacing face and bared teeth looked truly demonic in the torchlight, his hands on his stomach where my makeshift iron spear had gone straight through him and lodged into the mossy vaults behind.

"Oh Jesus fuck…" Dicey's voice began shaking, and the light beam with it.

"Give me the torch" I said, and took it off him, suddenly ordering him around like a child. His compliance amazed and vaguely thrilled me. I took the light and checked behind Tyro's shivering form. The spear had lodged itself into an ancient rotting timber beam, impaling him in an upright position.

"They'll be calling the police and ambulance, getting their dads onto us. Oh fuck, Larky, this is bad shit…" I spun the light around onto Dicey, his face was pale and tearful, a parody of its usual bravado.

"Shut up" –I said again, as I freed the spear point, then drew it rapidly backwards. Tyro let out a hideous yelp then sagged down onto the tunnel floor.

"I'm out of here!" Maxi wailed, and I heard her footsteps trotting off, her torchlight bouncing in front of her. I saw Dicey wavering too, desperate to follow after her.

"You chickening it too then, like a girl?" I frowned.

Dicey shook his head, and I saw his face was wet now, with sweat as much as tears, pouring off him. "You're totally psycho, Larky, utterly mental, for real".

"Yeah," -I laughed in a weird shaky sort of way at that, spooking even myself. "You called it, Dice."

He ran off. But suddenly I didn't want to follow him or Maxi anymore anyhow, as if I had moved on into some other reality that I could no longer share with them. I was blooded now. Logically, the direction they were retreating in would take them a full four hours to reach the end of, while I reckoned that the Saracen Street boys must have come down some entrance nearby which I could find, or failing that: grapple out somewhere else, at some air shaft along the way.

I moved away from Tyro. I reckoned his mates would be back with help soon enough, and I wasn't going to be stupid enough to leave my fingerprints on him or leave the weapon behind. There I was, thinking like a real criminal already, but not like a surgeon. I suppose I must have thought that the human body was a big bulky thing compared to an iron spear, and if I'd missed all the vital organs then a doctor could just patch him up down there. Nowadays I know better.

I moved off in my own direction, forward. I could see and smell distant air shafts, abandoned stations. I supposed I'd find a way and get out and up, melt back into the anonymity of the city above, throw my spear away somewhere dark and irretrievable, in a nice big puddle to wash away the blood. I walked for a long time. I heard distant voices a few times, spotted what I thought might be the Saracen Boys' way down, but I never found anything, no staircase or door, ladder or rope, so I just kept going.

I suppose I became progressively more scared, only numbly aware even of the enormity of what I might just have done. But the old man had got away, and somehow that consoled me, in my childlike logic. Killing Tyro, if indeed that was what I had done, felt like a much lesser sin. I felt as if I had seen evil, and in a moment of inspiration, turned it upon itself. But how could I have thought that, when the only true evil, in the eyes of the law, had just been done by me?

I was getting cold and in the few air shafts I passed, I could see that darkness was approaching, a red sunset filling the sky. I felt more alone than I had ever done before in my life. More alone than the times I'd tried to run away from home. More alone than when my father had beaten me to a pulp. More alone than my first day at school. It felt like a penance, although I probably didn't know that word back then, like getting lost in this huge hopeless tunnel was my fitting punishment, my fate, for what I had just done. But then something strange happened.

The tunnel slowly turned and a huge tree came into view, bathed in red sunset light, as its branches reached upwards through an air shaft, its bark covered in eerie green moss. Its roots were exposed and gnarled, grappling over the tunnel floor in fantastical ways like writhing limbs, like the blind intertwined bodies of the dead. Like those photographs of Banyan trees devouring the ruins of Angkor Wat.

In retrospect, I wish I had had a camera, but this was before the days of mobile phones and every child taking snaps of their mates with them. The scene was unearthly beyond belief, and infused with the weird and exhilarating feeling that probably no one had ventured this far or seen this spectacle in countless years, if ever. But my excitement was more than visual. I had the immediate impression that this tree presented an opportunity, that from its upper branches I might be able to find a way out, a chance to leap over the guarding barbed wire into whatever backcourts or yards lay beyond.

I strapped my failing torch against myself with my belt and began to clamber up the branches, moving like a tree myself, slowly and methodically towards the light. As I got higher, the uncomfortable thought occurred to me that if I fell now I might never be found until I was a skeleton. Then my guts lurched momentarily at the thought of the wound I had inflicted behind me, the lonely death I might just have dished out. Guilt was creeping in, as if some kind of anaesthetic, adrenalin or shock perhaps, was wearing off.

As I reached the upper branches, I emerged at last into what was left of the light of day. I surveyed the scene around me. I was in a backcourt just like my own, with tenements all around me. And there in front of me was the back elevation, four-storey and in blackened Victorian stone, of a tenement in every respect identical to my own parents' one, where I had grown up. I had to pinch myself to remember that I was in a different part of the city entirely, perhaps ten miles from my own home, and the resemblances were only the product of the methodical rigour with which our forefathers had constructed these city blocks to the same standard model.

Dismissing these resemblances, I looked around and down, and saw with increasing dismay that no matter where I looked, no safe opportunity presented itself for me to jump or clamber from the tree to the safety round about. Ancient barbed wire-topped fencing and railings, and broken glass-encrusted capstones, set there by railway officials and anxious mothers, had thoroughly ensured that the safe domain of normality was entirely isolated from the dangerous no-man's-land in which I hung like a scavenger bird. I was an emissary now from a demon world, part of what the good people would go to great lengths to exclude from the nightmares of their sweetly sleeping children.

I thought about my options; swung on a branch and nearly fell, contemplated the risks and visualised myself impaled on a rusting spike too, felt the trembling fear in my chest, then thought the better of it. It was no use. I would have to retreat back down into the tunnel, wrap myself in my jacket and spend another night there, this time without the ambiguous comforts of Maxi to warm me up.

Then I froze. A figure was looking out of a rear tenement window, apparently straight at me, and I nearly raised my hand for help, not necessarily a good idea. But the light went out, and the figure left the kitchen and walked into other rooms of their flat. I saw other lights come on and off, a wife and children move about.

My eyes slowly panned back and surveyed that whole façade in front of me, now filled with lights coming on. I saw it as a canvas of life itself, a portfolio of choices, and concurrent realities. In one window I saw myself as I would be in the future: a young man with a wife and child. In another: my own mother as a newly-wed with my then-sober father, singing to herself as she tied up her hair in the mirror. In another I saw my father staggering in late, lights thrown on, objects hurled across the room, shouts, screaming, hand raised, beating my mother and me, and worse. In one I saw a cot holding my newly-born self, my young mother bowing over me admiringly. In other, darker windows, I saw myself as an old man, dying alone. There were still other windows I didn't want to look in.

I had the overwhelming sense that every answer, every question, every choice was there. –That my life was part of some kind of matrix, an infernal machine for the production of something… but what? Me? I was the ultimate outsider now, an astronaut off-world, an explorer on the moon looking back at his first ever Earthrise, receiving his revelation. Then I knew I had to go back, and what I had to do there.

I spent the night back down in the lower branches, hidden from view, but suspended above the dank floor of the tunnel. Incredibly, I was awoken at sunrise by birdsong from the branches high above me; and, stiff as a board, walking like a wounded zombie at first, I set out on my long march home.

The second set of batteries on the torch were running low and I knew I had to conserve. Whole stretches where even the weakest daylight was permeating; I had to move through these with the torch off, always thumping each foot down to test the ground in front of me. I knew there were pits and sinkholes that I had seen on the way in, some dry, some flooded so that a careless step would drop you into a hideous bath of cold black slime. I looked for the place I'd left Tyro, but everything seemed different that morning, maybe I was confused, but I never seemed to pass it.

But then in a particularly dark stretch of tunnel, I came across something I'll never forget, or understand. It was the old man, I swear it. Except that when I moved over to touch or wake him, I found his hair was only a grey mop-head, his face a punctured leather football, his body an old sack of coal. I stared and stared, stunned, breathing heavily, blinking, wasting torchlight. Then I heard something behind me, a rat perhaps, and I lost it.

I ran and ran, blindly, stupidly, over rubble and cobbles, not using the torch properly. My worst fear came true: I plunged into a deep sinkhole, screaming like a child, black water gurgling into my mouth. I was out again fast, but for a heart-stopping instant I had been beneath the water, losing all grip of the ground above, tasting total terror and despair. I had lost hold of my blooded iron spear. Surely my penance was complete.

Shivering now, soaked through, I marched and staggered the rest of the way with increased urgency, determined to survive. The torch failed altogether in the end, and I had to grope the last mile in total darkness, hands feeling along the stone archways, my heart in my mouth. My final terror came when I reached the steel doors and found them locked. I beat and beat on them, yelling and bawling, *Please, God*, yes I think I finally said that. Perhaps I was finally ready to believe in him then, having seen how he could mess with his reality and my head, the trickery he was capable of.

Somehow, long after I had given up hope, I heard footsteps and voices outside, and I stood up and resumed my beating against the doors, and they were opened. It was over. The sunlight by then blinded me painfully, and I wept like a baby. For a moment I think I even embraced the bemused council worker who stood there with his compressor and

Kango Hammer, shouting over to his mates about the little Dickensian waif, a veritable chimney sweep's boy, who had just magically emerged from the tunnel.

They were laughing at me, and someone was starting to talk stern about regulations and trespass penalties. Something distracted them, a supervisor arriving perhaps, and sobering up in a fateful instant, I seized my chance and ran like hell. They never caught up with me.

So I went to my uncle's and got cleaned up, and told him I was leaving my parents' home. I came clean about all the bad stuff that had been going down, things he must have guessed but had never had spelled out for him. That's the worst thing about abuse, of course, the way everyone keeps quiet about it, particularly the victims, from utter shame. Suddenly I was over with that, and I was scared of this city for even bigger reasons. I had to get away.

I went back to my parents' house and found my mother bruised and unconscious on the bed with a bottle of scotch open beside her, my dad dead-drunk on the living room floor. God forgive me, but I got a bucket of cold water and threw it over him, then battered the crap out of him. I'd probably been physically big enough to do that for a while, but in the bowels of Hell itself I had finally found the spirit for it. I didn't kill him, I'm certain of that, but I gave him as good as he'd ever given us, and made damn sure he understood the lesson and who was administering it. I'd be lying if I didn't confess that I enjoyed it, particularly the punches to his big stupid face, and the look of astonishment in his frightened eyes. Then I kissed my sleeping mother's forehead and walked out, closing the door behind me. I never saw either of them again.

So who am I now? My uncle paid for my last two years at a different school, then university in a distant city. I never saw Dicey or Maxi again and neither they nor the police ever came looking for me, despite my sweat and sleepless nights. Maybe somebody just kept their mouth shut. That's the good thing about cities and their layers of opposing maps and truths: they allow us all to get lost at will sometimes, to each chase our own realities.

If Tyro died from his wound then I never heard about it, or saw any story in the papers. But the guilt and fear have stayed with me all these years, and the sense of pursuit and penance, of needing to make amends and start anew. I buried myself in books, in study. I gradually became the opposite of everything I disliked about myself, of how my parents had made me. Thankfully, such transformations are possible. I am a doctor now, a surgeon. And although I operate on almost every area of the human body from time to time, it's when I'm called upon to open up the stomach and cut in and around the intestines, that I always remember Tyro and that strange night, and then I wonder whether I dreamt it or not, or whether that man still lives and breathes with flakes of Victorian iron rusting inside him.

Like human intestines and veins, I know those tunnels still lie buried under my old city, where nobody ever goes for fear. Connecting and interlinking, undercutting and undermining, like dreams and nightmares, joining us all up in ways that nobody wants to think about. Their creators are long forgotten, dead or invisible, the ways in barred and blocked. But once I travelled them, and made myself their master.

Overnight Bus

by Marion Pitman

By one a.m. the bus that had been due at ten-thirty p.m. still hadn't arrived. There had been a couple of announcements, to the effect that the ten-thirty service to Kimberley had been delayed, but no suggestion of how much, or indeed that the announcer knew any more than the rest of us. Most of the passengers seemed resigned to an indefinite or even infinite wait – they sat around, eating biltong and roasted mealies, talking, sleeping on the wide wooden benches, with cases, with paper parcels, with huge laundry bags of luggage, with sleepy toddlers and fretful or somnolent babies; the air was hot, heavy and thick. A few obvious tourists slept against rucksacks in a corner.

The excitement I still felt simply at being in Africa was fighting against the need for sleep, and a feeling in the pit of my stomach that the bus might never come, which emphasised horribly the pointless and ludicrous nature of my whole journey. I should have given up this silly plan, and stayed with Anne's aunt in Jo'burg, or maybe gone to Cape Town for a few days as she suggested. Which would also have involved a long time on a bus, but at least with a goal I wasn't embarrassed to mention.

There was a queue at the counter, where the Indian clerk had been checking someone's ticket for at least five minutes, typing things into his computer terminal, looking back and forth between the screen and the piece of paper with a frown, and scribbling notes. There were six people behind the man with the disputed ticket, and I decided I didn't have the stamina to queue. Ian's face came into my head, but at the moment it was just a face, hardly more meaningful than any other. Hardly worth queuing for.

But I was here now. I curled up next to my bag and dozed for a bit; I was woken by another announcement telling me the coach to Kimberley was delayed. The queue was shorter now, and the clerk had gained reinforcements. I stood up and joined the line, and fairly soon was talking to a young African man with a wide smile and a very soft voice.

I said, "Do you have any idea when the bus to Kimberley will be here?"

"The bus to Kimberley is delayed."

"Yes, I know. It should have been here three hours ago. Do you know what has happened to it?"

He shook his head; "We know it left the last stop one hour late. We have not heard since then. It may have broken down."

"You haven't heard anything at all?"

"No. The driver should have a cellphone, but it may not be working."

"So, if it doesn't get here at all, how can I get to Kimberley?"

"There is another bus at ten-thirty in the evening."

"You mean there's only one bus each day?"

"That bus, yes, it runs once a day. There is another bus, which will leave at two-thirty, in one hour, but it is a local bus."

"A local bus? Where does it go?"

"It goes to Kimberley."

"So – sorry – what do you mean when you say it's a local bus?"

"It is for local people – not for tourists – it will not have the same facilities."

"Such as what?"

"There will not be any entertainment, and there will not be food or drink served."

"Will there be a toilet?"

"Yes, there will be a toilet."

It was two in the morning, I didn't want food or drink or in-flight movies. I said, "Can I use this ticket for that bus?"

He took the ticket and checked various things on his computer screen. "Yes," he said, "I can change this ticket so you can use it for the local bus. You are sure you want to do this?"

"Yes," I said, "I do want to." The thought of another eighteen hours in this bus station was not enticing. The seats were only comfortable for a fairly limited time, and there were strongish smells of people and food, and some of the babies seemed to need their nappies changing.

I said, "Is there any difference in the price?"

He shook his head; "I cannot refund any money. You understand there is a charge for changing the ticket?"

"How much is that?"

"You will not pay any more, you will not pay that. But I cannot refund. Yes? You understand?"

"OK. But – OK, that's fine," slightly puzzled by his insistence on no refund, when I had in fact been expecting an extra charge.

So he gave me a new ticket, and I trailed off with my suitcase-on-wheels to look for stand 174F. The coach was loading by the time I got there – I'd been half afraid it might be one of the peeling, rusty, highly unroadworthy-looking vehicles I'd seen a few times at the side of the road, apparently broken down, with luggage on the roof and resigned passengers sitting about on the ground, but this looked in good repair, just like the other "tourist" coaches I'd travelled on. The driver put my case in the luggage compartment, and I climbed up with my shoulder-bag, and looked for my seat.

I saw then why the clerk had thought I might want a refund. The bus was about the same width as usual, but instead of two seats either side of the aisle there were three; the leg-room was pretty limited too. I was the only white person on the bus, but I was getting used to that. I had a window seat, which was a bit of a pain, since it was pitch dark and nothing to see, and it made it difficult to get up if I wanted to go to the loo. Anyway, I would be moving, so it was better than a few more hours in the bus station.

It took a while to get everyone on, but eventually we started, and gradually I relaxed and felt again how dreadfully tired I was. The people beside me were talking, but no-one was speaking English, so it was quite easy to tune it out; the bus was a hive of activity, people eating, drinking, nursing babies, changing nappies; I heard an odd noise, and after craning round a few times I realised someone a few rows behind me had two chickens in a box. It wouldn't have surprised me if they'd had goats as well – perhaps not cattle, it was too small – but I couldn't see any. The smells of the food and the nappy changing made me slightly queasy; I found the bottle of water in my bag and drank a little.

After half an hour or so the driver dimmed the lights, and the noise died down a bit, and I started to doze. I was vaguely aware of movement in the near darkness; people went up and down the aisle; once I almost thought someone had brought a goat on, there seemed to be something going past that wasn't a person, but I was too sleepy to take much notice.

I thought, sleepily, about why I was here, and how stupid it was. OK, the holiday had been a good idea, get away from the English winter, see new places, meet new people; but a long cross-country journey, to a place where the main attraction is a hole in the ground, to see someone who really wouldn't be pleased to see me...

The woman beside me tapped my arm and said something, thrusting a plastic box in front of me; it took a moment to realise she was offering me whatever was in the box, presumably food. I blinked, and shook my head, and said, no, thank you; but she insisted, saying, "Please, please," and eventually I took a brown lump of something, smiled and said Thank you, and ate it, rather dubiously. It turned out to be chicken cooked in spices. I hoped desperately it wouldn't disagree with me.

I'd met Ian at a party, and we'd snogged a bit, probably because he couldn't find anyone better; and that should have been that, and would have been, except that a couple of weeks later I saw him playing in a county cricket match, and fell violently in love with him. How stupid is that? He was averagely pleased to see me, but no more; by the end of the season it was blindingly clear he was never going to return my feelings; and yet when I found he was going on an England A tour of South Africa for three months, the thought of his being on a different continent for so long was unbearable. Go figure – what difference does it make if someone's in Kimberley or Canterbury, if you don't see them? But it mattered. I had no money, of course; I wangled an invitation to visit the aunt of a South African colleague at work, who lived in Sandton, and scraped and borrowed enough for the flight, and a bit of a tour round. The aunt was astonishingly hospitable; I felt a bit guilty, although I was paying something for my keep, and had taken out a load of stuff my friend didn't want to trust to the post.

The woman beside me was now offering me a drink from a bottle of orange squash; I was even more reluctant to accept, but could think of absolutely no polite way to refuse. I took a sip, trying rather absurdly not to let the bottle touch my lips, wiped the rim and handed it back with more thanks.

So, I had been to a couple of tourist sights, and had spent a good deal of the week on buses; I didn't feel I could just go straight to the match, with no further explanation. Despite the embarrassment, though, I was utterly determined to go through with it. How Ian would react when he saw me, I didn't even want to think.

I slept for a bit, with horrible dreams of trying to get to Ian on the other side of the road, but being prevented by the huge stream of people and goats – huge goats – that was flowing between us. I woke up when the coach stopped, the lights went up, and everyone started talking again, and getting up and getting down luggage and gathering up babies and getting off. I didn't think we'd been on the road long enough to reach our destination – it was still pitch dark – but I got up and moved dozily to the front. The driver said, "We stop here, madam, for one hour. Make sure you are back before we leave."

I nodded and said Thank you, and climbed down.

It was much less hot now, and the air smelt fresh. We had stopped in a large open courtyard, with low buildings around it, and a great high building along one side. There were a great many tables and chairs and benches, and people seemed to be fetching food and drink from some of the low buildings, and sitting down. I wondered what time it was, but my phone had switched itself off, and when I switched it back on it wanted me to tell it the time. Whatever, the middle of the night seemed a funny time to start eating and drinking, but I thought maybe the bus company had to have a break in any journey of more than a certain number of hours.

I wasn't hungry, so I just sat down at one of the tables. There were dim lights in some of the buildings, and open fires here and there in the courtyard, but it was still tremendously dark; outside the circles of light I couldn't make out people's faces until they were right close up. Perhaps because I was still the only white person there, people kept coming up and looking at me, smiling, shaking my hand; they didn't seem to want to talk. A small girl came and stood beside me, smiling shyly; after a little while she put out a hand and touched my hair, first on my shoulder and then the side of my head; the feel of her tentative hand was strange, but rather pleasant – I smiled back, and she stroked my hair a few times, and moved on. A lot of the men were drinking some lethal looking local beer from a plastic barrel; one offered me a cup, but I shook my head, and then someone else gave me a bottle of Castle, which he took the top off of by banging it against the table. I thanked him, and drank; it was quite welcome by this time, although I was afraid it would send me back to sleep.

There was tremendous milling about: people sat and ate and drank, then got up and moved about again. A woman with a baby on her back came and sat opposite me; she unfastened the blanket that held the baby, and sat it on her knee, and then held a very animated conversation with another woman, who kept pointing across the courtyard. After a while the second woman looked at me, and said something to her friend, and the mother nodded, and stood up, holding the baby out to me – "Please," she said, "you hold my baby?"

"Uh – sure, OK." It seemed a fairly simple thing to ask. She put the baby on my knee, and I held it, while it gazed at me with large, solemn eyes. It was pretty well wrapped up, despite the warmth of the night, and its gender was quite unguessable by me. The two women went off, talking excitedly, towards the large building.

The baby seemed contented, or perhaps resigned. Perhaps it was still at that age where other people are undifferentiated, and so long as it was warm and not hungry it was quite happy. I confess to knowing little about babies. They seem to appreciate attention, though, so I jiggled it a little, and talked to it in a random stream of consciousness. "Don't know how long we're here for, baby, but I can see the bus, so if people start getting back on, I hope your mother comes back for you." I tried to check how long I had been there, but now the phone battery had suddenly died, so I made sure I was facing towards the bus, a looming shape against the slightly lesser darkness of the sky.

People continued to move past me, some smiling at me, some talking; some, not quite close enough to see clearly, looked extremely strange. Further off, I could have sworn there were people with leopards' heads, and something like a great snake with a strangely shaped head, towering over the crowd; but I'm sure it was a trick of the dark. Possibly someone in a ceremonial headdress – there were all sorts of clothes, from jeans and tee-shirts, suits and ties, and skirts and jumpers, to robes in brightly printed cotton, animal hide loincloths, exiguous skirts of fur, one-shouldered tunics in mud-coloured fabric, to practically nothing at all. So far as I could remember, the people on the bus had been mostly in – well, what I think of as ordinary clothes, skirts or trousers and tops, or the women in sort of swathed outfits of printed fabric. There certainly weren't all these bare torsos, and I didn't remember the leopard skins either.

I finished my beer, and someone came by and gave me another. He grinned at me, and didn't seem to want any money. I began to hope that the mother would come back before too long, as babies are astonishingly heavy after a bit. I shifted it a little on my lap, trying not to disturb it; it murmured to itself, but didn't cry or complain, only gazed at the world wide-eyed. I was beginning to feel a bit panicky – what would I do if the bus started off and I still had the baby? I could neither abandon it nor take it with me – would the driver wait while I looked for the mother? Could I hand it to somebody else? Perhaps she wasn't coming back, perhaps this was a way of divesting herself of a baby she couldn't afford to feed... And what was going on here, anyway? Who were all these odd-looking people? Fear of the unknown, which had been subdued by adrenaline for a week, came up through my tiredness and flared in my head. If this were a book or a film, I would be on the look out for the hidden agenda, the food and drink would be drugged, or designed to fatten me up for sacrifice to strange gods – and weren't those strange gods I could see in the dark, that great serpent – ? Was this some ceremony that outsiders might not witness and live? Or, was I to be the victim of a more mundane plot, robbed and murdered for my money and passport, maybe raped first – the baby grunted and wriggled, bringing me back to the actual, and I took the weight on one arm while I checked that my wallet was still in my bag, and my passport in my pocket. Of course, it could be that I would simply have to spend eternity in this courtyard, the bus would never leave, the sun would never rise... I used to have feelings like that often as a teenager, once I remember coming back from the loo at a party and wondering if everyone would have vanished while I was gone...

People were still smiling at me, and shouting incomprehensible greetings; someone put a small bowl in front of me with maize porridge and a dollop of tomato and onion relish, and encouraged me to eat; I thanked her, and rearranged the baby so that I had a hand free. I pressed down the thought of the food's being drugged, or fattening me for sacrifice, but I still hesitated, not knowing where the food had come from, who had touched it – I stared at the bowl, and at last I thought, rubbish, these people are just as clean as I am, this baby is clean, it smells clean; the food is no more likely to be dangerous here than anywhere, less so, it is all freshly cooked – I could see cooking pots on some of the fires, and people ladling stuff into bowls. I ate – messily, not being used to using my fingers so – and it was unexpectedly enjoyable, and I realised I was quite hungry after all. When I had eaten, I looked round, to check that the bus was still there, though really it could hardly have left without my hearing it.

I became aware that there were fewer people around me; the fires were still burning, the coach was still parked, but everyone was moving towards the large building on my left, at the head of the courtyard. I looked up – I had registered it when I got off the bus as a two-storey concrete structure, with a couple of lighted windows. What I saw now was a great stone building, three or four storeys high, its ground floor blank but for a wide doorway, but with windows above, and both doorway and windows blazing with light. It hardly looked like electric light; if it hadn't been steady you would almost have thought the place was afire, it blazed golden against the blue-black of the sky. As I looked around, the whole courtyard looked bigger; it stretched out on all sides, and instead of small iron or wooden huts, the space was defined by a wall, twenty feet high, immeasurably old, the light catching geometric patterns in the stonework. There seemed to be hundreds of people congregating in a wide open space in front of it – the tall building; as I watched, they began to sing.

Suddenly I felt a lift of my heart, a great surge of joy. I was in the middle of Africa, and I could be anyone, do anything. Suppose the bus went without me, I could find my way to Kimberley, probably recover my luggage. People would help. I know some people will rape and beat and rob you and leave you for dead, but a lot more won't. Even those who don't care will often help if you nag enough, like the importunate widow in the parable. And why should the bus go without me? Meantime, here I was, not having to be any of the things that were expected of me at home, entrusted with this quite delightful baby, and I felt that even if the mother never came back, the baby and I should manage somehow. I looked at all the people around me with extraordinary benevolence. Some were, I supposed, by their costumes expressing kinship with leopards or buffalo or snakes – if there is such kinship, then how much more between human beings, whatever their colour or language or name for God? We are all very much more like each other than any of us is like anything else. Even Ian, just for the moment, was simply part of humanity, and I loved him no more nor less than the rest.

I murmured some of this sudden epiphany to the baby, who continued to look around with solemn amiability, and after a bit gave a deep sigh, put its thumb in its mouth, and appeared to go to sleep, resting its head against my breast.

I looked back toward the crowd before the great stone building. Their singing was slow and chant-like, and to begin with it sounded strange and rather eerie, but I began quite soon to tune-in to the sound of it, and got a sense of strength and purpose, increasing in intensity, as though the singing were enacting something; the singers began to move in a slow, shuffling, very rhythmic dance, with hand clapping, hypnotic, compelling. It was scary and exciting; I chose to go with the excitement. Though I was more or less immobilized by the baby, I felt drawn in, as though somehow my energy was contributing to whatever action was being performed. At first this terrified me, but as it built up, the energy that filled me became irresistibly positive, a surge of goodwill towards the whole world – OK, it sounds corny, but I really felt as if I were connected to the whole human race, and could affect it for good or ill.

As I watched, the light in the building grew, and light rose behind it, like sunrise, except I was pretty sure that wasn't the east. A great figure rose against the light – it looked far too tall for anything human, it looked like a huge snake, with the head of a fish, but it was silhouetted against the light, and that could easily have been an illusion. In front of it, people with the heads of leopards, lions, buffalo, hippo, rhino, giraffe, elephants, danced and sang in a semi-circle; the energy rose from them, from the great snake, rose like the sunrise behind the building; whatever was being done, seemed certain of effect. My feet moved in rhythm with the singing, shuffling so as not to disturb the baby; my hand moved too, on the table.

The baby stirred and mumbled, and I looked down, and jiggled and murmured to it; and abruptly the light diminished, and when I looked up, the sky was dark, and only subdued gold lights burned in the windows of the great stone building. The singing died away, and people began drifting back towards me.

I finished my beer, and soon the baby's mother appeared; the baby woke, blinked up at her, and held up its arms, and I surrendered it, to beams and thanks and enthusiastic handshaking; her friend helped the mother to strap the baby to her back again, and they moved off. I saw the driver get on the bus, and put the lights on, and I stood up – rather stiffly – and made my way back. In a few minutes, everyone was in their seat – still no goats, but I'm sure I heard something bark at the back.

The lights stayed up for a while; the woman next to me was reading an English language magazine; I glanced over, and a subhead in a story or article caught my eye, "No love is ever wasted". I wondered vaguely what the story was about. I also wondered what the time could be; surely it should really be dawn by now, but the view out of the window was still of blackness. I was suddenly intolerably sleepy, no doubt the beer had a contributory effect; I drifted off and slept till we stopped, in the beginnings of dawn, at another bus station – Kimberley, this time.

I struggled off, retrieved my luggage, and found a taxi to take me to the cheap hotel I'd booked by phone. The memory of the night stop was fading, but I was sure it wasn't a dream. Still I didn't have much attention to spare for it now – I had something of a job conversing with the Lithuanian taxi driver, and then when we got to the hotel, they admitted I'd made a reservation, but said they had me down for the following week, and sorry, they were fully booked. I complained vigorously, waved my arms a lot, emphasised that I was a woman alone, with no transport and nowhere to go, and eventually they made some phone calls, and said they had got me a room at another hotel, at the same price, and called me another taxi to take me there. This driver was Polish, but we managed to understand each other fairly well.

The new hotel turned out to be part of a rather classy chain, three- or four-star, and rather bland and mass-produced. I didn't take much notice, being still somewhat bleary-eyed, beyond being quite pleased at the result of the arm waving and stroppiness, but when I had checked in, deposited my luggage, washed my face, and found out breakfast was still being served, I realised that I was in the same hotel as the team – there were cricket bags in the lobby, and as I went into the breakfast room, I saw Ian at the far end, carrying a bowl of cornflakes and a glass of orange juice back to a table full of scrubbed looking young men.

My first reaction was delight; my second was uncertainty – how would he react to seeing me? Could I convince anyone I was here by accident? For a moment I considered going back to my room for an hour; but despite eating in the middle of the night, I was craving food again, and more especially the stimulus of tea, so breakfast took precedence over not appearing a mad stalker. I was shown to a table, ordered some tea, and went to fetch porridge and juice.

While I ate, I thought, what am I going to say? Should I ignore him altogether, avoid speaking to him at all? That would look weird too. I was starting to panic, now he was actually in the room – Will he ignore me? Will he warn me off? He can hardly have me arrested. I can prove I didn't book into this hotel deliberately. Oh God. Why on earth did I come? I was keeping my eyes away from Ian's table, but I sneaked a sideways glance; he was at the buffet, putting bacon on a plate; I watched him as far as the toast machine and then managed to look away. I wondered if he'd seen me yet. The urge to go and make toast was strong, but I resisted. A waitress brought my tea; I poured a cup, and thought, come on, what's the worst that could happen? He *can't* have me arrested. If he's rude to me, I've made a fool of myself, but it'll be all the same a hundred years from now. I'm having a fantastic holiday, I had an extraordinary journey last night, which would never have happened otherwise; OK, I've irritated the poor man dreadfully, but if that's the worst that ever happens to him he won't have a bad life – I felt quite brutal for a moment, but after all it was true; God knows I've been irritated by enough unattractive men in my life, but I've survived. I'm here, eating breakfast in a four star hotel, and if he wants I'll apologise and go away. It absolutely isn't the end of the world. I can survive, I thought, even if I never see him again.

All the time, of course, the thought of him, the knowledge that he was in the room, was filling me with a singing delight, and the effort needed to keep looking away from his table was considerable, but I managed it. Later, as I spread honey on toast, I became aware of his coming towards me – I had developed a hyper-awareness of his presence over the last few months – and he said,

"Hi, Alison. Didn't expect to see you here." There was wariness in the tone, and uncertainty of reception, but he was obviously trying to be laid back about it.

"Hi, Ian. Yeah, kind of a last minute holiday, been staying with a friend in Jo'burg, and thought I'd come out here and watch the game."

"Oh right. Long way to come."

"Well, long way to come from London, but not so far from Jo'burg." I smiled, trying to keep it light.

"Yeah, guess so. How are you getting out to the ground, then?"

"Get a cab, I suppose."

"OK. Um, I'll see if anyone can give you a lift, if you like."

"That'd be cool. Thanks very much."

"OK. See you later. Uh – nice to see you."

"You too." I smiled again, hiding the completely gobsmacked feeling, I hoped, reasonably well, and he glided out. Well, I thought, finishing my toast, there's a thing. I went back to my room, got sorted out for the day, and went to hang about in reception. I looked at headlines on the rack of newspapers: "Breakthrough in Peace Talks", "Roep vir skietstaking", "Dictator Toppled". I looked out of the main door where a woman was walking past with a baby on her back; she smiled, and waved at me, and I smiled and waved back.

I drove to the ground with the team coach's Australian wife, a cheerful blonde in her fifties.

She asked me the usual polite questions, and said, "So, you're not Ian's girlfriend?"

"No! Oh no, just a friend."

"It's good that you came. It's a long time away from home, the guys really like to see friends. Oh, I nearly forgot – Ian's given you one of his comp tickets, it's in my bag. Why don't you come and sit with me, unless you're meeting anyone?"

“I’m not meeting anyone, no. That’d be great.”

“Be good to have another woman to talk to!”

I smiled at her, and looked in my bag for sunblock; it was already hot outside, with hardly a cloud in the sky.

Wake with the Light

by Jet McDonald

What Dave Morsby expected on redundancy was boredom. Instead he got the universe. He was sat by the "Hard Interchange", Portsmouth's harbour side travel centre, when the stars of the night sky sprayed onto the inside of his head like the spew of a billion mirrored disco ball.

He opened his eyes and saw Portsmouth Harbour, "Popeye's Snack Bar," and his own creased cup of coffee. He closed his eyes and saw galaxies. He turned his head to the right and the cackle of a hen party increased as it tottered past to Gosport ferry. But what he saw, with his eyes closed, was the constellation of Cassiopeia, the blaze of Polaris mid sky and the upended panhandle of Ursa Major. He turned to his left and the sound of the hen party diminished. But what he saw were the vertices of Virgo reaching towards the diamond of Bootes. And these were but the brightest stars of a billion points that lit the inside of his head.

"It's the numbers," said Keith, as he'd handed over a badly typed redundancy letter one month before, "they don't add up."

This was clearly not true. Dave had been a Maths undergraduate at the University of Southampton and the numbers always added up. In fact they bored him to tears and he'd ended up with a third class degree and a job at "Fratton's Family Furniture", a warehouse in Portsmouth three miles from where he lived with his wife Cheryl. He'd been there fifteen years. For each of those fifteen years he'd constructed up to five pine chairs a week for two hundred pounds each. Then, a month ago,

Wal-Mart began selling the "same" or "near enough the same" chairs for twenty pounds a pop. Presumably these "knock offs" were being sold to the very people who had once admired his own perfectly locking mortise joints. Somewhere on a container ship between Portsmouth and Beijing his working life had been lopped by about ninety per cent.

Keith patted him on the back. "Sorry mate. Hard times."

Dave ran down Fratton, Fawcett, Lawrence, Waverly and Clarendon Road, across to Southsea Parade, floundered across the pebble shore and let the letter fly out of his hands and across the Solent.

"Ha," he said to the sky, to the heaving ocean. "Ha." And then, landing with a rattle in the millions of pebbles, he turned and fell asleep.

When he awoke, the sun had set and stars had swung over the harbour. With the bleed of city light he could only see a few but he could still make out their simple geometries, shapes his grandfather had explained to him when he was a child. He roused himself and used the coin operated telescopes to bump from constellation to constellation, those few stars becoming brighter as the sun was lost to the world. "Welcome," the telescopes announced pointlessly in a looping commentary, "to Portsmouth."

The Job Centre on Arundel Street had blacked out windows. Its actual name in fact was "Job Centre Plus" as if it should be offering more than the traditional benefits black hole, an added "Jobness."

It was off Commercial Road, a relentlessly positive parade of department stores and glittering phone shops. But if Commercial Road suggested superabundance Arundel Street was a retreat, a subtractive step into an unforgiving reality of British Heart Foundation Charity Shops and plastic bucket stores.

Opposite the Job Centre there was a more enticing place called "U-NEED-US". The shop was faced in 1950's yellow tiles and underneath there was a slanted plastic sign "*A.G. Pearle and Sons.*" It seemed to suggest to Dave that Mr Pearle and sons would be waiting to service whatever broken dreams managed to limp into Arundel Street from the main drag. Dave pushed his hand through his widow's peak, felt the wood turner's callus against his forehead, and walked instead through the automatic doors into "Job Centre Plus".

He was funnelled to a "Job Point," a computer screen on a plastic plinth. He asked the machine what to do and it told him there were lots of jobs in the Armed Services, if, he were ten years younger, and that, if he were prepared to commute to Derbyshire he could get a job part time as a "furniture assembler" for the minimum wage. In fact what the computer was telling him, in a binary kind of way, was that the numbers didn't add up.

Dave zipped his anorak, walked out of Job Centre Plus and into "U-NEED-US."

It was clear that Mr Pearle was no longer in charge and "U-NEED-US" was being run by a buxom middle-aged woman from Birmingham. There were cardboard Fez's, rubber gorilla masks, wipe clean nurse pinnies, plastic machine gun bullets, inflatable willy balloons and laminate Union Jack flags.

"Mr Pearle?" he asked the woman hopefully.

"Oh no, duck we got the lease when he died."

"And what did he sell?"

"Old stuff. We sell fancy dress, hen parties, stag parties…" She stopped herself as she saw the defeat in his eyes. "There's still a few of the old man's boxes in the basement. Junk mostly."

The remains of Mr Pearle were interred in a cellar that smelt of patchouli and camphor mothballs.

He found a pewter candlestick, a gentleman racer, stacks of hats from the fancy dress overflow, a stuffed rabbit and some boxes of books on a shelf. He poked in one miserably.

And there it was… "The Amateur Astronomers Handbook by J.D. Sedgwick. 1st Edn. Pubd. 1958." The dust jacket had a picture of a crescent moon and a man with a pair of oversized binoculars.

"*Pasta*" said Cheryl. She was hunched over her class planning. She was always hunched over her class planning.

"Pasta?"

"You were meant to get pasta."

"Oh."

"Rice then. Rice."

Cheryl went to bed after food. Cheryl always went to bed after food.

This allowed Dave to pick out the binoculars he'd found in a charity shop, slump in one of his pine chairs and set about mapping the night sky with J.D. Sedgwick MSc PhD Oxon.

A week later he was able to map the major constellations of the Northern hemisphere. Arcturus was brightest with Virgo and Spicca marching after. More southerly were Alpha and Beta Centauri and the powdery spray of the Milky Way. When he ventured away from the city, into the fields along the Hamble, he saw galaxies; M51 and the Globular cluster of M3. "Galaxies," announced Mr Sedgwick on page 44, "are mathematical models of stardust that reflect our own earthly predicament."

But after a month Dave was bored. He had surveyed the heavens and was still jobless and motiveless. Sedgwick, however, had other plans. "See the monthly charts for more star facts," the book repeated on every page. Sedgwick wanted him to memorise more and more stars, more constellations, more galaxies, more clusters and patterns and vertices of feint nodes in the celestial sphere. And the more Dave tried to resist the book the more he felt compelled to read it, as if the corners of the mildewed pages had magnetised his fingertips, as if the fury of his redundancy had joined in some zealous pact with the astronomer. Even during the day he was aware of the guide shut away in the trunk under the stairs, transmitting a filthy radiation; Sedgwick on the cover, staring up at the sky with his oversized binoculars, neck crooked.

Dave watched television. He dusted. He spun between stations on the radio. But the book transmitted its dusty radiation.

"U-NEED-US" it crowed. "Andromeda, Antila, Apus, Aquarius, Aquila, Ara, Aries, Auriga…"

And finally he found himself at the "Hard Interchange" on Portsmouth Harbour, dodging hen parties, and clutching Sedgwick's Handbook.

He had come to the "Hard Interchange" because he knew he would see less of the stars and the moon and the galaxies. The harbour lights would drain the celestial radiance and Sedgwick, so he reasoned, would have no hold over him.

He tossed the book over the railings and it landed with a "thwuck" in the tidal mud.

He got a coffee from "Popeye's Snack Bar" and looked around for something more or less interesting than the night sky above.

To his left was the "Spinnaker", a massive public sculpture that was more of a darning needle, stitching up towards the clouds. To his right was "HMS Warrior", a nineteenth century warship, berthed towards the shore. It pointed towards the bedsits and the shopping centres, as if the reclaimed land was the new ocean, through which, set loose from its moorings, the "Warrior" might sail.

Revellers sloshed about "The Hard Interchange" like slops against a beer glass.

He took a sip of his coffee and closed his eyes. And it was then that Sedgwick burned the stars onto the inside of his head. The hen party toppled onto the Gosport ferry and he was left alone, star pickled, on the concrete.

"Hypnotism," he said out loud, "autosuggestion." But every compass point he turned to, he found another cluster of galaxies, far beyond the learning of Sedgwick's book. He tried to imagine something other than the night sky – the cup of coffee he was holding in his hands, the bowl of sugar on the table. But all he could see, behind his eyelids, was Ursa Major and the billion points of stars. He tried to visualise Cheryl naked. Still Ursa Major. He tried to imagine Cheryl's teaching assistant, Charlotte, stretched out on a chaise longue. But still the cocked panhandle of the constellation hung like an underhand taunt. He turned three hundred and sixty degrees with his hand pressed over his eyes and saw all the constellations and galaxies and planets of the night sky. It was as if an existentialist had discovered the immensity of existence was not without, but within.

Below, he could hear the tide lapping at Sedgwick's book, sucking at it, heaving it into the immense ocean.

He tried to tell his wife. He nestled against the warmth of her backside; he made a spoon for her spoon in their bed. He whispered to the pulse of blood at her neck. "Whenever I close my eyes," he said, "I see the Universe."

"Oh," said Cheryl as she tumbled through dreams. "Oh."

Zero is an indefinable number that only can be explained reflexively. It can be additive, where nothing plus a number equals that number, or multiplicative where nothing times a number is nothing. It can only be explained by reference to that which it is not. One and zero. Zero and one. Light and dark. Dark and light. Light and dark. Dark and light.

Dave could not sleep. He closed his eyes and there was the star field of the universe. He opened his eyes and knew that the night sky still pressed upon him, above this house, above this roof. Was it possible to sleep with your eyes open? Dave wasn't sure but he knew he couldn't sleep with his eyes closed, wherein the stars awaited.

And that was all he wanted. To tumble unanchored into nothingness. To fall and then wake with the light. But there was no sleep to wake from. He watched Cheryl's chest rise and fall. Who was this person he had shared his life with who now had this quality of separation, of which he was deprived?

He watched her dress in the dawn, brushing out her hair in the sunlight. She waved at him from the bedroom door and was gone.

The next day he went to an optician on Commercial Road. He wasn't sure if it helped that this optician was fifteen years younger than Cheryl and wore tighter fitting blouses.

"Miss Emily Dodson MCOptm" blinked at Dave over her clipboard as he sat crumpled into his anorak beside a poster of a man on a motorbike. Dave was clearly not the kind of shopper that bought three hundred pound spectacles.

"Moby?"

"Morsby"

She beckoned him into a windowless room behind cabinets full of v wing glasses.

"Headaches?" she said.

Dave looked at her from within his default sleeplessness. The woman had such pure skin it must never have touched the world, its UVA, its UVB, its greedy battering entropy.

"Headaches?" Miss Dodson intoned, a bit louder this time in case he was retarded.

"Nope. No headaches."

"Any problems with your sight at all?"

"Only when I shut my eyes."

"And when you shut your eyes…?"

"I see spots."

Emily bore down on him suddenly with a single-lensed magnifier.

This was all too soon, thought Dave. What about the letter charts? And the lenses. And the red light and the green light…

"Look to your left. Look up. Look down."

She smelt of jasmine.

"Stare straight at the light."

Moisturiser and scented bathwater.

"Oh." Miss Dodson was saying. "Oh." She twisted the instrument ninety degrees so it didn't touch his nose and peered into his eye so close he could taste her breath, the mints and cigarettes. "How odd it's…"

He leaned closer so his lips touched hers.

She cartwheeled backwards like a bomb blast.

"GET OUT!"

"I'm sorry I…"

"GET OUT." And then quieter, more hurt. "Before I call the police."

Dave ducked onto the road and pulled the lapels of his anorak up, fearful that anyone might see. Him. Moresby. Dirty mad old man.

He wandered instead in the direction of the coast, along the High Street, past Portsmouth Grammar School where Cheryl taught. He wanted to barge into one of her lessons. To say he was "sorry". "Sorry" he'd kissed "Miss Emily Dodson Copt." Sorry that when he closed his eyes he saw the universe.

But there was a gold leaf motto on the brickwork of the arches.

"Honours are the reward of virtue," and in invisible parenthesis, "You, Dave Moresby, are sick." Dave toppled down the road. Wretched with himself, wretched with carrying the night through the day.

He lurched to the sea's edge where Portsmouth had its memorials: The Falklands fallen, wilted paper poppies leaving only green plastic stems. Plaques to the first transportations to Australia and the colonies. This place a leaping off point for the wretched and the doomed.

Dave wondered whether he should jump and let the tides carry him. He closed his eyes and the night sky was unveiled, the triangulation of stars by which the new world was navigated from the old but which now led only to his own brain, his particular madness.

If they were to peel back his skull would they find a star spangled pitch inside, something of which Emily Dodson had found so strange? Would the ever-expanding night spill like stout from his cracked head and consume the day?

He opened his eyes and saw some swallows fighting against the wind, beating their wings, going nowhere.

He wandered back to Southsea along the sea front, found a bench on the common and looked past the trees, at the birds stalled in the wind. And then one plummeted and landed by the bushes.

Across the park there was a boy on a bench, cocking an air rifle. The boy slotted in a pellet and took aim at the birds battling the wind. Dave edged around the green and slumped beside the boy who ignored him and slotted in another pellet, rapping a song under his breath.

"Why," asked Dave eventually, "are you shooting the pigeons?"

"They're not pigeons," said the assassin, " they're sparrows."

The boy pulled the trigger, the rifle jerked back.

Dave tried a different angle. "So why aren't you shooting the pigeons?" He pointed at the fat grey birds pecking at some crumbs a hundred yards away.

"Dirty. And bad insulation."

"Bad insulation?"

"Who are you anyway? A copper?"

"No." Dave offered him his hand. "I'm Dave."

The boy gave him the rifle and unzipped the brown leather jacket he was wearing. The lining was made of small brown feathers, each sewn at the shaft, so they overlapped like a wing.

"Pigeons have shit on and they don't keep the heat."

The boy zipped his jacket back up to the neck and retrieved his rifle.

"Shouldn't you be at school?" asked Dave

The boy cocked the barrel, slotted in a pellet, and snapped it shut.

"Shouldn't you be at work?"

Together they watched in silence as the birds dipped and rose.

Dave did not sleep. He did not rest. He watched Cheryl doing her lesson planning and wondered what it was like to be preoccupied with something other than your own head.

Cheryl said they were bringing in a "virtual blackboard" at work and she had been appointed as the lead teacher. You could press on any part of a large flat screen and the references came up immediately. She could manipulate objects and join them into other objects. Everyone was expected to use the things and they had to "get with the program." She allowed herself a little laugh and turned to the index of the manual.

Dave closed his eyes. In the direction he was looking he could see the star cluster M13 between the two western stars of the Keystone of Hercules

"How's the job hunting?"

"Good," he said, "it's going well." He saw Mercury beginning its slow arc at twenty-two degrees separation.

"Interviews?"

"Lots… Lots."

"Good." Cheryl picked out bits of pepper from between her teeth with her fingernails.

That night, as she slept, he lay with his hands cupped around the back of her head, wondering if you could control a mind like that, like a virtual blackboard. And then he tried to calculate zero into one using abstract proofs based on real numbers and infinity. But he'd forgotten how the proofs worked and instead the decimal points added up in his head 0.9, 0.99, 0.999, 0.9999, 0.99999, 0.999999…

The symbol for infinity can be used to solve mathematical models that cannot be enumerated in longhand. The set of whole integers 1, 2, 3… are countably infinite whereas fractions and decimals are uncountably infinite. But crowbar the symbol for infinity, ∞, into an equation, instead of these numbers, and you can make pretend infinity lives in a box, which can be as large, or as small, as you make it.

Dave watched Cheryl wake, and dress, and go. He opened the window and gazed at the saucers of lights around the bird droppings on the conservatory roof. Every time he blinked the night sky flashed into his head like the pits and nicks at the end of a black and white film.

When he was a child he would spend hours hunched over dot-to-dot books, joining them into rabbits, frogs and dinosaurs. When he went to University he spent days hunched over graphs where "vertices" or points were connected by "edges", mind lattices of the outside world. But somewhere between here and there the universe had intervened, it had slipped under the carpet of his brain so that the outside was in, a super complex dot to dot within his head. All he had to do, he reasoned, was get it out again.

Dave found a marker pen, closed his eyes and dotted his forehead with the brightest stars. Looking over the spatters of guano and the conservatory roof with his eyes closed, he saw Cassiopeia and Ursa Major. He tried to mark them as he saw them on the outside of his head but was prevented by his hairline and by the blotching point of the marker pen. The sense of spherical space within his mind could not be represented on the outside of his head without the marking being cramped in a way that ruined its relative geometry. To be able to represent the vertices of the stars inside of his head outside of his head he would have to extrapolate their position from his skull to a distant point near the ceiling.

Dave found an old trimmer and shaved off his hair to a grade one. Using a biro with a tiny nib he did a basic representation of the Northerly constellations on his forehead and hairline. He then sewed a cotton thread to each constellation point and attached the other end of the thread to the white bathroom ceiling using drawing pins, until his frontal scalp was a spray of cotton threads leading to a thumb tack constellation on the plasterboard roof above the boiler.

Dave hung from the ceiling by a spray of cotton threaded pimples, peering through them to divine the star chart he had made, a cackhanded replication of the universe he saw inside his head.

And then the doorbell rang.

"Bollocks," said Dave.

The doorbell trilled continuously.

Dave swiped about him, found Cheryl's cosmetics bag, plucked out a pair of nail scissors, clipped the cotton threads till they hung like a weed from his forehead and made for the door.

"Brrringgggggggggggg"

Behind the mahogany door there was an old man with a walking stick. He had his finger hovering over the black spot where the bell used to be.

"I'm parched," said the old man.

"I'm not sure I…"

"Just a tiny cup of tea." He elbowed past Dave and into the corridor. "Two lumps. I know it's naughty but at my age what difference does it make?"

"Who are you?"

"A better question would be: how am I? And the answer would be parched. Far too long in that box."

"What box?"

"The one they put me in. Just a splash of milk. Enough to make the china pale."

"*So who are you?*"

"Jonny Sedgwick."

"You're J.D. Sedgwick?"

"Well I've always insisted the tutors called me Jonny." He stared at the kettle as if it might defuse the peculiarity of the situation.

"But you're dead?"

"A dying star still emits light."

"And you've come here to help me?"

"Help you? They only let me out of the box as a treat."

"What box?"

"*The one they put me in.*"

Dave decided to get straight to the point. "I read your book… 'Astronomy: A Guide for Beginners'…"

"Rather pedestrian I'm afraid but the university insisted."

"…and the night sky was transplanted into my head like a planetarium."

"A bit far fetched, and, if you don't mind me saying, *a bit unscientific.*"

"Look. In my head." Dave bent down and the old man peered in.

"I'm afraid my eyesight isn't as good as it used to be Mr…?"

"Dave."

"All I can see is an extremely tired young man… I say, you don't have any biscuits do you?"

Dave propped himself on the edge of the sink and stared across the garden, where a bird was pecking at the lawn. "I'm forty," he said to no one. "I'm not young. I'm forty."

"The solar system was made four and a half billion years ago," said Sedgwick, "so that makes you about the same age as… well nothing at all. Now about that cup of tea…"

Reluctantly Dave made him a brew and watched him dunk his biscuit.

"I really wish I could help you," said Sedgwick, "but I've got to get back in the box." He gestured vaguely at the front door and slurped Earl Grey through his gums. "…in fact I ought to be off." He levered himself from the table using his stick.

"What about my head?"

Sedgwick wobbled down the corridor with his walking stick.

"At least tell me what to do," said Dave.

"Have you got the correct fare?" said Sedgwick.

"Fare?"

"The number 19. Driver short changed me on the way here."

Ten minutes later Dave found himself on the Number 19 bus to the sea front.

"Is this the box?" said Dave incredulously as they sat huddled together on the disabled seat.

"Oh no, old chap. I just wanted to get a bit of fresh air before they popped me back in the box. Awfully stuffy in there you know."

Out on Southsea promenade the old man looked like he was about to be blown away until Dave took his arm and they tottered along together. At one point Sedgwick turned towards the sea, towards the glottal stop of the wind, "Makes… you… feel… alive."

Dave squinted at the salt spray. "Yes, I suppose it does."

They walked as far as Clarence Pier, took the number "19" back on its loop into town, stepped off at Commercial Road and walked past the department stores, the mobile phone franchises and the boutiques with Sedgwick flailing through what little puff he had remaining.

"Just here…old chap…" They shuffled along Arundel Street to "U-NEED-US"

"This is your box?"

"Mr Pearle's, actually." Sedgwick pointed at the plastic sign and climbed through the door with Dave following close behind.

"Oh no," said Sedgwick. "It's not your box. In fact you wouldn't fit at all." And with that the door closed behind the old man and Dave was left alone on the street with the fag butts and crisp packets.

He paused and then barged the door of "U-NEED-US" with his shoulder but it was now locked with a "Closed" sign swinging from a piece of tack.

Behind him there was a "zip" and Dave spun round to find the "Job Centre", with its automatic doors parted. Crisp packets danced around his ankles. "The job you want. The help you need," a poster announced in the lobby. It flapped in the febrile breeze.

One week later Dave was working in a warehouse in Fratton called "Funky Evolution." He was on a production line soldering together circuit boards that made "the brains" of soft toys offering a reasonable approximation of pond life.

Dave was in charge of Toads. He connected the linking pins to printed circuit boards from China using a binocular microscope, tweezers and a superfine soldering iron. He then stuck the completed unit in the head of an acrylic fibre toad, clipped the wires to the lithium powered motor in the gut, and gave it a test run on the concrete floor. It would belch and hop in time to his shouts.

Dave made fifty Funky Toads a day, each priced at twenty pounds. This made his working life approximate to one thousand pounds every shift or five thousand a week before expenses.

Every time Dave spot-welded a connection pad through the binocular microscope he closed his eyes and one of the constellations would disappear. Dave was spot welding the Universe from his head, star by star, constellation by constellation, planet by planet, by making synthetic frogs. When a frog was finished he would sew in a label that said, "This Funky Toad was made by Dave."

Beside him the toads hopped and burped and burped and hopped with their perfect unthinking brains. And when they were done he would put them in a box and send them out. Ready to be born into the world.

Somewhere in the fields beyond Gosport real frogs hopped beside the River Hamble, starlight reflected in the water as they mated. There would be bundles of spawn hanging beneath fallen leaves and branches, some of which, given a shove and a good roll of the dice, would make it into adulthood. Good luck to them, he thought. Good luck. Then he turned to the binocular microscope, pressed the click button hanging from the ceiling, and burned the stars from his eyes.

Future Prospects?

by Geoff Stevens

Dungeness
and I've begun the walk yet again
in the cloying air
the warm May sun.
Derek Jarman's cottage is -
over there somewhere
look out for the black house
with the yellow window-frames
the station master said
and if you reach the Pilot Inn
you've passed it
so one more try
down the concrete roadway
past the sprawled out row
of wooden huts
and left turn
the sea way out to my right
beyond a vast flat open space
dotted with rusting tin shacks.

Strain the eyesight
and there it is
black house with yellow window frames
still a way to go.

Prospect Cottage at last
take a breath
love the garden
shingle and more shingle
some shaped into swirls
lots of different lavenders
the odd dog rose
cornflowers and poppies in bud
and strange pieces of driftwood
stuck upright in the ground
like a wooden Stonehenge.
And there's a boat
tilted on its hull
a wooden lugger
overlapped planking weathered by the wind
bleached grey by the sun
and growing lichen.

The house seems empty
but all the houses do
and everywhere is so still
so quiet.

I'm round the back now
where time seems to be having a snooze
and there's a picture window
with a huge white duvet
rolled up inside
as still as death
which somehow shocks the mind

into moving away
so I go round the side
and there's more wooden posts
with rust metal attached to them
and they seem to me to be planted
by Eric Von Daniken or the like
as guidelines to the shore
for extra-terrestrials perhaps
giving another view
of deserted space
dotted with rusting asteroids
and in the far distance
the sun
hovering over
the trembling lip of the sea
as it offers a possible exit
from this place.

But I'm no astronaut
no sailor either
and in 30 minutes
the last train will be leaving
so time to start walking
or might get stranded here
like so many before me.

Entanglement

by Douglas Thompson

> *"...Then all at once he came to understand*
> *the dead through her, and joined them in their walk,*
> *kin to them all; he let the others talk,*
>
> *and paid no heed to them, and called that land*
> *the fortunately-placed, the ever-sweet.-*
> *And groped out all its pathways for her feet."*

– Rainer Maria Rilke, *The Death Of The Beloved.*

1.

A hundred years ago, the great tides of probe-spores were unleashed from Mother Earth, and for several weeks she looked like some exploding puffball of seeds, a dandelion head unfurling in the solar wind. Within all the apparent chaos of fuel and hardware however, there was precise purpose, which has become apparent over time. Each probe was aimed on a separate trajectory, each to travel out towards a different candidate among our nearest neighbouring star systems, each known to hold planets likely to harbour life.

No human being travelled in these devices, nor did any need to, for each carried a chamber of quantum-entangled sub-atomic matter, whose twin remained here on Earth among the space future travel bank, the Telepedrome, as it has become known, the purpose-built NASA base in the Nevada desert. By a simple method of displacement upon entry and exit, whatever is added to one chamber is instantly created in the other, whatever the distance. The principle was well-known centuries ago, even by Einstein, who called it "spooky action at a distance". Only immense patience and hard work has been necessary to make theory reality.

This year the first of these probes reached their destination, the planets orbiting the Gliese 581 star system, a red dwarf sun, and I finally received my orders to report to the Nevada Telepedrome and prepare for insertion into one of the Gliese-twinned chambers, and thereby to instantly "travel" to the surface of an alien world twenty light-years distant, from where robotic messages and images have already been revealing a rocky surface with liquid seas and signs of microbiotic soil life.

But "teleport" is strictly speaking a misnomer, and "dupliport" would be a better neologism. My self on Gliese 581g will be physically identical to me, but unable to move or think, essentially a zombie, a golem, a mandrake man, until my self back home on Earth is made to enter deep and carefully-maintained sleep, to enter a coma, in other words. Then and only then, will I open my eyes on Gliese 581g, sniff the air (so to speak, through my elaborate breathing apparatus) and be able to walk around and look for new life forms.

So, contrary to centuries of science-fictional speculation, there is no space travel as such, no need for suspended animation and travelling bio-domes, whole communities in space. Only one science fiction writer got one thing right: Ursula Le Guin, with her concept of the "Ansible", whose name the real device now carries in her honour. The Quantum-Entangled matter chamber is pretty much exactly what she envisaged, delivered by the strange miracles of sub-atomic particle interactions, except that it can *dupliport* not just information, but objects and even life, but with one mysterious qualification: life arrives, but minus its soul.

<u>2.</u>

We have given this planet a new name already, myself and my colleague Lieutenant Pleznick. We hope NASA will adopt the term as official some day. To us this world is "Somnos", a sleeping planet, where paradoxically, since it is tidally locked, in all probability no life-form sleeps at all. An orb of brown swirling gases, nitrogen oxide rain and yellow sulphur rocks. The sky is pink of course, ruled over by a blood-red sun and a host of irregular-shaped moons, evidence perhaps of an asteroid collision a few million years ago, the jagged edges still not smoothed by time and gravity.

The probes reported a city-like construction about seventy-five miles from here, and "tomorrow" (I use the term loosely, my spacesuit's chronometer still splits time into terrestrial twenty-four hour segments) we will investigate. Perhaps it is some kind of mushroom field or mineral crystalline accretion, and we will be disappointed. Or perhaps it is something even more unthinkable or unimaginable than the wonders we have already seen: the settlement of living beings, as intelligent as ourselves.

We comfort each other, only half-jokingly, that the dangers are only half here: if these bodies are injured and die instantly in some accident or attack, then our minds will "magically" find themselves back on Earth and wake up startled in our original bodies. But we both also know that this is not strictly true. The rules of Entanglement dictate that if I lose an arm here, that arm back in Earth would be destroyed at the exact same instant, and that if my body were burned to a crisp here before the Telepedrome operators could be alerted to douse my body with suitable coolant (making me "magically" non-flammable on Somnos) then I would simply die, with no body left in either world to contain me.

The bigger question of where such a soul, deprived of any body, ultimately migrates to, remains a mystery, even to our so advanced and enlightened civilisation, who are now conquering the stars at last.

<u>3.</u>

My colleague Pleznick is beginning to concern me. Last "night" I went home, by the simple trick of sleep. I was awoken on Earth, where I could greet my family through the glass walls of the Entanglement chamber. My wife and I spent several hours joking and playing with our children, and although I wish I could have held them in my arms rather than merely gesturing through glass, the experience was restorative. Pleznick, on the other hand, refused to "travel" home and take "shore leave". How can NASA approve of that? It can't be right for any man's mental health. He says he slept but that he told NASA not to wake up his Entangled other self. I quizzed him and he said that he has no family that he wishes to see. This sounds very sad I know, but I somehow found it hard to believe: not a brother, sister, or parent, friend, nobody that he would enjoy talking to in person back home? I'm sure NASA know what they're doing, but I feel like I need to know this guy more, and dig beneath the surface. I don't want anyone losing their marbles on my watch. He only joined this assignment at the last minute after Mark Selwyn's illness, and I haven't had the customary lead-in time to bond with him as a "partner".

4.

"Today" we reached the "city" and that is just what it is. Incredible to think of millions of people back on Earth watching this through our helmet cameras in real-time, the first contact with another apparently intelligent race. I say apparently, because their language and gestures are so unintelligible, it's like listening to dolphins or whales, but computers on Earth are now already working around the clock on de-encryption and translation software for us.

The *Somnons* (Pleznick and I are happy that people back home seem to have latched onto our colloquialism and embraced it) are brown-skinned and on average about four feet high, with long fish-like vertical mouths and large blackish eyes on the side of their heads, more prey than hunter, to follow terrestrial anthropological assumptions. They seem to eat root vegetables, and a lot of red mushrooms, and indeed their architecture to our eyes at least, seems almost a homage to the mushroom form. Scientists on Earth are getting very excited about this. First thoughts are that the architectural mushrooms that form their houses and palaces are a hybrid of natural and Somnon design, like coral reefs back on Earth, some fusion of mineral and biological, whereby they have learned to divert and expand a living form into a building material, while still keeping it alive.

Early "days" and first impressions, but compared to the rape we inflicted on our own planet, this seems like an impressively gentle and renewable technology, and consistent with the hypothesis, touch wood (to coin an old Earth phrase) that these natives of Somnos are very peaceful and consequently accepting of our presence among them. It seems a little patronising of me to say so perhaps, but my impression is that this society is a primitive agrarian economy, akin to Aboriginal or Polynesian races on Earth before collision with the white man. But we have strict rules. We will do no harm to these people or their culture. Only study them and try to understand, then leave them alone again.

Did I forget to mention their bodies? Despite walking upright the Somnons have four crablike lower limbs and three arms, one central one of which seems to function like a trunk or antennae, with which they incessantly touch as they chatter to each other and tentatively explore us.

Pleznick seems to have been particularly taken with these locals, and they to him, and it's been good to see his spirits lift today, and him forget whatever has been the source of the melancholy darkness I've seen within him.

<u>5.</u>

Unbelievable progress and new wonders. I feel like Howard Carter stumbling upon Tutankhamun's tomb with his torch and famous pronouncement: "wonderful things".

The Somnons led us "today" to a great central palace where we met what appeared to be their rulers, an inner circle of particularly thin and old beings, wrinkled with age and connected to various bubbling tubes, whether carrying life-giving elixirs or information, we were unable to tell.

The "mushroom" architecture of this hall was hugely elaborate and decorative, on a par with any of the great cathedrals of England or France, and the walls were full of what we think are books or records, semi-transparent crystals that the Somnons place into a kind of slot on their abdomens and then attach their third arm to until it glows. The effect is bizarre, as if they are living record players, turntables of the old twentieth century variety.

We have the disorientating impression that these beings are much more intelligent than we at first thought, and that our value-system is too Earth-based to be able to evaluate them properly.

<u>6.</u>

Speechless. A paradox. The translation software came through from Earth along with devices to help us create Somnon sounds from smart-boxes on our chests. Suddenly a veil is lifted on a whole ancient culture and two worlds look at each other and gape. We are now able to show them live images of people and cities back on Earth and to begin to explain ourselves and learn from them. We constantly emphasise that we will leave their world in a few weeks and that no colonisation is ever intended. I'm not sure yet that they understand our Entanglement technology or the implications of that, both good and bad: that we need not arrive in huge spaceships holding many people, but that provided they never destroy our Entanglement chambers here on Somnos, then we can theoretically return at any instant, with no warning.

*   *   *

<u>7.</u>

Listen. This is Pleznick now. I have taken over command. My sincere apologies firstly, to his wife and children and to planet Earth in general, for my having killed Walters. It was however, necessary, since he would not agree to allow what I plan to do next. Likewise, the destruction of the full-size Entanglement chamber was necessary to prevent you from sending other astronauts to interfere and stop me. Thus, I can no longer return to Earth nor you send anyone after me, for another hundred years. Only the "Ansible" still connects us, that miniature miracle, as predicted by the great seer Le Guin. I know you won't disconnect it or attempt to blow it up or set the probes against me. I know that much about human nature, about the defining characteristic of our pernicious little species: that we are insatiably curious and nosey. And here you all are, peering into Somnon culture like fevered peeping-toms, lapping it all up, terrified that I will cut the transmission. Well, don't worry, I have something to show you. Something important for you to try to understand.

In the meantime however, and for the rest of my life, you have my twinned body in a permanent coma back on Earth. And as an extra precaution, I don't intend to fall asleep, just in case you have some extra trick with which to wake me up and trap me back there. Don't worry, I "packed" a lot of coffee!

I know I am in no particular position to make demands (threaten to kill myself and thereby cut off this flow of information?), but please take my twinned body out of the Telepedrome and place it in a bed next to my beloved wife Julia in her intensive care ward in Westland Hospital in Maryland. She is in a permanent vegetative state, since the car accident, and thus it seems rather appropriate that our two "zombie" bodies should lie there together, keeping each other company, however uncommunicatively.

<u>8.</u>

My understanding of their language and culture is increasing by the hour, exponentially. Maybe some of those liquids they keep offering me, the ones you told me and Walters were nearly safe to drink after that last analysis, -maybe they're doing things to my brain, good things, expanding my cognitive capacity. They certainly seem to stop me requiring sleep. Genius! How did they know that's exactly what I needed? Did I actually tell them that? I don't think they're telepathic (how could they be when we think in mutually incomprehensible languages?) but they do seem extraordinarily empathetic.

<u>9.</u>

Their planet being tidally locked, as our astronomers predicted two centuries ago, means we have only seen the light side of their world so far, the Red Realm as the Somnons call it, which always faces the sun, no nights or days, no seasons. But a hundred miles beyond here, across what they call the Mouth-Eye Mountains, the other hemisphere begins. The moonlit, hidden world of perpetual night, of brown nitrogen-dioxide cyclones and constant rains and sulphur sand-storms. The Somnons tell me that this land contains their souls, that it is where they each go when they die, and sometimes unhappy souls come back. You might think this laughable superstition, but they devoutly maintain that sometimes wraiths are seen wandering through their mushroom-cities at night, strange white ghost-like beings who have become disorientated and drifted back across the forbidden border from the netherworld, the Grey Realm. They are said to be disturbed and disturbing, unable to rest, tortured spirits, those who have died prematurely or violently and come back to seek answers, or closure.

You think this is primitive and religious, but an astounding similarity with our own folk-myths surely, in a culture so distant from our own? And more to the point, they have shown me these creatures. Twelve hours ago I touched one with my own hands before it fled away. I am told that sometimes wraiths will seek out the house of a particular citizen, and stand over his body because…. here's the crunch: Somnons have coma victims too. And when that happens they send a priest traveller out under special license, over the border to search in the Grey Realm for the lost spirit of the living person, and then lead this wraith version back over, bring it home, and when it touches the body of its sleeping twin, it fuses with it, passes into it, and the patient wakes up and recovers.

So you see? For Julia, for hope, for the love of God, I have found a new mission here. This is why I had to mutiny. Walters just wouldn't understand.

10.

My native guide for the journey seems to be a female, but what am I saying? The term is meaningless here of course, so why am I using it? She is merely one of the two apparent sexes of Somnons, both vastly different from men and women, but I already like her immensely. Her name I will translate as *Lanyleirtis*, although half the actual sounds are more like clucks and sucking noises to human ears, so it's all a bit arbitrary. She must be some kind of high priestess. To the Somnons, travel to the Grey Realm is a religious rite, as much a passage of the soul and mind as a physical journey. She is puzzled by the weight and cumbersome packaging of the Ansible that I'm carrying with me, curious about its function, but tolerant of its intrusive presence.

The landscape is beginning to change, the yellow deserts and red mushroom forests of the Somnon heartland giving way to lusher, wetter vegetation, brown and purple trees and a kind of leaf-creeper ground cover like seaweed. Terrifying lightning strikes rage on the mountain tops ahead in the dark shadow of the Nitrite storms. Clouds change from brown to yellow as Nitrogen Dioxide cools to Dinitrogen Tetroxide then back again. We have to climb up and through that maelstrom to reach our destination.

11.

I don't know the rules of this culture, and that is very dangerous, albeit that the Somnons seem so peaceful and friendly. Too friendly. Has Lanyleirtis been assigned to me as a wife or something? As we rested fourteen hours ago (no sleeping of course!), she started caressing me with her third arm and kissing my spacesuit with her voluptuous fish-mouth, while emitting a weird song through some kind of tendril-lined gills on the side of her chest, followed by puffs of an odd pink gas. I found the effect bizarrely enchanting and nearly relaxed so much that she was about to take my breathing apparatus off. I would have died within minutes, of course. I had to explain to her very carefully after that how different my physiology is and how different our two planets are. How the cold temperatures and nitrogen-rich air are beyond the range of human adaptability.

I am confused to have to admit that I found her two large blinking eyes, filled with sadness as I told her how alien I am, enormously attractive. But of course, nothing can assuage my sense of loss, my love of my Julia, frozen, sleeping icy princess lost on a distant world, beside my other body, as I hope you have arranged things.

12.

This is Pleznick, Earth. We have a wraith here, Lanyleirtis is appalled, screaming hysterically and keeping her distance, but I've trapped the thing and I'm holding the Ansible instrumentation up against it, scanning. Can you analyse this thing? You need to work out what its chemical and atomic composition is. Don't you see? This is a soul, a ghost, a spirit. Solve this enigma and you may very well have the key to life on Earth also. If souls migrate here to a darkened hidden hemisphere, then where might they go on Earth? Perhaps they live all around you there, but simply cannot be seen in our atmosphere. On this so-different world, somehow they are both visible and corporeal. You have to try to understand and learn from this.

13.

Earth, why have you remained so silent? Still working on it, or don't you like what you've found out?

Reluctantly, and although still shaken, Lanyleirtis has led me deeper into the Grey Realm, a forbidden world. An entire year on Somnos takes only thirty-seven days. We must have orbited the red sun twice already and yet remained plunged in perpetual night. Only the orange light on the moon fragments give us a clue as to what we're missing, as they drift through the clouds, throwing dappled changing light patterns, like nightclub strobes.

About forty hours ago as we rested, Lanyleirtis told me about one of her people's myths about the origins of those nine irregular moons. Somnons tell their children that they are jigsaw pieces (I translate loosely) that one of their Gods (the "monkey god" although I have yet to see their equivalent of a monkey, a less intelligent version of themselves living in the hottest regions of the Red Realm) created by smashing up the Orb of Knowing, a sort of crystal ball, in a rage of frustration because he could not understand the meaning of the universe. It was the supreme God-being, "Zea" who had given the monkey this privileged opportunity for enlightenment, and when the monkey threw away this chance, Zea condemned the monkey to confinement on Somnos. This is why there are so many storms and thunder and lightning, the children are told. This is the rage and despair of the monkey god as he travels the world repenting and regretting, tearing his hair out, alternately begging with Zea and railing against him, pleading for another chance to see the crystal ball put together again so that he might have another opportunity to understand the universe. But Zea always refuses.

Somnons seem to put great stall by the concept of knowledge, by which they mean spiritual understanding, not just the scientific accumulation of facts, which they see as a kind of vanity. Their monkey god festival is celebrated every ten years by an exchange of small puzzle games and telling to each other of enigmas and riddles. Lanyleirtis tells me that it's not the solving of these puzzles which Somnons cherish but the opposite: the sense of mystery and unknowing which creates in them a sense of humility, a character trait they admire above all others.

14.

We have reached the first wraith city. Astonishing. Instead of mushrooms it appears to be made of semi-transparent crystals that flicker with electric pulses, in some way related to the lightning perhaps. The inhabitants are silvery translucent versions of the Somnons themselves, and Lanyleirtis insists that they are each equivalents of the living beings we left behind in the sunlit world. She has begun talking to them, overcoming her fear, asking them directions. She says she intends to take me to meet her dead mother, to prove her point and make me believe.

Everywhere we walk, spidery white cobwebs blow and accumulate over us, from the branches of some kind of black leathery trees. I am sending you a sample to analyse.

15.

It may be true. She has found her "dead" mother, and although these creatures have no tear glands, I think I now recognise their equivalents: a shivering in their upper limbs, accompanied by a sweat of green moisture on their hind legs. The "gills" also palpitate, just as they did during what I took to be amorous or sexual arousal.

16.

Am I going mad? "Today" I thought I glimpsed humans among the crowds in the wraith city. I pursued them, on three different occasions, but never caught up with them. How could such an insane thing be possible? I killed Walters. Does that mean that Walters' soul is here? Insanity enough. But I thought I saw more than one. I have asked Lanyleirtis to ask a question of her mother or of one of the leaders of the wraiths. There's a lot here I don't yet understand, but I feel a kind of panic at times, as if logic itself is slipping away from me. Is everyone here all the Somnons who have ever lived? –Or do they each in turn return to new bodies, when babies are born on the daylight hemisphere, like reincarnation?

17.

Yesterday we travelled "all day", to use the term loosely, to meet the wraith's leader in the eastern hills. I say "east", but what is west or north or south in a world such as this? North is here, away from the red sun, and south is where I came from, to me at least.

Exhausted, I unwittingly dropped my guard and fell asleep for a moment, but was not returned to Earth. I take this as a good sign and am very much relieved. Have you given up the idea of tricking me, back there on Earth? –Followed my instructions regarding my other body? -Not burned it and destroyed me out of spite at least, I see.

The wraith leader told me to my astonishment that there are indeed humans in this realm. He says that a few began appearing around the time of the arrival of our first probes, and being a polite race (like their daylight counterparts) they ignored the probes and accommodated the new people. How can this be? The probes only contained Ansibles. Can human souls (invisible on Earth) somehow migrate through these devices, and were they somehow attracted to them like moths to a flame?

Who are they all and can I meet them? –I asked excitedly of course, but my question puzzled the leader. Wraith-Somnons have neither names nor fixed abodes apparently, they merely wander endlessly, talking to themselves. They find each other only through feelings, strong emotions like love or hate, and thus Lanyleirtis had found her mother. Can the method and effect work for me I wonder, or for my fellow humans in this alien place? Of course, nobody knew the answer.

18.

An answer. Wraith-Somnons like Somnons themselves, only live for their equivalent of fifty of our Earth years, and then their souls instantly re-emerge as newborns on the sunlit hemisphere. Thus is this peculiar world held in equilibrium.

Why are you still so silent, Earth? What did you find out about the wraith data I gave you? Are they made from Muons and Higgs-Bosons, anti-matter or electromagnetic plasma, dark matter? What might their equivalent be on Earth, and how would you detect them?

Well, it's you that needs to find out now, not me. I resigned myself to death here the moment I destroyed the Entanglement chamber, I understand that. I only hope that you will have the sense to use the data I sent you and… and what? Find the soul of my beloved Julia and re-unite her with her sleeping body? Unless…. What if…?

19.

Yesterday I tripped and fell from a sulphur rock outcrop and a sharp fragment tore through my survival suit and pierced my chest. I was unconscious for four hours, and yet I am alive. I threw myself off another cliff this morning, to check an astonishing hypothesis. I am immortal. I have dispensed with my survival suit and breathing apparatus, I no longer seem to feel cold. Am I breathing nitrogen? It feels no different. The white cobweb-filaments that drift everywhere here have been slowly accumulating on me, I can no longer brush them off.

20.

I have made a calculation. The surface area of this hemisphere is 11,822,510 square miles. If I walk 50 miles a day for the next 236,450 years I can traverse it all in search of Julia or the other human spirits. If I am immortal, such a task is easily feasible. I no longer seem to have to eat, just as well since my protein pills have been running out.

21.

I walk endlessly every day now, across dark wastelands under electrically-flickering storm clouds, lashed by brown rain, travelling between white crystalline cities. Above me always, the jigsaw pieces of the fragmented moons slowly twist and interlock and pull apart like luminous sad birds, indolent fish in the depths of a bored eternity. I am no longer afraid to sleep and dream, and when I do I sometimes imagine myself putting all those pieces back together again, reconstructing the puzzle and at last finding out the sublime meaning of all this, these strange torments that I live through in these darkening days, so far from all sunlight and understanding.

Somewhere at last I may find my beloved Julia, or at least another human soul as lost as I am, if God wills it. But which God, and over what realm? –Or are all realms the same one? –Now and always?

And why are you so silent, Earth? You who put me here, sowed me like a seed, casual casting of a handful of life, spattered across the universe like milk or honey? I killed my brother and I have a long time to reflect upon it. Is this my punishment, how you ostracise me, cast me off into the black abyss of space? Am I now disowned and disavowed? I cannot bring my brother back to life, though his spilled blood cries out from this alien soil. Will I meet him here again and will he and you forgive me? –Or I: forgive myself?

22.

Lanyleirtis is getting old and frail. I think she may die soon. But she is not sad or afraid as a human would be, but jubilant, overjoyed at the prospect of returning to the sunlit world. Does that mean she died when she came here? –And have I then also?

She has been a good companion, my dear friend these last long months and I will miss her terribly. But my own journey has no such end in sight. I walk and hunt and search through every land and all the many faces that I meet, each day, looking for an answer, for recognition, for hope and hope returned.

And meanwhile I know I live, not just here but somewhere else, on another world, where I sleep peacefully, I must trust, side by side with my Julia, my Queen. *Et in Arcadia Ego.*

And have you still nothing to say to me, Earth –my mother, my father? Are you ashamed of me? Or are you proud? Or are you no longer there? –an emptiness, an absence, empty void?

Have you solved my puzzle yet?

Signing off,

-Walter S Pleznick.

Brief Author Biographies

ALLEN ASHLEY

Allen Ashley writes short stories, novels, poems and lyrics. His novel "The Planet Suite" (TTA Press, 1997) was highly acclaimed by Brian Aldiss as "The course for the future". Allen's debut collection of stories "Somnambulists" (Elastic Press, 2004) was shortlisted for the British Fantasy Society award as was his recent collection "Once and Future Cities" (Eibonvale, 2009). This is Allen Ashley's fourth full-length editorial project. His first "The Elastic Book Of Numbers" (Elastic Press, 2005) won the BFS award for Best Anthology. "Dreaming Spheres", his collection of poems with Sarah Doyle, is due from PS Publishing later this year. www.allenashley.com

GARY BUDGEN

Gary Budgen grew up in London where he still lives with his partner and two children. He has had fiction published in various places including "Interzone", "Dark Horizons" and "Jupiter". He has stories forthcoming in: "Aoife's Kiss"; "All Hallows"; "Morpheus Tales"; and the "After the End" anthology from Static Movement, edited by Shane Collins. Occasional musings and further information can be found at garybudgen. wordpress.com

ANDREW COBURN

Andrew Coburn is the author of 13 novels, including "Birthright" (Simon & Schuster), a speculative re-examination of the Lindbergh kidnapping. His work has been translated into 14 languages. Three novels have been adapted into French films subsequently subtitled in German and Italian. He's the author of numerous short stories which have appeared in such publications as the "Massachusetts Review", "Consequence Magazine", "Rio Grande Review", "J Journal", "Decameron Annual" and the collection "Men From Boys" edited by John Harvey published by Dark Alley, an imprint of HarperCollins. He was nominated for an Edgar Award in 1990 for his novel "Goldilocks".

DANIELLA GEARY

Daniella Geary is currently a mature student of Behavioural Psychology at the University of London, enjoying a second life now that her two kids have left home. She has always dabbled privately in poetry and philosophy, but "Underpass" is her first published story, based on wildly distorted memories of her childhood in Edinburgh and Liverpool.

TERRY GRIMWOOD

In the real world, Terry Grimwood is no stranger to Eibonvale, who have recently published his first novel "Bloody War". Also, wearing his publisher's hat, Terry's Exaggerated Press is on the verge of unleashing "The Monster Book for Girls" anthology. In the dream world Terry pays the bills by teaching at a college and maintains a tenuous hold on reality by writing chapters for a new engineering text book. He is married to the poet Jessica Lawrence.

ANDREW HOOK

Andrew Hook has had some 80 short stories published in the past ten years, many gathered into three story collections. He also writes novellas, with the most recent, "Ponthe Oldenguine" (Atomic Fez) – a comic / surreal media satire – launched at FantasyCon 2010 by Andrew wearing a rubber penguin mask. He describes his life as curious… not surprisingly, perhaps. Look out for Andrew's next collection "Nitrospective", due soon from Dog Horn Publishing.

A.J. KIRBY

AJ Kirby is the Leeds-based author of three novels, "Perfect World" (TWB Press, 2011), "Bully" (Wild Wolf Publishing, 2009), and "The Magpie Trap" (New Generation Publishing, 2008), as well as one volume of collected short fiction, "Mix Tape" (NGP, 2010). His dark shorts have won, or been short-listed for numerous awards, including runner-up in the Dog Horn Publishing Fiction Prize 2011, and have appeared across the web and in print, including, most recently in "The Horror Anthology of Horror Anthologies" (ed. Des Lewis). Creak open the door at www.andykirbythewriter.20m. com to find out more.

JOEL LANE

Joel Lane lives in Birmingham. His recent publications include a collection of short stories, "The Terrible Changes"; a novella, "The Witnesses are Gone"; a chapbook, "Black Country"; a collection of poems, "The Autumn Myth"; and a booklet of crime stories, "Do Not Pass Go". He recently co-edited (with Allyson Bird) an anthology of anti-fascist and anti-racist stories in the weird and speculative fiction genres, "Never Again".

ALISON J. LITTLEWOOD

Alison J. Littlewood lives in West Yorkshire, England, where she hoards books, dreams dreams and writes short fiction – mainly in the dark fantasy and horror genres. Alison has contributed to "Black Static", "Dark Horizons", "Not One Of Us" and the charity anthology "Never Again". Her debut novel, "A Cold Season", will be out early in 2012 with Jo Fletcher Books, an imprint of Quercus. Visit her at www.alisonlittlewood. co.uk.

JET MCDONALD

Jet McDonald is a writer and musician. His debut novel "Automatic Safe Dog" was published by Eibonvale Press in 2011. He has written for "The Idler" and "Boneshaker" magazine, has published many short stories in the alternative press and in 2008 won the Missouri Review Audio Fiction Award. In May 2010 he cycled from the UK to India and is currently writing a book on cycling and the imagination. He is lead singer and songwriter in a folk pop band called The Woodlice. You can find out more about his writing at www.jetmcdonald.com

RALPH ROBERT MOORE

Ralph Robert Moore's fiction has been published in America, England, Ireland and Australia in a variety of literary and genre magazines and anthologies. His latest short story collection, "I Smell Blood", is available through Amazon and other online venues. Mario Guslandi, reviewing the collection in Horror World said, "Ralph Robert Moore's second collection confirms the excellent qualities displayed in his previous book 'Remove the Eyes', namely a powerful imagination, an extraordinary degree of originality and a great storytelling ability... A highly recommended book."
Moore's website SENTENCE at http://www.ralphrobertmoore.com features a wide selection of his writings.

STEPHEN PALMER

Stephen Palmer first came to the attention of the SF world with his Orbit Books debut "Memory Seed" and its sequel "Glass". Further novels followed from Wildside Press and Prime Books, then in 2010 "Urbis Morpheos" from PS Publishing. Stephen is best known for his environmental SF, but also for the "tribalpunk" novel "Muezzinland", which, with the music novel "Hallucinating", has been published as an ebook by Infinity Plus. The ebook of "Urbis Morpheos" was also published in 2011. He is currently working on new material.

MARION PITMAN

Marion Pitman (www.marionpitman.co.uk) has been selling short stories and poetry at intervals since 1977, most recently to "The Eighth Black Book of Horror", Mortbury Press, 2011. Like most people, she spends too much time on Facebook, and is trying to sell a novel. A Londoner now living in Reading, she deals in second-hand books on the internet, and has no car, no television and no cats. If she won the lottery she would avoid winter altogether, go to more folk festivals, and watch a lot more cricket.

FRANK ROGER

Frank Roger was born in 1957 in Ghent, Belgium.
His first story appeared in 1975. Since then his stories appear in an increasing number of languages in all sorts of magazines, anthologies and other venues, and since 2000,

story collections are published, also in various languages. Apart from fiction, he also produces collages and graphic work in a surrealist and satirical tradition. These have appeared in various magazines and books.

By now he has a few hundred short stories to his credit, published in more than 35 languages. Find out more at www.frankroger.be

IAN SALES

Ian Sales has had short stories and poems published in "Postscripts", "Jupiter", "M-Brane SF", "Alt Hist", "New Horizons", and the anthologies "Catastrophia", "Vivisepulture" and "The Monster Book for Girls". He is currently editing a new anthology of hard SF from Mutation Press, "Rocket Science", which is due to be published in 2012. He reviews books for "Interzone", and DVDs for "VideoVista". He is represented by the John Jarrold Literary Agency. His website is at http://iansales. com.

It doesn't have to be right... it just has to sound plausible: http://iansales.com/
A Space About Books About Space: http://spacebookspace.wordpress.com/
Sferse: http://sferse.wordpress.com/

IAN SHOEBRIDGE

Ian Shoebridge has reported insomnia, unusual dreams, restlessness and a feeling of being about to remember something important, but lack of clear physical symptoms make diagnosis difficult. He lives quietly in Australia and writes short fiction, some of which has appeared in "Bound For Evil", "Electric Velocipede" and "Subtle Edens".

GEOFF STEVENS

Geoff Stevens has been editor of "Purple Patch" poetry magazine for 35 years. His own poetry is published worldwide and often and he loves reading to audiences. His latest book is "Islands In The Blood", from Indigo Dreams Publications. Website: www.geoffstevens.co.uk

DOUGLAS THOMPSON

Douglas Thompson's short stories have appeared in a wide range of magazines, most recently "Ambit" and "Albedo One", and in two of Allen Ashley's previous anthologies: "Subtle Edens" (Elastic Press) and "Catastrophia" (PS). His novels, "Ultrameta" and "Sylvow", were published by Eibonvale Press in 2009 and 2010 respectively. A third novel "Mechagnosis", is due Autumn/Winter 2011 from Dog Horn. http:// douglasthompson.wordpress.com/

www.ingramcontent.com/pod-product-compliance
Lightning Source LLC
Chambersburg PA
CBHW061540210726
48287CB00006B/2033